Obstacles

By
Christopher Michael Reardon

Edited by
Brian Cavitt

Cover Art by
Tiara Mehic

Cover Design by
Jason Humphreys

Published by
Alpha Wolf Publishing
© 2012–2013

ISBN-13: 978-0615897783
ISBN-10: 0615897789

*Chris
Reardon*

Chapter 1
Coward

A swift slice of the blade almost severs my head. I gasp, ducking with enough speed to evade the onslaught. I swear this man doesn't just want me dead. He plans to wipe my existence from the universe.

His failed assault leaves him vulnerable, allowing me to kick his shin with full force. He wails upon impact. A flame ignites in his soul. I've transformed this beast into an all-out monster. I dart away from my enemy, desperate to find safety. Alas, the blow does not impinge on his agility. He charges with outrage.

Thankfully, before he arrives I'm able to rise into fighting stance. I aim my sword's tip directly between his eyes. He mirrors my action. We commence circling each other. How in the world did I get here? I'm no sword fighter! I'm a doctor for goodness sake.

My memory blurs with reality. Both become a mesh of the same. The only thing I'm sure of now is that I'm about to be killed. Not willing to trust my defensive skills, I lunge forward to stab my attacker. The man parries this pitiful attempt with ease. He smirks at my naivety.

Casting my blade aside with his own, he juts forward and clocks my face with his fist. The intense blow demolishes me. I crash into the hard mountain dirt. The bombardment hurls my sword across the stadium to vanish into abyss. It's not such a big loss. I mean it's not like I can use it well anyway.

It's as if the world knows my fate. Pitch black sky

transfigures into reddish hues. Blood flows down my cheeks, meshing with my dark mocha skin. All hope is lost for me. There's no doubt about that now.

Inhaling my last gulps of air, I contemplate if death will hurt. The man strides to my location. He savors his kill with each footstep. A stroke of luck suddenly arises as I detect a sturdy stone beside my leg. Never breaking our locked eyes, I maneuver my arm to the rock. Intense darkness shields my plot. His blissful stride indicates complete ignorance.

Grasping the stone, I adjust my legs into leaping position.

"Alcott…" my attacker wheezes. "You're a dead man." The words don't faze me. He whisks over with eyes blazing murder. Just as he raises his sword to annihilate me, I hurl the rock at his face.

"Ahhh!" he wails, dropping his blade to the ground. Immediately upon the smash, the red sky evolves into a cobalt blue haze. The color alteration allows just enough light to portray his shock. Eyebrows rising, he sprints to his abandoned sword. I'm still too petrified to locate my blade. I don't even know where to start searching. My chance instantly fades. He retrieves his weapon in no time.

"You've done it now," the man proclaims into blackness. What did I think chucking the rock would accomplish? Perhaps I wanted to show him I'm not going down without a fight. Either way I've done nothing but ensure my demise will be hell. I guess I could reason with this monster. Despite that being my only chance, I'm just too fatigued.

He sprints to my helpless body, excited to end me. Abandoning all confidence, I can do nothing but accept defeat. I've never felt so worthless in my entire life. Without warning, a high-pitched screech pierces the night.

The man's blade halts in mid-air.

It echoes against each mountain. A ghostly hawk dives into the stadium. With another wail it barrels into the man at full intensity. Blue atmosphere vanishes leaving a shimmering orange fog in its place. The hawk's wings spread wide, enveloping the man's face in a sea of sharp feathers. Could this really be happening?

My avian soldier bombards him. It drills with its lethal beak. The spectacle floods my veins with adrenaline. I actually thought I was done. Summoning stamina I rise despite my half-asleep limbs. I stride to him with new-found fire.

The hawk senses my approach with a screech. It abandons the man entirely. With him now vulnerable my clenched fist bashes him in the face. The punch is far more powerful than anticipated, smacking his body against the dirt. He's clearly frantic, cursing everyone and everything that ever existed.

This universe approves of my frenzy. A bright yellow atmosphere appears. He hops back up in no time. This monster's not going down easy. I panic once more as I still remain weaponless. Delving into the shadows, I inspect the darkness for my blade. All I can locate, however, are patches of dirt with occasional pebbles and weeds. If I don't find it fast, I'm out of all options.

Scrambling amongst the gravel I make no progress whatsoever.

"Where is it?!" I moan into the murk. I cringe as a raspy voice responds.

"Gone," the man wheezes into my ear. I wail in utter horror. Turning to defend myself, I realize it's too late. He stomps my torso into the dirt with ease. I can do nothing but cough out all my strength.

"Hiss…" my ears detect to the right. What could

this be? The man shares my confusion. His beady eyes scan the ground. A rattlesnake barrels through the gravel, slithering my sword amongst its coils. My terror transforms to hope as I lunge for the blade and creature. Grasping them both, I block the man's attack. The serpent hisses at the man with a glare. Its allegiance must lie with me.

I can't help but grin as he leaps back in bewilderment. Though I'm just as clueless, I smirk at the circumstances. Venom spewing amongst its fangs brings him to insanity. He slashes the reptile, chopping it into two slimy halves. The tragic killing of my new friend charges my nerves. I spring up determined to end this evil once and for all. Our blades clash in metallic uproar. Both of us lose all balance.

I attempt to jab his chest. Yet, he detects this in my eyes. He grasps my arm like a grappling hook. My skin stretches until blood rises. His strength surpasses any I've ever seen before. Despite every force in me saying to keep fighting, the grim reality is impossible to ignore. My life might actually be over.

Chapter 2
Death Lurks

"Please! No!" I whimper like a mule. I'm a complete fool, ashamed of this behavior. Despite how much I plead, no mercy is shown in return. The man's blade twirls along the gentle gusts. It accelerates every second. My heart beats with unstoppable energy. How does it not burst out of my chest?

I close my eyes, waiting for whatever fate may be dealt. I'm certainly not strong enough to battle anymore. This man has conquered me.

"No!" I howl across the living room. I plummet off the shaggy tan bedspread. My body smacks the fuzzy carpet, causing my head to throb like crazy. Inhaling a few deep breaths, I attempt to discover what happened. The view of my apartment and blaring television reveal the obvious. Another idiotic nightmare overtook my subconscious once again. I can't summon the strength to rise. I truly thought my life was over. Tears cascade down my cheeks. My eyesight blurs into a watery mesh.

This has to stop.

Sunbeams delve through the blinds causing me to squint. At least morning has arrived. That's the little blessing in this. I knew I shouldn't have fallen asleep with the television on. I can be such an idiot sometimes.

My limbs still shake as I raise myself off the floor.

"Dr. Alcott!" Antuna's shrill voice wails from outside the door, "Are you alright in there? I heard a thump."

"Yes," I call. "I'm fine. The table just fell over." Despite my attempt to appear calm, my breathing is still rough. I hope the white lie will suffice.

"Oh," she shouts. "Well, breakfast is ready!"

These night terrors have haunted me for quite some time. You'd think I'd get used to them after a while. However, it proves more the opposite. Every night just gets worse. With death lurking so close in the household, there's no mystery why I'm paranoid.

"I'll be down in a minute!"

My head gets extremely woozy. I slump onto the bed. Staring at the ceiling fan, I wonder why this keeps happening. Does everyone else go through this? Death has always horrified me. People say you grow out of these fears. I, however, just seem to grow back into them.

The fan twirls round and round. Anybody else would just see a household appliance. My brain transforms the blades into knives waiting to slice. If I stare long enough, I might even convince myself it's true.

Breaking from the trance, I whisk out the door. It slams shut behind me.

"Hey Dr. Alcott!" my patient, Gari, stammers whilst devouring bacon. "How did you sleep?"

"Wonderful!" I'm surely getting good at this lying thing. Besides, I have to be as positive as I can for this little guy. I may not have many chances left. "What about you?"

Antuna glides past the wooden table. A fresh plate of delectable eggs is deposited. I take a seat next to Gari. Eying the plate, I can't help but be hypnotized.

Sizzling bacon lies next to wheat toast. Slimy jelly oozes off onto the plate. The sheer sight makes my stomach grumble. I do not hesitate. Plunging my fork in, I shove scrambled eggs into my mouth.

"It was awesome! I had a great dream about ice

cream!" Gari chirps beside me. At least someone's having good dreams around here. Given the current situation, his blissful attitude shocks me; a more correct statement would be, terrifies me.

"Gari," Antuna chimes while washing dishes. Her cheery tone is complete hokum. Anyone can see through that. This woman is about to collapse. "Would you like to go explore the beach today? I'd like to spend some time with you."

"Sure," Gari says with nonchalance. "I'm going to die soon; might as well have some fun."

Antuna slams the dishes in the sink. The clang of metal jolts my heart. A tsunami surely approaches.

"Don't you dare joke about that!" She twists around with fire in her glare. Gari's too frightened to respond. I also freeze with wide eyes. "You're not the only one affected here!"

"I'm sorry," he stammers. He lowers his bacon strip back to the plate. Antuna circles back to the sink as if afraid to make eye contact.

She begins washing the dishes. Seconds of utter silence ensue. Nobody knows the proper thing to say, and no one is going to attempt it. The rush of sink water drowns out all thought. Suddenly, Antuna drops the plate once more. It bangs against the sink. She doesn't seem to notice the crash. Tears barrel down her cheeks as she rests her head in her palms. I can't watch this sight any longer.

Chapter 3
The Horizon

"Gari," I state with a grin. We need to dash out of here, and fast. "Let's go take a walk to the cliff."

"Okay." Gari's tone suggests complete relief.

Both of us dart out the door without hesitation.

This type of behavior is not new to me. I'm a doctor; I've seen all types of people around deathly situations. Antuna and Gari are actually more on the tranquil side.

I have been residing here for roughly a year now. Being a live-in doctor, I really take my work home. Perhaps now the work takes me with it.

Long story short, Gari is going to die. His little body can't stand the trials and tribulations of this universe any longer. Nothing I can do will change that.

After a few minutes, we reach the magnificent cliff view. Billions of people are scattered across the sandy beach below. It appears as if I'm looking at an ant hill.

Of course, heights aren't my favorite thing in the world. My mind starts to become hazy. Flashes of plummeting to my death enter my mindset. My trembling feet barely have the strength to step back.

Seagulls soar in the distance, off to their next destination. Many dive bomb the people hurling food to them. Once one finds out about the smorgasbord, the whole colony bombards. Seagulls aren't the most courteous of creatures.

Right below us, a pelican thrusts its beak in the

ocean to catch some fish. A big gulp indicates a successful venture. The waves crash against the shore, bringing the many surfers in.

Gari then begins to speak, almost startling me.

"I probably got like a year, huh?" he states with eyes glued to his feet. "It's a little scary, but I guess I'm okay with it. You've worked in a hospital. What have the people there done when they knew they were going to die?"

"Well," I attempt to give the best answer I can, "some of them are really scared, and some are just... excited. Another cool thing is that, usually just down the hall from where someone dies, there's someone else being brought into this world. I don't know exactly what I'm trying to say here," I continue into uncharted territory, "but it just is supposed to happen, you know? So, don't worry."

"Yeah," he stutters. "I just...don't think I'm ready for it to end yet."

That shatters my heart. Reality punches me in the face. Life certainly isn't fair. His foot plays with a nearby pebble, kicking it back and forth between flattened grasses. I'm terrified of death, yet this little guy is the one who has to face it head on.

"You know," Gari continues, gazing at the ocean waves. "When I look out at the horizon, I just feel like there's an adventure for me to go on. You know? Maybe something out there waits for me. That feeling comes every time I come up here. I just don't want death to take that away."

"It won't," I spark back. There is no millisecond of hesitation. Though I am not quite sure where I am going with this, something tells me I'm right.

"It'll be that adventure."

Chapter 4
The Obscure Incantation

As I enter the hospital, the bustling chaos overtakes me. Each doctor, nurse, and patient purposely carries out their task. I look in awe at their determination.

I discover that I am not really needed anymore. My main job is away with Gari now. Even so, I have too many friends here not to return. A lot of people aren't exactly mentally there, but they love seeing me, and I surely love seeing them.

One elderly man upstairs has no roommate. Many have been saying he's lost his marbles. Perhaps being alone that long can cause that. For a while now, he has been ranting on about ancient magic. Secret scripts and books flood his conversation. The man literally thinks he can bring back the dead! His utter belief in this stuff frightens the other patients. This man is very well known. Few in the hospital haven't succumbed to his rambling.

He goes by Mashilto. This man has actually surpassed ninety years. That is certainly an accomplishment on its own. Nonetheless, he remains mobile and social as well. He is always very kind to me. I certainly enjoy spending evenings talking to him. He always has something interesting to say, even if most of us didn't believe it to be factual. I keep him up to date on Gari and everything going on with him. He seems almost overly interested. Empathy is surely present in those shimmering eyes.

"Dr. Alcott, how are you today?" Mashilto yells with gusto as I arrive with some lunch.

"I'm wonderful Mashilto! How are you? What have you been up to?" I ask with a bright smile.

"Oh, I've just been watching my game shows." He grasps the remote firmly. "Learnin' lots a' new stuff!"

"That's awesome! Game shows are pretty entertaining."

"How is that little boy you is lookin' after?" Mashilto inquires.

This brings my mood down a bit. Gari's health has been decreasing dramatically. I am in no good place to talk about it. Not that there would ever be a good place to talk about it.

"He's not…as good as I would hope." I look at the floor tiles. "But I guess I can't change that."

Gazing back at him, I detect a slight twinkle in his eye. Here we go. Knowing what is undoubtedly coming, I regret my choice of words.

"Can't you?" Mashilto replies. He shuts the television off. His mystical tone indicates where this is going.

"What do you mean?" I say. I'm aware his mental state is pretty much lost. What harm would humoring him cause?

"Well, look at this here masterpiece." He points toward the floor to the left side of his bed. I maneuver around to get a better look. There lies a gigantic old book entitled, *'Altering Fate'*. The enormous tome appears as if it has lived longer than he has. The cover is very durable. Many pages are crammed inside.

Just as I reach down to pick the monstrosity up, the sky outside flashes. My heart jolts as light explodes. I stop and peer out the window. It looked practically like a lightning burst, yet there is no storm. No clouds float in the sky either. Dashing over to the window, I check to discover

13

the source of the explosion.

Everything seems to be completely normal. Blackness stills the atmosphere. Whatever that was, vanished. Could I have imagined that? I will admit that is a little creepy. Mashilto doesn't seem to notice the flash, or doesn't even care to mention it. He then continues…

"Please take it; if what my mother says is correct, you can save that little kid."

"I wish that were true, Mashilto. But I doubt even this book can save him now," I respond in hopelessness. It's really kind of him to want to save Gari. That's what we all desire. He is even willing to attempt this magic book thing. Crazy man or not, I know it is the thought that counts.

"You listen here!" he explodes out of nowhere. It shocks me so much I even trip over a floor tile. Mashilto yelps in the same haunting voice…

"This book works! My mother wouldn't have given it to me if it didn't. I've never had the courage to ever try it, but something tells me that little Gari deserves another chance." He bursts into tears. His knees shift up to catch his falling head. I'm used to this kind of behavior daily from patients. Something, however, is peculiar about this man.

"I've lived far too long in my opinion, Alcott. That kid deserves more than what he's got. Please just give it a chance." His rage startles me so much I'm speechless. That outburst took a lot out of him. His eyes fade shut. The man abandons the world, dropping into slumber. The eerie hospital room terrifies me.

I've never seen him get like this before. My heartbeat still races. I continue to stare at the man. Mashilto survived so long, irregular behavior is normal from time to time. The things he rants of, however, do make sense. I can fully understand where he is coming from. Despite the obvious insanity, I guess I owe it to this man to take a glance at this thing.

"Alright, I promise I'll look at it," I reply. His snores indicate I am merely speaking to myself.

The weighty book is difficult to lift. It's as if I'm lugging around a boulder. Dust clouds each page. For all I know, there could be ten million pages in here! Whoever wrote this thing needs a hobby.

As he snoozes on his bed, I decide to sit down and sift through it. A lot is written in languages almost prehistoric to me, while much is in English. Maybe this thing is a sort of a Rosetta Stone type deal. Why would they bring together such varying languages? I'll give Mashilto one thing; this book certainly is creeping me out.

Perusing through, I realize there is much I can't decipher. I'm definitely no archaeologist or whatever. The pictures of deities and spirits frighten me. Other images contain various witches hurling things into cauldrons, to gods arguing around a table. They are very elaborate drawings. Why in the world would people take so much time to create this stuff? Thinking of the illustrator startles me. I'm playing with some messed up people. Perhaps I shouldn't do this alone.

Suddenly, I reach the chapter Mashilto had been raving about. This chapter reads, 'Bringing Back the Dead.' It is surprisingly in English, despite the odd languages preceding. Skimming through, I detect only vague ideas about the process. You apparently have to go to a secluded area at night. A specific inscription or chant must be recited ten times. The statement is…

'I challenge fate, to change its course, for what it's done, needs to reverse.'

It must be deliberately chanted, also with eyes fixed on a shining star. Any star will do, but the reader must view one star and one only. That is very weird and oddly specific. I can't imagine the reasons. After that, the only statement left in English is that 'it' would then begin. What 'it' is, neither I nor even the authors of this thing know. Neither could the translator in the book it seems. That is right where the English part ceases.

Everything else seems to be printed in some ancient text. Beyond that is nothing but unknown gibberish to my eyes.

It is getting really late now. The light above Mashilto's body swings. Even that renders chills in me. I've got to get out of here.

All of this supernatural stuff is freaking me out. Of course, I know it to be fiction. Mashilto doesn't seem to think so. It can be kind of horrifying being alone with someone who puts that much faith into magic. Despite my best judgment, I lug the book home with me. I need something scary to read. What could it hurt? Plus I think it would break his heart if I didn't.

Heading back to Gari and Antuna's place takes some time, but that is okay with me. A long drive can be enjoyable. It is certainly relaxing. It also feels wonderful to have some alone time. As I rumble down a now secluded dirt road, something incredibly spooky happens. All the tranquility is gone. I'm shaken to my very core.

Out of the darkness, there is a sudden whisper in my ear. It comes out of nowhere, causing me to swerve the car. I almost cause a deadly accident. The voice sounds like that of a very old person. Are they right in the car with me?! The voice wheezes one word…

"…Alcott…"

Chapter 5
Terror

My heartbeat accelerates. A swift gasp follows. Literally, someone has spoken directly into my eardrum. Rotating with haste, I find no one there. Empty seats glare back at me. Up front I sit with *'Altering Fate'* to the passenger side. What's wrong with me?! I instantly freak out. I haven't really gone insane?

I need to get my head back on straight. Peering around, I look for the first stop. Luckily, a gas station appears up ahead. Breathing excessively, I pull in and dart out of the car as if a tiger hunts me. In my burst of terror, the gigantic book falls off the seat onto the car floor. Hopefully no pages are damaged. Not that I remotely care at the moment; I'm getting out of here!

I can't remember when I have been this terrified my whole life. A few yards from the car, I calm myself with deep breaths. No other vehicles are in sight. Standing in the parking lot alone, I'm aware I'm a lunatic.

It must just be stress, I tell myself. Just stress. Just stress. No more Mashilto for a while; that's for sure. All of that ghost mumbo-jumbo must be getting to me. As I peer into the bright gas station, the attendant glares at me. She probably thinks I'm crazy, not that I would disagree.

Now settling down a bit, I go in. If I pretend everything's normal, maybe it will be. A delicious snack will clear my head. Entering the store, the worker eyes me with caution.

"You okay?!" She looks at me with horror.

"Yeah," I answer trying to at least appear sane. "I'm sorry; I just had a freak-out for a minute."

"What happened?" she inquires, abandoning her post.

"Well, I…" I stammer as she glides over, "I thought I heard someone call my name when I was driving, but there was nobody around. I just panicked and pulled in here."

"That's pretty scary," she replies. "I'd be freaked out too. Where did the voice come from?"

"From the back seat," I respond. Thank goodness she's empathetic. "It was like a whisper. I'm sorry if this sounds crazy to you; I'm sure I'm just stressed out from work." After I speak, I head over to the coolers. An icy soda should wash my troubles away.

"You want me to go check your car for you?" she asks with a grin. That is extremely courteous of her. I in no way want to be a burden. Frankly, I am too scared to get back in; hence me stalling so long with all the drinks.

"If you could," I sheepishly respond. "Thank you so much."

"No problem." She strides out into the darkness. As she reaches my vehicle, there seems to be nothing out of the ordinary. The attendant opens up all the doors. She checks every seat. Lifting the trunk, her eyes gaze into every nook and cranny. Nothing.

The worker comes back into the store. A ding signifies her arrival. I know I really look insane now.

"Your car's clear." She returns to her spot behind the counter. "You must have just been imagining things. I do that all the time. It can get pretty scary driving by yourself at night."

Suddenly, I begin to think of Mashilto's book. The monstrous tome crashed onto the floor. In my petrified state, I may have damaged it. Mashilto is really fond of that thing. I would feel terrible if I messed any of it up.

"Yeah." I rest my soda on the counter. "That must be it. Is the book okay?"

"What book?" The attendant's eyebrows lower.

"The gigantic, ancient-looking one," I respond. How could she miss that? "It's a friend of mine's, and I think I damaged it when I rushed in here."

"There was no book in there," she states, regaining her curious look from before.

Extreme panic sets in my heart. The book was definitely on the floor before I charged out. This woman couldn't have taken it. She strode in empty handed. What in the world is going on?

"What?" I'm seriously about to faint.

"There wasn't any book." She looks at me. Her eyes portray deep empathy. I feel like complete crap now. "Maybe you left it back at work or something?"

She obviously believes something is wrong with me. She isn't the only one. Maybe I am going crazy. In an effort to sound somewhat normal, I drop the subject entirely.

"Yeah." I muster the brightest grin. "You're right, I remember now. Thank you so much for checking that for me."

She rings me up with a smile, shielding her unsteadiness. I whisk out with my new soda. Taking a few deep gulps, I attempt to return to sanity. *Maybe I did leave the book back at Mashilto's room. Yeah, I left it there because it freaked me out too much. That's what I did.* Don't get me wrong; I wholly know that isn't true, but I have to convince myself that's what happened.

I wave to the gas station woman one last time. She returns the motion as I depart. Looking all through the car, I discover that she is completely right. *'Altering Fate'* has vanished. Lifting up the front seat along with all the other ones only assures me of that. No book to be found at all. I close my eyes and begin to take a few, steady breaths. *Yeah, I left it at the hospital. That is the only rational answer.* I force myself to believe that to be true. A stressful day distorts the mind.

Leaving the gas station, I cruise along the dirt road. I wipe everything from my mind. It didn't occur. Any thoughts of the book are cast aside. That was a daydream. The rest of the drive to Gari and Antuna's place is fine. Everything is the same as always. I pull up in the driveway by the house.

They ask me what took so long. I parry that question. There is no way I'm telling them anything. I am the house guest. Hinting that I'm insane is not on my to-do list. When they inquire what I was doing all night, I stammer that some of my patients just wanted to talk for a while.

"I couldn't get away without being rude." The lie glides off my lips. With some light chit-chat I avoid the truth at all costs. Going into my bedroom, I prepare for a haunting night.

Chapter 6
Gari's Time

Sleeping is a hellish experience. A disappearing book floods my nightmares. Sadly, as I remember when I wake up, the gas station incident was a reality. I know I took the book in the car. It definitely disappeared. There is no question about it, no matter how much I wish there to be. I have to go back and see Mashilto about this immediately.

So, before Gari and Antuna even awake, I jump in the car. My destination is the hospital. Answers are needed once and for all. Eventually making it to his room, I find another nurse darting out. As I attempt to go in, she stops me.

"He needs to rest right now," the nurse sparks. "Could you possibly come back later?"

"Oh." I attempt to think up an excuse. I can't go another minute without knowing what that book is all about, and why it went missing. I am about to say that we're related, but, by my black skin, that may be hard to believe.

"He really wants to talk to me about something important. Can I just ask really quick? It will take two seconds."

"Well..." the nurse ponders the request, "I guess so; head on in."

I graciously thank her and rush into the room. Mashilto is, as expected, ignoring doctor's orders and watching television.

"Mashilto!" I wail into the room. I don't care how loud my voice is.

"Hello Dr. Alcott," he says with charm. "Such a pretty morning today; what can I do for you? How's Gari?"

"That book," I yell. "*'Altering Fate'*. You gave it to me yesterday, but then it disappeared! What's going on?"

"What book are you talking about?" He portrays utter confusion. My jaw drops at that statement. I know this guy is old, but he cannot possibly have forgotten all of last night.

"Yesterday," I state with defiance. "The one with magic, bringing people back from the dead."

"I don't know what you're talking about," Mashilto whimpers. He scratches his head to jog memory. "I'm very sorry, I've never owned a book like that in my life."

By his expression of complete confusion, I know he is telling the truth. Something is not right here. I stare at him for a few more seconds. Maybe if I wait a bit longer he will remember. Alas, he just sits in bafflement.

This silence is getting me nowhere. "It must have been someone else who gave it to me. Don't worry about it."

After more light-hearted conversation about Gari and television, I exit the room. I then schlep out of the hospital. My sadness is almost tangible. *The man's really old*, I tell myself. *That age is the premium time to forget important things. Amnesia is practically mandatory for someone like that. There's no other explanation*. At least, there's none I'm willing to accept.

So, over the next few days, I continue going to his room. Each time I inquire about the book. Every time without fail, he has no idea what it is. If he did, Mashilto said, his age must be causing memory loss.

I keep returning because I believe eventually

something will click. He has to remember something at some point. He agrees that magic and bringing back the dead are things he loves to discuss, but nothing about any book. Nobody else knows of it either. Not wanting to burden him anymore, I cease mentioning the situation. It was a dream. That is the end of it.

Over the next few months, things return to normal. The vivid hallucination departs my thoughts.

Gari is the one thing I have to concentrate on now. He does not have that long left on this planet. Everybody is aware of it. A crazy doctor is certainly not the last memory I want him to have. So, as the next few months pass by, everything returns to the way it was. These days are filled with wonderful times. Gari and I do so much and play so many exciting games. This is truly the life for me. Any haunting thoughts fade to bliss. That is, until today.

Gari has to be taken to the hospital. Though it is just a routine checkup, I hold no optimism. Neither I nor Antuna have seen anything obscure within him for quite some time. I have always done my job, making sure he is thriving and healthy at home. If ever an issue arises, I usually know exactly what procedures to take. Occasionally, I have to call the hospital and ask for minimal assistance. Eventually, everything works out.

As the three of us sit in the waiting room, I contemplate all the wonderful times we have been through. That happens every time we take Gari to the hospital. You never know when, of the three of us, only two will make it out.

Though pretty dark, it is a threatening reality. Antuna seems far more nervous than I am, tapping her feet nervously in the chair. She almost jumps when we're called. The person at the desk waves us in. Being his live-in, I am allowed to go into the room the whole time. In fact it is mandatory I do so.

I have to answer many questions about his living conditions and what I have been doing for him. It is all same old, same old. Nothing is unusual. However, something terrible occurs next. Once Gari finishes the x-rays and scans, the other doctor demolishes all hope.

"Gari," she whispers with compassion, "could you please head out with Nurse Terry while I talk to your guardians?"

"S…sure," he stammers, grasping the nurse's hand. The two stride out. Antuna and I know what is coming. This certainly is not going to be pleasant. We had originally been told a year, at most.

"The scans," she continues, "indicate, maybe, a week at the most. I'm very sorry to have to tell you this." Being a doctor as well, I need no explanation. I'm wholly aware what the scans indicate. Antuna glares at the ground. She's stunned with no escape. Her soul almost seems petrified. Gari knows it as well, despite him not hearing it directly. We can tell he is fully aware the end draws near.

Over the past few weeks, he has almost seemed excited. I would give anything for that courage. No negative attitudes from that boy. That is what I like the most about him. I wish Antuna and I could have that state of mind. It seems just the opposite for the both of us.

After some more medical mumbo-jumbo, we leave the hospital. She encourages us to make his last days the best they can be.

Don't even show an ounce of sadness, she advises. That is going be much easier said than done. Nonetheless, the effort has to be made. I have to try even if I can't succeed. Antuna and I act as chipper and joyful as possible. On the drive home, we sing along to the radio. The two of us wail at the top of our lungs. Gari sees through the transparent charade.

We finally arrive home. The darkness possesses an eerier feel than usual. Silence pierces through any courage. Gari rushes in to go use the bathroom. I am just beginning to get out of the car when Antuna bursts into tears. I knew this was coming. I am just surprised it took this long.

"I can't do this. I can't lose him. What am I going to do?" she cries into the night. The woman is demolished. Antuna then just sits there with her head planted in her lap. I just don't know what to do. Despite being a doctor, consoling was never my strong suit.

I have no idea how to respond. Pain pangs at my soul. It's like a monster manifests inside me with no way to break out. He's really going to die.

Chapter 7
The Decision

Washing my hands in the bathroom, I decide something. No matter how distraught I am, I'm pushing it aside. Gari deserves a true friend. I'm going to give him that. If that means watching him pass away it's what I'm going to do.

When I enter my room, everything in me comes to a jolting halt. The horror freezes time itself. Hairs on my neck stand on end. Bewilderment overwhelms all I know to be true. This cannot be happening. Not again.

'Altering Fate' lies on my bed. It rests adjacent to a fluffy pillow, perhaps lost in slumber for my arrival. I have not seen that thing for months. I was so sure that had been a dream. Now, that nightmare manifests once more into reality. The sight horrifies and distorts my senses; I begin wailing with all my might. Curling up into a ball, I break down on the carpet. I have truly lost my marbles.

Just then, Gari's voice echoes from down the stairs.

"Alcott!" he yells, dashing up. "Dr. Alcott!"

My jaw plummets. I'm petrified. He can't see me like this. Getting off the floor, I lunge for the book and grasp it. I will not have him thinking I'm insane before he goes. I turn my head swiftly contemplating my next move. Pitter-pattering of footsteps draws near. Eying the bed, I shove the thing under. I'm just in time as the door creaks open.

"What's wrong?!" he screams charging through the room. His wide eyes indicate sheer terror. Though I'm still freaking out, I attempt a nonchalant smile.

"Oh, nothing." I slump with false composure. My breathing is out of control. This does not help the situation at all. "I swear that sweater looked like a person in my room. I can't believe I'm so stupid." *Please buy it, Gari.*

"Don't do that to me!" he barks. "I thought you were hurt or something."

After both of us relax, he jumps up and rests on the bed with me.

Gari then speaks to me in an eerie tone.

"I'm really scared about dying. Where do you go when you die? Does it hurt? I know everybody does it. I'm sure I'm just being a baby, but when you're here," he pauses as tears well up, "I'm not really scared anymore. With you here, I can do it. Don't leave me now."

I'm literally speechless. What can I possibly say? How can I portray courage? I'm more scared of death than this kid! Thankfully he continues before I utter a response.

"Antuna said she wants to take me to my favorite ice cream place," Gari states with a happier expression. "It's pretty close by. Do you want to come?"

"I…" I respond, attempting to make up an excuse, "I think I need to rest for a bit. You guys should be together now."

After immediate protests from him, I finally convince him to leave without me. It kills me to decline the invitation. With that, he exits the room. I'm alone.

Right now, I guess I have to try. Despite waterfalls of sweat cascading from my forehead, I find strength. I drop to the ground. Crawling under the bed, I grab *'Altering Fate'*. My eyes scan through the chapters. I re-locate my destination, 'Bringing Back the Dead.' The same confusing directions flood the page. Various languages scramble my brain.

'I challenge fate, to change its course, for what it's done, needs to reverse.'

Ten times in a row this must be recited. I can't believe I'm actually doing this. A little kid is about to die and I'm playing with magic. The book creeps me out, especially the ghastly illustrations. Demonic images lunge at my soul. Once again, everything appears extremely vague.

The passage insists on journeying to a secluded place at nightfall. Well, I'm all by myself. So, with the book in hand, I march down the staircase. Piercing silence indicates I'm safe. Since I am the only one here, I feel no need to conceal the book. *How long has the book been there? Have I known about it, but have been repressing it? I'm surely out of my mind, so I've got nothing to lose.* Perhaps that mindset accelerates me forward.

So, I dash out of the house, knowing exactly where my destination is. It is quite spooky at night. Wind gusts as the mysterious cliffs beckon. If there is ever a place to do this thing, it's up there. As fast as I can, I dart up the dark forest path. Impulse motivates me alone.

I repeat the phrase to myself. It must be ingrained in my mind. Opening the gigantic book again would prove far too much of a nuisance. Trudging up the pathway, I panic. What if this spell actually does something?

I stomp over various sticks and stones. Despite my heartbeat, nature proves to be quite tranquil. I'm disrupting the peace of the land. Finally, I arrive at the top. It's now or never. Gazing up at a star, I chant the phrase.

About the fifth time of repeating the phrase, I'm surely insane. Many night-walkers on the beach would probably attest to that. I don't really care.

"I challenge fate, to change its course, for what it's done, needs to reverse." Still the eighth time now and nothing seems to happen. I'm already a complete psycho; might as well keep going. What have I got to lose?

Chapter 8
Impossible

I recite it ten times with perfect enunciation. Nothing happens. Everything remains eerily still. No insect screeches sound, and the wind suddenly fades.

A microscopic wave crashes against the sand. All turns to silence. I never expected anything would occur. Still, I feel the universe stabbed me in the heart. All of that is for completely nothing. I stride back down the path, chastising myself for not spending every moment with Gari. I should've gone to the ice cream store with them. Yet, here I am chanting into the soulless abyss.

However, something strange solidifies. As I stride, the wind immediately picks up. Delicate gusts evolve into whirlwinds.

Trees sway uncontrollably with each gale. Could a tornado be brewing? Being up this high is not wise. Leering back, the sky thunders out of nowhere! Rain slams down, almost like a flash flood type of deal. The weather channel stated clear skies all night. I don't know what could possibly be going on.

There is no way that I, nor this book, could have really set this off, right? That book is just fiction. I only tried it because I promised Mashilto. This is all a dream; there is no way it magically appeared on my bed anyway! I'm so stupid! It's time to wake up now, though for some odd reason I remain. *Wake up now!*

A voice whimpers in the unknown darkness…

"Alcott…" The tone mirrors the time in the car. A

creepy message is practically implanted in my ear. I lose grip of the book. It crashes into the dirt. Crumpled pages whirl up in the wind. It sounds as if a little child has whispered my name. Then, a new voice emerges in an uproar.

"Alcott!" it yelps, almost that of an elderly person; this time sounding as if on top of the cliff. This completely contrasts the first. I'm frozen in my tracks.

"Alcott," a third voice repeats in an infant's cry. The baby shouts my name in a diabolical giggle. A million voices immediately follow, chiming in sheer rage across the crisp air. I'm trapped in a nightmare. My sanity is chipped away with each new shout. Cacophonous lightning bolts flash above me in the black sky. Covering my eyes, I huddle down onto dirty ground, abandoning myself in the screams.

"Wake up!" I continually wail. It just will not seem to happen. After about five minutes of holding myself there, I decide to peek. Lifting one hand from my eye, I realize everything is frozen. Just as before, all is muted. The little insects I detect on the ground aren't moving, while the trees appear fake. They are merely artist creations painted into the landscape.

Time itself no longer exists, if that makes any sense at all. At that moment, I realize that the book is gone. The ruined pages have vanished as well. It lay adjacent to my feet one minute, and now is nowhere to be found. You'd think I'd be used to that by now.

Rushing to the cliff once more, I realize the ocean has become a dark blanket. Each white foam pauses in mid-crash. On the horizon, a shimmering gold dot hovers. Squinting, I see the dot growing in size and luminosity. It is definitely coming towards me; there's no doubt about that.

The gold dot materializes. It undergoes an immense

evolution. Arriving on the cliff is a woman dressed in gold attire. She stands in elegance and dominance, as if portraying her status above my own. The woman gazes off at the ocean, as if mesmerized by the way she herself arrived. There was certainly no one there before.

Did the book speak of this person? I stumble up for a better view. My legs shake with fear as she never averts her stare.

The only thing I can do is watch. I gaze in utter bewilderment. The hair on my neck stands on end as the woman swings around. Her gleaming white eyes peer right into my soul.

"Hello, my child!" the god wails at high volume. Half the city must hear her. "I am one of many Jauntla, guardians of life within the universe. You have called upon my powers, have you not?" My mind is blown right now. The little speck from across the horizon is actually talking to me! Maybe I really have gone completely crazy.

"I...I..." I am rendered speechless. I can't even form any words in my brain, never mind from my mouth. What should I say to that?

"It's okay, child, I'm not evil. I'm good. I'm not going to eat you, unless you have some cocktail sauce of course...everything tastes better with cocktail sauce!" She bursts into an uproar of laughter at her own joke. I smile as well, beginning to feel a bit less woozy.

I wobble about, almost standing up once again.

"I know why you called, Alcott. Gari's passing is not something you're willing to accept, is it?" She does not beat around the bush.

"Life is unexpected and many times...unpleasant," the Jauntla states, eyes locked with an ant on the dirt. "Creatures just go."

"But..." I stammer my words. "It's just not fair;

he's so young and has so much to do for the world."

"What makes you think you have the power to challenge fate, Alcott?" The Jauntla glares fire.

"I don't know what I'm supposed to do." I honestly have no idea what I'm saying. "The boy is so young. It just doesn't seem fair." I look down at my feet. Look who's the shy one now.

"Well," she responds. "Changing fate's course is… a tricky thing. It isn't something one does without serious thought and determination." She gazes back off at the horizon. "To change fate's course, there's something you're going to have to know."

"What is it?" I ask.

Her tone ascends to hellish decibels.

"If he is granted a full life, you're going to have to take his place."

Chapter 9
It Begins

"Give up my own life?" I stammer to myself. The five words send chills up my spine. The whole notion is surreal. Am I really ready to give up my life? Already?! My forehead throbs with stress.

"You must decide now, Alcott," the Jauntla proclaims with crossed arms. Gold shimmers off each slight jerk of her shirt. Each speck hypnotizes.

She horrifies every ounce of me. Peering directly at her, I feel my chest shake in terror. My watery eyes hover. This is just far too much, and I can't handle the situation anymore. I burst into tears, tumbling to the grass with a thump.

"I don't...know if I can do that," I reply through sobs. I feel like a kindergartener who just got detention.

"Well, then. Gari must pass. Unless you agree to surrender your life to me, I cannot let you compete in the Obstacles."

"The Obstacles?" I mumble.

"Yes," she barks. "The Obstacles are testing trials for those who wish to challenge death. If you win enough, the death cycle will be reversed. The victorious competitor must then take the victim's place. It is the only way."

"Alcott," the demon peers into my soul, unraveling every bit of my fortitude, "will you give up your life or not?" Lightning flashes in the darkness. Her outrage is obvious and nature portrays it. She expects an answer now.

Memories of Gari flood through my mind. His face

lights up with a fresh piece of pie. The smile contains hope and happiness, something uncommon for many. My terror suddenly transforms into self-contempt. *I'm in my thirties. Gari is a nine-year-old kid. I haven't lived a long life, not by a long shot. That little guy, however, doesn't even get to live a short one.*

That reasoning could be the main cause of my next response. Perhaps I'm sick of being a pathetic coward. My horror of death has always embarrassed me. What good is life if all I can do is worry about losing it? My mind trails back to me in that dream. *I was a feeble mess. That person makes me physically sick. If I can help it, maybe I can actually save two people here.*

"Yes," I rise with eyes closed, "I'll give up my life." The words glide off my tongue.

A strange sensation manifests in my heart. Could this surge of energy be relief I'd given an answer to the Jauntla? Maybe this feeling is fear. After a few deep breaths, I figure out what's going on. This must be bravery. I've never felt it before, and I can't help but grin at the notion. I'm actually proud of myself right now.

The Jauntla must notice this as well. She half smiles with rising eyebrows. "Alcott, you're now a competitor in the Obstacles."

Now comes all the rules and regulations of what's going to happen. It seems pretty complicated, and very strict indeed. These Obstacles are to prove that I am a worthy warrior and can truly challenge fate. She goes into deep detail, constantly stressing they are for the best of the best.

"There are six Obstacles," she states with confidence, "and you are only allowed to fail three. If you fail four of the six, everything goes back to normal and time resumes from the moment the phrase was repeated.

You will have no memory of any of this. Life will just continue. The person you were trying to save will die as planned."

"Time has stopped," she states in a somber tone. "It will resume when you have either passed three of the six obstacles, or failed four of them." *That's pretty tough odds. How can I possibly pass these Obstacle thingies?* Nervousness creeps into my heart, and fear returns. Positive, once again, that this is a dream, I calm myself down. Now I can interpret what she has to say.

"Four others have recited this phrase within the past year, and are exactly in the position you are now. Each of them wishes to save the life of someone, too. The Obstacles cannot begin until five people summon me; that day is today. You, Alcott, are the fifth."

This is all getting too much to handle. I can't even process what is going on at the moment. Who would these other four be? Would I have to compete with them? How does anyone else even know about this spell thing? So many questions need answers. I'm just too petrified to ask any of them.

"These four will be your Allies," she says. "They will fight alongside you for some of the challenges, though much must be accomplished on your own."

I am a little relieved at this point. Mostly for not finding out I am crazy by chanting a spell to the night sky. Other people seem to be in the exact same position. At least, this is what she says. Apparently, I will not have to make this journey alone. I am almost excited, in a way, to see who my fellow fighters are going to be. Of course, throughout most of this I think I will wake up soon. However, there's an equal amount of hope there too. What if I don't?

"I do not understand. When do these Obstacle

things start? Where do they happen? Where are these other four people?" I bombard her with tons of questions, those just being the top four. Instead of going into deep detail, she just instructs me to relax and take deep breaths.

"All will make sense to you in time. For now, prepare yourself to embark on an amazing journey. It will require extreme fortitude, strength, hope, and determination. Not having one of these qualities will surely lead to failure," she sparks, not shying away from the reality of the situation.

"So, what happens if I fail?" I implore her to answer. "I don't understand."

"As I've told you," she continues. "Everything will go back to normal as if nothing had ever happened. Your memory will be wiped, and you will remember none of this, not even the book. Who you are trying to save will, indeed, die."

"Can I go back and see Gari and Antuna one last time before the Obstacle things start?" I ask, rubbing my forehead.

"No, Alcott," she says without hesitation. "Time has frozen; you couldn't see them even if you tried. I'm terribly sorry to spring all of this on you at once, but, as you know, you are the one who read the chant. Now, it is time for us to go on a wonderful journey. Prepare to endure and battle, for every force within you will be required."

That last statement frightens me. These challenges sound like they will be extremely horrifying, maybe even impossible. How in the world am I possibly going to do this? I feel ashamed for being so scared.

"Okay," I sigh, despite everything in me advising to dart back in the house and crawl underneath the bed. "I guess…I'm ready."

With that, she lifts up her arms emanating the

brilliance of her majesty. An endless amount of sparkles fill the sky. Her index finger extends to the horizon. There is a stark determination in her eyes.

She shouts into the ocean breeze…"Let the Obstacles begin!"

Chapter 10
Embark

Immediately, the whirlwind rises once more. Where the Jauntla had stood, I view literally nothing. She was there a second ago, but now completely vanished. Looking all around, I realize I'm the only one. There is no way I imagined that scenario. The apprehension begins to overtake logic. My mind battles between fear, strength, courage, and confusion.

"Alcott, Alcott, Alcott." Voices chant, to my astonishment. *What did I get myself into? How can I even trust this Jauntla? She may be a demon or something; how am I supposed to know? Perhaps I should have read 'Altering Fate' more carefully. Just because it magically appears in places doesn't mean it is all good. Did Mashilto know all of this was going to happen? There is no way this is what he had been ranting about all that time.*

I pray for any trace of her jaunting up to the cliff. The whirlwind's intensity increases. Without even noticing, my eyes dart around to discover I have been lifted off the ground. What seemed like a millisecond had gone by and I am fifty feet in the air. I stare into the darkness wailing at the top of my lungs! I glance all around. All I can detect are the tops of trees. The voices are becoming way too much for me to handle. I can't even concentrate on what is going on anymore.

As I look around, the sky transforms into an eerie cobalt blue magic. Everything around me alters as if I am traveling inside a star. Colorful waves of blue and pink surround me. There is no top, bottom, or any sides visible. I am in nothingness at this point.

Floating through this unknown, I discover a small square type of object. It rests under me quite a ways away. I am somehow levitated closer. The square materializes into a huge platform. It appears glass-like and transparent. Descending quickly, I see other people on the platform as well. Could they be the Allies, or whatever that the Jauntla is talking about? These are the four I assume I shall fight alongside.

My body slows toward the platform. Each of them retains a fixed gaze upon me. By the same calm demeanor they have, it is safe to assume my arrival is expected.

All four of them continue their firm stares. I take a swift drop to this glassy platform. I have never seen any of them before; they are complete strangers. One of them appears to be very young. She portrays a pureness and longing in her bubbling eyes.

"Nice to meet you!" some burly guy shouts. I rotate toward that direction. "My name is Travis. We're all so happy you finally arrived." This man, Travis, looks to be in his twenties. He seems quite tall and confident. A belly bulges underneath a t-shirt. A beard and mustache overtake his face.

"Thank you, it's very nice to meet you all too," I reply, immediately becoming anxious with all of them watching. "I am Alcott. What are all your names?"

"Gretchen," utters what looks like a thirty or so year old woman. She's extremely welcoming, while still containing a hidden side. Gretchen appears older than Travis and the girl. Bright red cheeks and short blonde hair make her prominent.

"How do you do?" she squeaks with a delightful tone. The positivity is contagious.

"Fine, thanks," I reply. Based on that statement, I assume she is proper.

"And what's your name?" I bend down to the little child.

The little girl's scared to death of me. The fact that a child is here astounds me. I can't imagine this little kid is doing what I am. Could she really give up her life? The idea baffles me.

"Vit...taly..." she whispers. This girl is ashamed of her stammer. "Vitaly."

"Well, it's wonderful to meet you Vitaly." I gleam a bright smile. I attempt to imitate how I greet patients at the hospital.

"What's your name?" I ask another girl. She has her back turned to me. Her crossed arms indicate extreme hostility. What did I ever do to her?

"That's Marya," Gretchen chirps. "She's not in the best place right now. Please don't take her behavior seriously." She shoots a glare at Marya, embarrassed she must speak for her.

Despite her attitude, I am very pleased with these people. Aside from my initial fear, they appear a pretty awesome bunch. It's so much more comforting to find other people.

"So," I inquire. "When did you all get here? You guys are my Allies...or something, aren't you?"

"Yes," Gretchen responds, strongly smiling again. "We are doing the exact same thing you want to do; save somebody's life. We're all...willing to die to do so, even the little kid. We've been on this platform for quite a while now, anticipating your arrival. We were told that a fifth person had summoned the lifesaving spell, and that our adventure is about to begin."

"Really?" I ask, surprised at that. *Hadn't this*

happened moments ago? At least, I'm pretty sure it was just a little while ago. Nothing makes any sense anymore. Guess that's not going to change. "So what have you all been doing before I arrived?"

"Well, after each of us said the, you know, chant thing ten times," Travis states in a gruff voice, "we were immediately taken to a beautiful mansion to await the rest of the challengers; a spectacular place to be. I was the first to arrive and have been there for four weeks."

"It is truly wonderful," Gretchen adds, supporting Travis' claim. "I came second and didn't ever want to depart. A full staff attended to breakfast, lunch, and dinner. All of this is located by a spectacular beach. It is a sort of waiting ground until five people recite the spell. Now that you're here, I guess we're ready to start."

So, apparently there is this mansion where they all were waiting for the fifth spell chanter. Since I am the fifth one to do so, their wait has now come to an end.

"Why don't I get to go to this mansion?!" I ask with jealousy. *It sounds like paradise there. I don't even get to go?*

"Oh well," Gretchen frowns. "It wasn't all it was cracked up to be. It is more nerve-racking than anything, Alcott. Just waiting and waiting patiently every day, terrified of whatever these Obstacle things will be. I would've taken your place in a heartbeat."

"Still, maybe I'll just be the number one for the next five people," I attempt to make a stupid joke. "You guys can wait for another one." Jesting seems like the best way to make friends. It seems to have worked because everyone laughs.

"I doubt that's an option for you," Travis still smiles. "Besides, I, for one, am ready for this to begin." He's obviously the most determined of the group.

"Don't be sad, Alcott," Vitaly whispers, tugging on my leg. "I've only been there one day; it's not that great."

"Oh, I'm only kidding, Vitaly, but thank you," I tell her with a joyful tone. She's the nicest person in the entire world at the moment. It really scares me that this little kid is going to enter this thing.

"So, did everyone else talk to a Jauntla in gold or am I just going crazy?" I still am convinced this is all a dream. I don't even know what's real anymore. Might as well see where this goes.

"Yep," Gretchen responds first. She's obviously the chipper one of them. "She appeared to all of us out of nowhere at all. None of us thought that what we are seeing is real, but," as she twirls her hand around, "looks like it is."

"Yeah," Travis adds. He seems more the logical one as well. "We all spoke the same spell and she soared in from the horizon. Gretchen's right, though, I never expected anything to happen when I said it."

"Huh, that's interesting," I say. "It's just great to find out everybody else saw her too."

"Mmmhmm," Vitaly states. "We've all been there. It's pretty scary."

"Well one thing is for sure," Travis adds. "We're all here for the same reason; we want to reverse the course of death."

"And one other thing as well." Gretchen glares at Marya once more. "If we succeed, we must take the place of the one we are trying to save."

They obviously had all been through the same spiel. I wonder why I am not waking up. *My life may seriously be in jeopardy. Despite how welcoming all of them are, being reminded that I could die is just too much. This can't really be happening, can it?!* The extreme insanity of the situation demolishes every inch of me. All fades. Darkness overtakes my falling eyelids.

"Oh no, fainting again," Gretchen states before the endless haze.

Chapter 11
Preparation

Darkness abandons me. Consciousness returns. The platform seems to have disappeared. We are somewhere completely new now. No more blue magic type of deal surrounding every ounce of sky. Swerving and rotating around, I take this scene in. An armrest juts into my torso, causing me to grimace in pain. Two other seats rest to the right of the one I'm in now.

All are crammed in tight together. To the left of me a long aisle extends. I realize I have been transported to an airplane. Blinking to affirm my new location, I see the other four sitting near me.

"He's up!" Gretchen yells from the seat across. Her blurry form becomes slightly more visible. "Fetch him some water, will you?"

"Got it!" Travis shouts in response. I detect the fuzzy image of him jaunting up to me with a bottle in hand. "Here ya go, Alcott. Drink up!"

My mind is clouded with delusion. It doesn't seem to be subsiding at all. *Why are these people still here?!* Everything is going out of control in my head. This can't possibly be real, but I'm not waking up. *Get me out of this dream right now!*

"Thank you," I drowsily stammer. "So this isn't a dream, is it?"

"Nope," Gretchen sparks. She seems to be the realist. "Took us all a very long time to realize that, Alcott. Every one of us thought we were crazy at first; don't worry yourself."

I crawl over the seats to view an enormous body of water below. Purple clouds hover in navy sky. Hawks soar valiantly through them. The sight is breathtaking. Breaking myself from the trance, I attempt to answer some questions. *Who is in charge here?* So, I summon the strength. My shaky limbs walk down the aisle to the cockpit.

Distancing herself from everyone else, I find Marya sitting. She rotates her head away as I pass. This girl is really not a kind person. I shake my head and continue on.

Against my better judgment, I barge into the cockpit. Alas, I discover nothing in any flying seat.

No pilot is in here; nobody. It appears similar to any other aircraft I have viewed, with endless dials and gadgets. Just seems like there is nobody here to fly it. I guess nothing makes sense anymore; better start accepting that fact. Stumbling back to my original seat, I rub my forehead in bewilderment.

"Where are we going, now?" I inquire to these people.

"To the contract room," Vitaly replies. Her swift answer startles me. "They said that we have to firmly state our cause of what we are going to do before this all begins."

"A contract?" I ask, a bit taken back. "What are they going to do if we disobey something, throw us in imaginary jail?" Even the idea of signing anything strikes a new fear. There always seems to be some dreadful loophole in these things…

"I don't know," Travis says, shifting his shoulders upwards. "We know just about as much as you do at this point." He appears angry at not being told any proper information.

"If she transported me to the platform thing by

magic," I wonder, "how come we are in a plane? This seems a little low tech, compared to magic travel. Can't we get there the same way?" Oh no, it seems I've already become accustomed to this fantasy.

"A strange voice said," Gretchen turns towards me, "during your little fainting incident, that this plane ride is supposed to be a bonding experience for all of us. We need to learn each other's strengths, weaknesses, reasons for getting into this, and so on."

"Well that makes sense, I guess."

"Most of us know each other somewhat well, Alcott," Gretchen adds. "It's you we know nothing about. You appear to be in the best shape of all of us, so I'm assuming we'll be relying on you for most of these uh… Obstacles."

"Oh, I hadn't considered that." My eyes shift to the floor.

I do seem to be in the best physical condition of the group. That stacks pressure on my shoulders. I don't enjoy pressure. *What are they going to do if I don't succeed in these challenges?* I'm not fond of criticism either.

"So, Alcott," Travis lowers his eyebrows. "Who are you?"

"Um, I don't know." Wow, there's the answer of the year. I can never find the right thing to say. My eyes travel to the floor again, hoping my shyness will make them all disappear.

"Well," Gretchen lightens the mood with a grin. "What's your job?"

So, I attempt to tell my story. I don't enjoy telling strangers how much I'm afraid of death. However, I guess that's a pretty important aspect. It's difficult revealing Gari's life, nonetheless I do the best I can.

"That was really nice of you Alcott," Vitaly's eyes

water. "He's got a great doctor."

"Thank you so much," I respond. A spooky fact suddenly dawns on me. This little girl does not appear that far off from Gari's age.

"What could you possibly be doing here? You're just a baby?!" My shock bursts into an uproar.

"Her story is pretty complicated," Gretchen raises eyebrows. "None of us can really understand it. I'm not sure I even believe it."

"Well," Vitaly glares at Gretchen, obviously upset by the doubt. "My dad is the ruler of a large country on Neptune." She speaks so nonchalantly. The tone suggests this is elementary information.

"Neptune?!" I scream, flabbergasted. "There's life on other planets?" There's a new batch of insane information.

"Oh yeah," Vitaly turns towards me. "I forgot you just got here. But yes, you guys just haven't discovered us yet. Even though we are both human, I can just survive under slightly different conditions than you. I'll explain more later. Well, my dad is the king of Nepothria.

"Other countries aren't exactly happy with us, for many reasons. I'm still really young, so I don't know too much. However, I know that my dad is an excellent diplomat. He's the only reason we lasted this long," she frowns.

"It might have been over invasion or lack of food, but they are very upset. My dad is the only one keeping them at bay."

This is all insane. There's life on other planets. They have rulers. They are human. I can't believe what I am hearing from this little kid. Well, life can't get any crazier at this point, so I might as well just listen for enjoyment. What could it hurt? I'll wake up and forget all of this soon anyway.

"Well, a rebel shot him." Her icy words pierce my heart.

Deep silence envelops the plane. Nobody knows how to respond.

"Oh no, I'm so sorry." I can't imagine losing a parent that young.

"It's okay; I mean I always knew it was an extreme possibility. Even when I was six years old I could tell. After he was murdered, Nepothria was bombarded. In only a day, rebels flooded the city and burned everything. It was then some street magician beckoned me over. In the darkness, he offered me the book, *'Altering Fate'*. I cast it off as insanity. Even when I tried to get rid of the book, it had a way of… coming back to me, you might say."

"That's what I used!" I yell with utter bliss. Travis leaps back at my high volume. "It disappeared and appeared magically on me too!" I am relieved to be affirmed, again, that I am not alone. The ancient book had done its tricks on her as well.

"It's what we all used," Vitaly states. "Apparently this book lies across the solar system…and seems to certainly have a mind of its own."

Gretchen peers out the window, as if the unknown terrifies her.

"Yeah, well this magician believed it could bring back the dead. So, I thought I might as well try. If I can't save my dad, the entire country will be demolished."

Well, that is an eye-opener. I can't believe it. She has a whole country at bay.

"Wow, are the rest of you…aliens too?" I ask, getting a bit…just a bit more alarmed.

"No, we're earthbound just like you. She's the only one traveling from another planet," Travis assures me.

"Yeah, the book had its little vanishing act with me, as well. Alcott, I can't say I'm charging for a whole country," Gretchen spoke, "but I am fighting for something pretty special; my sister, Sharia."

Travis and Gretchen then give their stories. Gretchen's sister, Sharia, had down-syndrome. She charged after a squirrel hoping to rescue it from oncoming traffic. The squirrel darted away just in time. Sharia did not.

Biking along the cliffs, Travis and his father encountered tragedy. All it took was two seconds of not paying attention. His dad's body now rests down amongst the scattered rocks.

"You've never told us your story, Marya," Travis says, trying to alter the subject. Speaking it obviously made his mood grim.

Marya hadn't spoken this whole time. She made no attempt to display her existence. Something must be severely upsetting this young woman.

"I don't want to talk about it," she sparks back. Marya doesn't even turn to make eye contact. She seriously has an attitude problem.

"Marya," Gretchen's angelic voice proclaims. "It would be better to talk about it. We're here for you."

"I don't want to talk about it!" Marya wails this time. The uproar shocks us all, and I can't even comprehend what just happened. Gretchen's jaw drops wide open in shock.

"Well," Gretchen snarls. "Fine then!"

She turns back to the window, her blissful attitude demolished. Everyone is speechless at this point.

"Drunk driving," Marya mutters. The dark words hover across the aisle. Nobody attempts to get anything more out of her.

Chapter 12
Signing Everything Away

The plane spurts a peculiar gurgle. Descending with increasing acceleration, it pauses on an instant. After the turbulence subsides, a raspy voice wails over the intercom.

"Please exit through the door to the right of the plane, challengers. Thank you very much for your consideration."

"Walk out onto a cloud?" Gretchen's lowered eyebrows indicate abhorrence. "What are they talking about?!"

"Doesn't look like we got a choice," Travis jerks up immediately. The side door opens, revealing a pathway outside. The glassy substance does not look promising. I'm almost positive now that it contains the same material as that platform. Still, I'm not fully willing to walk out onto that thing. Travis glides out first.

"Well, let's go." Vitaly jaunts out the door after him.

I depart last. With one last glance into the deserted aisle, I leap out. Gusts of wind brush against my cheeks.

The airplane's engine buzzes. The uproar causes my eardrums to throb. After a few seconds, it soars away on its own. The lack of any pilot still freaks me out. It heads directly back whence it brought us.

As we stride along, a shimmering stairway manifests in the distance. I close my eyes in terror. Heights and I are not chums. A few deep breaths only make the situation worse.

Clouds block most visibility around me. Still, we all

just keep climbing. Each time I raise my foot my heart panics. One false slip and I'm off into the atmosphere. My body will plummet below to demise. Nobody else exhibits this fear. That makes me feel great.

We eventually arrive at the top of the stairs. An enormous platform juts out from the final step. I let out a sigh as I step onto it, relieved to be on steadier ground.

Five giant parchments hover throughout. Each stands about five feet tall, equally spaced apart. The sight of them pierces my soul. They resemble five alligators waiting to devour us. Upon further inspection, I realize these are contracts. Each of our names has been written at the top. As I suspect, my contract is the fifth from the start. I was the fifth to summon the Obstacles, after all. My eyes lock with the cursive 'Alcott' at the top of the parchment.

An uproarious bird call pierces the air. All of our eyes dart up. A colossal falcon soars into the vicinity. Its shimmering wings glide through gentle gusts. Specs of gold trail its flight. I've never laid eyes on any creature so breathtaking. The beast's eyes are slits with no visible pupils. It could be looking anywhere.

It almost bashes Marya's head gliding past the five of us. My eyebrows lower as I peer under it. The sturdy talons carry something. Opening them, five objects plummet to the platform. Vitaly rushes over with wide eyes. Examining the things, she draws a conclusion.

"They're pens!" she calls with a click of one. I charge over to her confirming it. Each black pen contains white writing near the cap. I grasp one and rotate it. The name "Vitaly" is carved in cursive.

"Alcott," she whimpers almost afraid to interject. "I think you have mine."

"Sorry." I hand her that one. Reaching for my designated writing tool, I can't help but examine it with awe. I can't believe this is actually happening. My name is actually on this thing.

Glancing around, I believe the other Allies have the same sensation. Pens in hand, we move to the hovering contracts. The enormous paper leers down at me. Various law terms and legal mumbo-jumbo flood the thing. I don't understand more than half of it. My heartbeat accelerates as each line I skim appears as gibberish. Breathing gets swifter. *Oh no*, I inwardly chastise myself. *Not another panic attack.*

Finally, my eyes reach the bottom. A long dotted line extends from one end to the other. Despite my ignorance, I surely know what this part means. *This is where I sign my life away.*

"Succeed in three of the six Obstacles, the death cycle will reverse. They shall be granted long life, and you, death. Fail four of the Obstacles and life returns to normal. Your memory shall be wiped clean. None of these events ever occurred. They will die."

The last three words are like poison. Glancing over at Vitaly, I pray someone else is as terrified as me. However, she portrays nothing but utter bravery. She practically carves her name into the contract. I peer around to the others, discovering them signing as well. Nobody, apparently, has any hesitation but me. Closing my eyes, I summon all the fortitude within.

I've lived a good life, and I suppose it doesn't have to be long. Who's to say I'm even going to win anyway? Besides, I'm in too deep now.

Despite my hand shaking into oblivion, I write my name on the dotted line. A silver hue illuminates my name. It gleams like a tranquil lake in moonlight. The contract whisks off into the sky before I blink. This happens so swiftly I barely realize it. Rotating around, I discover every other contract vanished. That's it, then.

"Thank you for your patience, warriors," a mysterious voice echoes in the distance. All of us glance around to find no source of it.

"The time to test your strength is almost at hand. All of you are signed and bound to your decision; there is no turning back. The Obstacles are now ready to begin. The first one will be done individually. It will be a test of strength, determination, and skill. Of course, each of your tests will be different, corresponding to your life experiences and hurdles."

What could that possibly mean? They are going to delve into my childhood. How much can these people know about my life? This is all starting to freak me out, as usual. I have to keep my mind steady if I'm going to have a chance at all. Besides, the fear in Antuna's eyes was just as terrifying.

"Good luck to all of you; we will meet again after the Obstacle. Begin!"

Begin?! It's actually already starting. I thought there would be more time to prepare. Guess I get none at all. I hyperventilate immediately. Darkness envelops every bit of the world around me.

Could I be asleep? Will I wake up? Perhaps I'm fainting. Maybe I'm just dead. It could be any of those possibilities.

"Vitaly, Travis, Marya, Gretchen!" I scream into the unyielding abyss. I receive no answer. My Allies are gone. Whatever's going to happen, I'm facing it alone.

"Alcott, Alcott, Alcott," voices chant. They alternate between boisterous wails and soft whispers. The combination is far too haunting. Roars continue, taunting me no end. It feels as if a new voice joins each second. They show no sign of subsiding. Suddenly, I feel myself plunging into some sort of liquid. As the water hits my thighs, everything is silent. My hands paddle to keep me afloat.

Extreme light pushes into my closed eyes. I delicately open them to find an entirely new world. An ocean breeze caresses my cheeks. Tiny waves splash onto my face. Blackness no longer remains. Glancing around, I discover that I am swimming. My toes can detect no sense of a bottom. Turning in a swift circle, I find no land around in any direction. The dark realization is impossible to evade. *I am alone in the middle of a vast ocean.*

Chapter 13
Monster

What am I supposed to do? Do I have to swim somewhere? Am I going to have to cross an entire ocean?

At least ten minutes pass by, and nobody tells me anything. Blue water chips my sanity away with each wave. The delicate splash in my face drives me to madness. So far, my only course of action remains floating and kicking. My eyes scan the puffy clouds. Something appears a bit peculiar. One cloud appears slightly different than the others. It hovers in the sky away from the rest. Raising my hand to block the sun rays, I detect a message. Bulky words are practically carved into the cloud.

'Kill the thing that hunts you down, to beat this test and win the crown. But if the hunter does you in, forever shame you'll earn within.'

A hunter? Something is going to attack me. Part of me wishes I never read that. Perhaps I could've been devoured in peaceful oblivion. Now, I know what's coming. How can I possibly defeat it without any weapons? My helpless body flails in the water. Peering all around, I see nothing but me and the never-ending water. Where will this hunter come from?

Something manifests a little ways away. This thing definitely wasn't there before. I would've noticed it. I quickly realize a large rope extends from above. It ends just above the surface of the water. Waves delicately crash below.

Looking up, it appears to hover in mid-air. I'm

certainly not complaining despite all laws of physics being thrown out the window. A strange box at the top contains a flashing message.

My heart lifts at the opportunity. At least I have some hope now. Hopefully this thing can hold me. If not, I'm pretty much doomed.

Using all my stamina, I paddle. I extend each arm with all my might. Swimming has always been a fun activity; now it's hell. The ocean is now my enemy, keeping me away from my one chance at safety. Anything can snatch me and eat me. Shoving water back with each kick, I actually make it.

My limbs tingle in discomfort. Without any hesitation, I jump for the rope. My hand misses by a few inches. My body crashes back into the ocean waves. It was a pathetic attempt anyway. Part of me knew it to be in vain.

I somehow manage to keep my head above water. Flailing a bit, I paddle back to the location. This time I refuse to miss. Eyes squinting with determination, I lunge for the knot.

No sign of any hunter yet. My right hand grasps the rough knot. Success! Pulling as hard as I can, I raise my body out of the ocean. Water drips from my soggy shirt and shorts. One hand replaces the other as I ascend the rope.

Horror then manifests once more. An eerie tail fin emerges from the clash of waves up ahead. The triangular slit swerves through the waves with ease. This is a sight any beach dweller cringes at. I'm no idiot. I know what lurks underneath the water. A dark terror arises in my soul. *Can I really conquer a shark?*

Chapter 14
Courage

Trembling fingers clutch the rope tighter than ever. I dart toward the top. The agility of this beast strikes a near fear in me. It swiftly eliminates the distance between us.

The sharp curve of the fin could tear me open in a heartbeat. That's not even thinking about the body attached; no need to think about that. A murky shadow lurks on the surface. It grows more enormous by each second.

Breaking myself from the trance, I continue up. My brain depends on the 'out of sight, out of mind' tactic. However, that proves to be useless. Not looking only makes everything worse. I'm about halfway to the top now. I let out a sigh of relief despite the fact I'm probably not safe.

The box at the top becomes clearer than before. Bright green numbers illuminate the box. It doesn't take long to realize what it is. Every second, a number decreases in value. This must be a timer of some sort. The discovery brings on a whole new worry. *What is going to happen when the numbers run out?*

The timer states one minute and thirty-nine seconds remain. *What could that possibly mean? What's going to happen after the timer goes out? Is the rope going to move or something?* In the midst of my panic, the fin maneuvers around the bottom knot. It appears even more giant this close. A very taunting shark shadow is now slightly visible through the water. I am not excited to see the rest of the body up close. This animal looks so enormous; I wouldn't be surprised if it surpasses fifteen feet in length. The shark circles around the rope. Each new revolution feels like a demonic attempt at hypnosis. My eyes are locked with each swerve it makes.

I can do nothing but hold on for dear life. I'm utterly powerless. All I can do is wait patiently to become dinner. Just then, something comes into view at the top of the timer. Despite the horrific circumstances, I can't help but grin.

Sheer joy courses through my veins as I detect a weapon. Upon further inspection, I discover a deadly knife. The blade's tip sticks out from on top of the timer. Thankfully, I finally have some hope, even though that hope is microscopic. The timer now states one minute and ten seconds. At least now I can acquire a knife, but I somehow doubt this will be enough to take on this creature. I finally pull my body to the top. My arm lunges for the knife. Grasping the handle, I gaze back down. The shark's speed has accelerated. Each revolution causes me to grab the knife tighter. It's getting impatient with me.

One minute left.

I'm certainly not going to leap out and attack this thing. All I have is a measly knife. That course of action has nothing but death written all over it. I have no other choice but to wait for this timer. Once it counts down to zero, we'll see what happens.

My heart has never beaten so fast in my entire life. If there was ever a time for a nervous breakdown, it's now. Again I pray that this is all a dream. Sadly, that hope is completely vanished now. I wrap my other arm around the timer box.

Twenty seconds left, the green numbers flash. I close my eyes. *This isn't real! Come on!*

I wail into the winds, "Get me out of here!" Maybe one of these Obstacle people can get me out. There's no way I can win this.

"I can't do this!" Alas, only silence ensues. No one's coming to help me now.

Ten seconds left. The creature splashes around the rope at an even faster pace now. It is almost as if it knows something is up. How can I possibly fight something that intelligent? I begin to scream and yell at the box, as if that will change anything in the situation. Beating it with my fist, I try desperately to make it stop. To no avail, the numbers continue counting down.

Five seconds left. The bright green numbers flash to a fearsome red. I know what that indicates; the deadly warning of what is to come. With each drop of a second, the timer releases a piercing horn.

"Errrrrnnnn!" it roars like an alarm clock. However, there's no snooze button for me this time. My eyes open wide as I prepare for my worst nightmare to come true.

Three…Two…One…

The rope vanishes into thin air, taking the timer with it. I'm literally airborne above the vast ocean. The swift rush of gravity grips at my stomach. I can't decide whether to scream or throw up. My body plummets to the deep. Crisp wind barrels my cheeks.

Great white shark facts flood my brain. I do my best to remember every tidbit of information. They are indeed terrifying creatures. I've always been obsessed with them. Well, how can you not? They are the largest predatory fish on Earth. I know few who aren't mesmerized by the sight of one snatching a seal. Facts, websites, books; all of them cloud my mind. Hopefully I can remember something important. Immediately, a very important fact dawns on me. Every book and website I have ever viewed stated the same thing.

The eyes are the ultimate weak spot; this is my only

shot.

I wail at the top of my lungs. It's time for me and the demon to meet. Now its entire body fills my view. The true nature of the creature becomes evident. A great white shark springs out of the water. Enormous white waves crash behind it. Its massive body leaps at full force towards me. Deadly rows of teeth invite me into its stomach. Sharp black eyes resemble two worm holes. I can't help feeling as though I'll be sucked into oblivion.

Our eyes lock. All fifty billion of its teeth come into view. They are in direct line of my face. My shaky fingers continue to grasp the knife. I thrust the knife in utter terror. With my arm extending, I stab the gigantic black eye. My stomach shifts with gravity's unrelenting tug, overpowering any chance of breath.

Despite every doubt the situation shows, my knife does not lie. I feel contact as my knife slides into the black oval. Unyielding pain jolts my entire body as well. Peering down, I realize one of its teeth had dug deep into my arm. The sight horrifies me. Screaming is my only way to deal with the agony. Both of us plummet to the open ocean.

"Ahhhh!" I yell, overtaken with pain. My vision becomes hazy and almost nonexistent. The biggest splash of the world occurs as both of us slam into the ocean. Unrelenting water crashes into my lungs. My stomach lurches forward in an attempt to cope. Immense whiteness clashes above the surface.

Chapter 15
Overwhelming

The deep water engulfs my body. All the forces of the deep clutch me. My strength completely fades. I don't think I'm going to make it back up. Despite the salt burning, I keep my eyes wide open. Glancing at my arm, I find rivers of blood flowing out. The murky sight clashes with the water.

Just then, an urge of adrenaline kicks in. Perhaps I'm just terrified to the maximum. My feet kick water with full intensity. Arms shove water down to propel me. Blocking out all the pain, I put all my energy into swimming. Kicking with all my might, I somehow break through the surface.

Taking the biggest breath of my life, I look around to check my surroundings. There is nothing but ocean as before. The giant shark is nowhere in sight. It requires a few long exhales to calm myself and think rationally. I am totally exhausted. Blood pours from my arm against gentle waves. Each paddle causes a new burst of agony.

The next sight I see brings a glimmer of hope.

Another rope!

Taking no time to think about it, I plunge toward it. The gift from heaven makes me completely forget about my bleeding arm. I finally reach it with a few breast strokes. I yelp when I detect a dorsal fin jutting out a few yards away. Grabbing the rope, I hoist myself out of the water. My ascent begins once again. The sight of the shark inspires me to climb faster, knowing it isn't afraid to leave the ocean when it pleases. Maybe my imagination plays tricks, but I swear its speed increases. *I don't think it wants to eat me anymore. It wants me dead.*

The shark, to my horror, mirrors its previous strategy. I yell out into the horizon. Its enormous body jumps out of the ocean. Its fury is tangible. The white water it created crashes into my face. Luckily, I keep a firm grip on the rope.

Its teeth reach for me, but I have climbed too high. The beast plummets back to the water. Another magnificent splash crashes water into my eyes. Sharp stinging gets even worse. Using everything within me, I lock my legs around the rope, holding on with every ounce of courage.

This rope appears the same height as the last one. Glancing up, there is no sign of a box or timer. There is what seems to be a platform type of deal. Floating in mid-air as well, are what look to be weapons of some sort. I am ecstatic to discover crossbow and arrows. Yes! I can finally attack this thing from afar. Maybe I can actually do this after all.

My hand reaches for the top of the rope. The dorsal fin circles around the rope again. Rage increases with each revolution. The shark is antsy to kill me. Swinging up, I leap onto the platform. The joy of seeing no timer in sight is wonderful. My happiness, however, surely doesn't last long.

As I land on this glassy platform, its transparent form changes into opaque sky blue. This platform senses my presence. The borders of it hover gently. Each edge illuminates a pure white gleam. After a few seconds of this, I finally figure out what is going on.

Borders are closing in. The platform is slowly vanishing into nothing. It looks like there is a time limit after all. The knowledge of that demolishes any sense of tranquility. From what I'm able to judge, I don't have many minutes. Fear grips my soul. Unless I work fast, I'm going to plunge into the ocean again.

I lunge for the crossbow. My shaky fingers shove an arrow into its place. There are very many lying about. Thankfully I won't be running out any time soon. Setting it in place, I lift the bow into proper shooting position. My feet waddle to the disappearing edge. I aim with eyes glued to the shark. This is certainly going to be a challenge with the animal's velocity.

My first arrow is clearly a miss, shooting into the waves. The shark takes no notice that anything even happened.

I attempt two more, frequently checking the status of the disappearing platform. Both shots are misses, just as off-target as the first had been. I don't seem to be getting any better. Concentrating, I lay a fourth arrow into the bow. By this time, I have somewhat of a handle on the shark's tactics. I release the arrow. It flies directly toward the deadly dorsal fin. Happiness fills me to the brim as it pierces through. The shot is perfect. I know that I have got it.

The shark immediately stops dead in its tracks. I waste no time in admiring my accomplishment. As its body emerges from the sea, I've already released another shot. The shark flails around in pain, giving me more of a target.

In all this excitement, I haven't remembered to check the platform. To my extreme alarm, the shining borders have almost met. There isn't any time to dawdle. I have to keep shooting, and hitting my target occasionally might help. My sudden burst of accuracy fades. All my shots are evaded. The creature has not given up. I only hope I don't either.

If I don't kill it soon, I'm doomed.

A few more shots only result in scattered misses. *What am I going to do?* Blood continues to waterfall out my arm. The pain mirrors my terror.

The platform definitely closes in. Time no longer sits on my side. The gleaming borders are inches from meeting. Now frantic, I barely have time to even look at where I'm aiming. The absence of any focus renders utter failure. Every arrow enters the ocean yards away from the shark.

Complete hell envelops my heart. I attempt to reach another arrow, but it's now impossible. The platform vanishes, abandoning me airborne above the monster. Discovering this fact, the shark leaps at me once more. Could it have been waiting for the platform to disappear? Bursting out of the ocean, along with a gigantic splash of white foam, it collides with my falling body.

My crossbow's hurled out of my hand. It flies away from my grasp.

"No!" I yelp. *That's it; I'm done.*

Gravity's force demolishes my senses. Whirlwinds slam the remaining arrows all over the place. I can barely even comprehend the razor sharp teeth entering my torso. Blood rushes every direction. I swear the shark smiles at my demise. That's probably just my imagination.

Both of us slam into the ocean once more, mirroring the last. This time, the pain is much more brutal. The horror is so intense, it's almost as if I can't feel at all. My eyelids shut.

Chapter 16
Failure

My eyes dart open. *What happened? I'm pretty sure I should be digested right now.* Peering around, I find myself in what looks like an enormous hotel room. Elaborate paintings flood tangerine walls. Each displays a vivid landscape ranging from oceans to mountaintops.

Gaining the strength, I lift the blanket off my legs. My mind is incredibly hazy. Feet thumping on the floor, I discover a spotless bathroom through the side door. The sink is pure gold. I swear it sparkles when I enter, though that's probably my mental delusion. I splash water in my face.

This is obviously a ritzy place. Returning to the bed, I contemplate the extreme battle that just occurred. That whole fight was surreal, yet it actually happened. Parched, I head to the mini refrigerator. It's inside a large, wooden cabinet. My fingers grasp the first soda in sight. I'm not picky. As I gulp the ice-cold pop, my body relishes the taste.

After casting it in the nearby trash can, a knock sounds at my door. Who in the world is this going to be? I whisk over and open it. My eyes must be deceiving me. A dark sphere of gas hovers outside. The sight mesmerizes me. If I have any chance at regaining sanity, this thing destroys it. This 'spirit' doesn't have eyes or any features that I can tell. Purple flames trail off the manifestation. How had it even knocked on the door?

"Alcott," the spirit whispers. The voice has a

haunting tone. "I'm sorry, but you have failed the first Obstacle."

It's not like I didn't know that. I was eaten by a shark! Still, the words cut like a knife.

"Yeah," is all I can muster. I certainly have a way with words. "What the heck are you?"

"I am a Sphream. We are servants to the Jauntla who brought you here. Each of us toils to assist competitors in the Obstacles. We wish only to serve you."

Utter silence ensues. My mind is blown, and I can't speak a word. I gaze at its body, bobbing in the air. It senses I will not respond and continues.

"You are the first to arrive back," the Sphream adds. Its spooky form hovers up and down. "The other four are still in the midst of their challenges. Do not be discouraged; your strength and determination have truly impressed us all. The first Obstacle is always difficult. Feel free to come down to the lobby for lunch. You must be starving."

"That sounds wonderful. Thank you!" I haven't eaten in quite a long time. Food sounds like the best thing in the world.

"Great, now if you'll please follow me." The Sphream floats down the hallway.

It guides me down at delicate pace. The magnificent hallway has billions of photos. Bronze sculptures of animals rest in front of each door. There are exactly five rooms in this hallway. This must be purely for us Obstacle competitors.

Decorative paintings rest along the gray walls. Each contains shadowed relics of ancient times. I could lose myself for hours at their captivating features.

At the end of the hall, an elaborate circular stairwell comes into view. I'm a bit disappointed. I wanted to explore the hallway more. As we continue down each step,

I determine never to leave this place. That statement is confirmed as a lobby emerges. The marvelous room fills my heart with wonder.

"Is this the mansion everyone was talking about earlier?" I'm desperate to find out everything about this new-found paradise.

"No, Alcott, that was the preparatory mansion awaiting five people to begin the Obstacles," the Sphream answers. It in no way slows its swift glide. "You, sadly, never get to see it."

"Oh well," I say, my mood not shaken. "Getting to stay in this seems awesome enough to me!"

"I'm very glad you like it," the Sphream replies. "This is the hotel you will be staying in throughout your journey. I suggest you familiarize yourself with the establishment. You will be here for most of the Obstacles."

As we descend the last few stairs, I see a glorious restaurant at the end.

It is completely deserted for the time being, with only the Sphream and me inside. I have never seen anything as marvelous as this. Everything is decorated, extravagant, and fancy. Classy, gold napkins rest upon each of the plates. I detect wrapped up silverware in special napkins. Sparkling glasses stand on every table.

No flaw is visible anywhere, as if the restaurant is completely perfect. There are certainly many booths up front as well. Every one of them seems luminous and colorful, ranging from shiny gold to dazzling cobalt blue. While I admire every part of this place, the Sphream guides me to a booth directly by the kitchen. Sneaking a peak in, I discover the chefs are also Sphreams. Each directly mirrors my guide. Three of them emerge upon my arrival.

"We can prepare anything your heart desires, champion," one of them whispers kindly. Its creepy form hovers closer. "What would you like?"

Whoa, the Obstacles may be the best decision I ever made. I can't believe I'm given the title of champion even though I lost. Maybe it's out of pity or something. After thinking for a while, I decide on what food sounds perfect.

"I would love a chicken sandwich with ranch dressing, if you could." I salivate at the mere mention.

"Then the best chicken sandwich with ranch you shall receive," the Sphream replies in its dark voice. "It will be up shortly; please be patient."

"Thank you for being so kind to me," I respond. Wondering about how these Sphreams discern themselves from each other, I ask my original guide, "Do you have a name?"

Immediately the Sphream whispers, "I can't reveal that information, Alcott." It descends to soft decibels. "I must apologize."

I guess they really like their secrets around here; that seemed to cross some sort of line. It seems awfully strange that it can't even reveal its name to me. Oh well, those thoughts begin to disappear. I dream about my sandwich's arrival. My stomach definitely growls hungrily.

"Oh I'm sorry," I stammer. "Well, thank you very much Mrs. Sphream."

"Enjoy!" It departs as another Sphream serves me a soda. The first scurries up to the rooms, perhaps waiting for everybody else to finish their challenges.

"Thank you," I smile, "Sphream Number Two."

"You are most welcome, Alcott."

As it travels into the kitchen, I have to ask... "Excuse me, when do you think I will know how the others have finished? They're coming to this hotel too, right?"

"That information cannot be revealed now," it swiftly states. "They are all still in the middle of their

Obstacle. When an Ally has returned, someone will inform you immediately. They will stay with you in the hotel as well. Now, your meal shall be up very soon."

"Oh, okay. Thank you very much." I very much hope everybody passes whatever challenge they had.

I spend the next ten minutes reliving the extreme giant shark moment. *Surely they all couldn't have had to do something so insane. I didn't think that I was ever going to get through that myself.* As I guzzle down my second soda, the Sphream brings me my meal. The glorious chicken sandwich causes my mouth to water. Heaven crafted it right there it seems.

"I'm never leaving this place," I yell to the Sphream chefs with delight. "I hope you all know that."

As I praise their work, dark smog suddenly manifests on the other side of the lobby. I can't believe I hadn't noticed before. Five enormous statues stand there. They are replicas of the five of us Allies, Gretchen, Marya, Travis, Alcott, and Vitaly. All of our statues look exactly the same as our true selves; I can even discern that from the far distance.

Right above my personal statue the murky haze hovers gently. The sight makes me drop part of my chicken. Resting there for a moment, the smoke transforms into a very long parchment. Upon it simply reads, 'Challenge Number One Failed.'

After that spectacle, everything is peaceful again. Lobby lights illuminate as if nothing ever happened. There rests a tangible sign of my fate. I have lost the first Obstacle. My mood plummets in an instant. Eyes drop to the floor tiles.

As I take the last couple of bites of my sandwich, the original Sphream returns. It approaches my booth. "Marya's challenge is almost complete," it says hoarsely.

"She will be dining with you shortly."

"That's wonderful!" I shout, so excited to have a friend to talk to. "What did she have to do? Is she doing well? Has she passed?"

"That information can only be revealed at her arrival," it replies. Part of me knew I would get no answers. "Which…it appears, is right now. Excuse me if you would, Alcott, I'll be right back."

The Sphream then heads up the same elaborate staircase to the hallway. I am extremely ecstatic to see one of my Allies again. It is interesting to wonder what the other challenges could possibly be. After brawling with a shark, anything could be possible. *What in the world could Marya have had to do?* As I contemplate this, I hear rough sounds of someone jaunting down the stairs. Marya's face indicates sheer abhorrence. The girl is not in a happy place.

"Hey, Alcott," she whimpers. Her eyes travel toward the floor tiles.

"Hey," I respond, extending a welcoming wave. "How was your challenge?" Her expression pretty much tells me everything. I almost think she's about to cry.

"Not the best." She plumps down across from me.

"Hello, Marya," a Sphream hovers. "What can I get for you today?" It sounds very enthusiastic, completely contrasting the girl. The idea of food makes her mood uplift slightly.

Marya appears very intrigued. She cannot decide between all the wonderful entrees. This kitchen definitely is breathtaking, and it is an Obstacle in itself selecting just one thing to eat.

"Hmmm," Marya contemplates. "What do you recommend here? It seems like a lovely restaurant if I do say so myself."

"Why thank you very much," the Sphream slurs.

"We have all of the basics from pasta, steak, fruit, vegetables, ribs, chicken, fish, hamburgers…you name it."

"Well, I suppose I would like baby back ribs if you have them," her eyebrows rising.

"Coming right up." The Sphream rotates towards the kitchen.

"Well, Alcott." Marya turns toward me. "I saw your statue. I take it your challenge wasn't all that great either huh?"

At that moment, the eerie smoke returns. This time, it heads now for a different destination. Its actions mirror the same for her as they did for me. Hovering calmly above Marya's statue, it morphs itself into a parchment. The new manifestation has the exact same statement.

'Challenge Number One Failed.'

Chapter 17
Continue

"Yeah," my eyes float across the room. "Let's just say it wasn't a cake walk. What did you have to do?"

"Well," she glares at the table in frustration. "I started freaking out on the platform. I screamed and thrashed with all my might. Suddenly, I found myself inside an ocean. A strange voice whispered in my ear. It instructed me on techniques to operate a submarine.

"I tell you, Alcott, all my confidence slipped away. They gave me a list of extremely complicated directions I doubt most scholars could interpret correctly."

"That sounds incredibly difficult," I say, taken back a bit.

"I had a very little amount of time to locate a rare species of fish. It lived deep under the ocean where little light touched. I guess I knew I was going to fail from the start. The various instructions were gibberish in my mind."

"I thought mine was as bad as it could get."

She looks directly into my eyes. "So what did you have to do?"

Despite the horror of recollecting the experience, I tell every detail of my epic battle with a great white shark. Magical ropes hanging from the sky, a very sturdy knife, and the disappearing platform all mesmerize her. Wide open eyes portray her utter shock. Frankly, retelling the story jars me. My legs start to tremble once more.

"Well then," Marya leans back, flabbergasted. "I'm a little speechless. I never had to worry about fighting any creature, not something that terrifying!"

Just then a voice booms. It explodes out of nowhere. The source emanates from somewhere across the restaurant. I know immediately who it is, as I could never forget that voice anyway. A few tables away, a figure of a person becomes visible that certainly wasn't standing there before. Dressed in the magnificent gold outfit, there is no doubt that this is the Jauntla from the top of the cliff.

"Congratulations to the both of you!" she screams, portraying the cheekiest grin. Her attire is still lavished in sparkles.

"Hello!" I yell back.

"Wonderful to see you two!" She paces a few steps closer to our booth. "You two started off the Obstacles greatly. You took your nearly impossible challenge head on. Winning isn't everything."

That statement seems very contradictory. My eyes once again linger on the statues. Our parchments certainly don't say, 'Good job for trying!'

"Never be discouraged. This is what the Obstacles are all about; believing in yourself despite the darkest odds." Her joyful expression entirely alters. She peers off into the distance. "I just wish I could say the same for the other three."

Oh no; does that mean Travis, Vitaly, and Gretchen are not doing well in their Obstacle? That statement saddens me to wonder what kind of horrible situations they must all be experiencing. Each of them deserves to save their loved ones so much. I can't imagine what circumstances they all must be going through right now.

"What's going on, if I may ask? Are all of them failing?" Marya quickly inquires. Her expression appears to contain just as much apprehension and concern as mine does.

"I'm sorry, Alcott and Marya, I've already revealed far too much as it is," she replies, showing a more stern face. "They will have to tell you themselves when they arrive back at this hotel. You will just have to wait and see."

A dark cloud hovers over all of us. It's really challenging to have developed such a bond with someone, and hear about them about to lose something so important. Vitaly, Travis, and Gretchen are all pretty courageous, intelligent people from what I can perceive. Whatever Obstacle they had to face, I believe they can accomplish it in a heartbeat with the right mindset. That's the hardest part though; believing that they can.

"Well," Marya says, looking directly at me now with an attempt to change the subject. "At least your little scamp has a true fighter willing to never quit. He must be pretty special for you to be doing this for him."

"Thanks a lot, Marya."

We enjoy each other's company as we patiently wait for our fellow Allies to finish their tasks.

Marya's scrumptious baby back ribs arrive soon after, dripping with barbecue perfection; I think I know what I'll be ordering next meal time. The food at this place is undoubtedly delectable. Throughout this, the Jauntla has been nowhere to be found. She seemed to vanish after our little conversation regarding the others.

Suddenly, what seemed like out of nowhere, she announces from directly behind me, causing me to gasp, "Gretchen's trial is complete. Would you go and get her for me please?" she asks, rotating toward a nearby Sphream.

That scares me half to death! It is as if she has been hovering there the whole time, yet could not be seen until she had spoken. Anyway, the Sphream politely obeys her request without any hesitation…"Certainly."

It immediately heads toward the large staircase once more. Neither of us are very hopeful for Gretchen's challenge, based on the Jauntla's obvious statements. At least she has two friends waiting down here for her, no matter what her grim fate may be. Our suspicions are confirmed when we catch a glimpse of Gretchen inching down the stairs with her eyes drooping toward the ground, wearing a transparent frown. The sadness becomes clearer as she arrives at the restaurant.

"Hey Gretchen," I yell in the nicest way I can, hoping to bring about some positivity. "Are you okay?"

She doesn't answer, just shakes her head and looks away. Obviously, she has failed whatever her Obstacle may have been. It isn't difficult for me to empathize with what she must be going through. Gretchen is battling to save her little sister Sharia, and she feels like she has let her down. That part is surely obvious, despite her unyielding silence.

"It's just the first challenge, Gretchen," Marya says, addressing the elephant in the room. "There's plenty more, and from what Alcott and I had to do it's a miracle anybody can pass any of these."

"Thanks," she replies, attempting to form a little smile.

Once again, a dark puff of smoke forms out of nowhere. It delicately hovers above Gretchen's statue for a moment, and then transforms itself into a parchment, just like ours had. It doesn't take long for any of us to realize what it is going to say. Blatantly, the parchment reads loud and clear, 'Challenge Number One Failed.'

I then ask the inevitable question, "So, what did you have to do?"

Through soft wheezes she wails, "I had to become a fighter pilot!"

Both of us are in complete shock at that statement;

these tests just seem to be getting more insane by the minute. Gretchen goes through all the details of her terrifying flying tale. When we inquire how she could have done that task without any training, she replies that there was a computer quickly coaching her through all the steps. Her mission was to take down three other aircraft in the air, before they retaliated of course. Though apparently she had no problem shooting one of them down, the other two were a different story entirely.

"So what happened?" Marya stares directly into her eyes.

"Well, after getting a hang of the controls, which took far longer than it should have, the other two aircraft flew below and bombarded me from behind. I went down spiraling into the ground within seconds flat. Just as I thought all hope was lost and that I was really going to die, I found myself sleeping in a hotel room."

Fighter pilot? Wow, that strikes a new fear in me that I didn't know existed.

"Well, I doubt I could've been able to do that," Marya shouts, sitting back in awe.

The Jauntla suddenly chimes into the conversation, "Do not be discouraged Gretchen, this is your first challenge. Now that you know what to expect, I guarantee you will be stronger in the next one. There are six Obstacles after all, Gretchen. You only have to pass three in order to save Sharia; never give up." The Jauntla attempts to offer up a smile, whilst still seeming hidden in some aspect.

Gretchen nods despite drooping her eyes back down to the ground. To break the silence, we then shock her with our insane challenges, hoping she might feel a little better. For some reason, every time I speak about the giant great white shark, it doesn't frighten me. *Maybe these challenges are supposed to make you stronger, as well.*

"Well, this isn't insane, or anything," is her first reply to our stories. It did in fact sound berserk as we repeat them once more to her.

At that precise moment, the Sphream states that Travis and Vitaly have finished their Obstacles. Gretchen's failure has brought on so much bleakness, I can only hope each of them has done well. Travis and Vitaly quickly dash down the stairs with the Sphream. Neither of them looks too thrilled with themselves, showing the exact same demeanor that Gretchen had. Both of them continue walking to the restaurant with the same glum look.

Just then, all of us glance back at the statues as something stirs by them. Two dark smogs again manifest over there as the lights fade. We all are well aware what that means. As it now states over each of their statues, we clearly know that the two of them have failed.

As what is evidently tradition, everyone exchanges stories and offers comfort. Vitaly and Travis had apparently both been given the same challenge. It involved intent literature skills to answer complicated trivia of some sort. They each got thirty minutes to read as much of this passage as they could, and then they would have to answer difficult questions about it. They both reveal that you had to get ten out of fifteen correct to pass the Obstacle. When Travis and Vitaly met up in the upstairs hotel room, they both figured out they had been given the same one. Travis, however, answered nine of the questions correctly, and Vitaly had only gotten four.

"I've never felt so stupid in my entire life," Vitaly screams in the midst of a tantrum, obviously embarrassed. "I read the stupid story so carefully and then I just had a panic attack. Only got four right; I can't believe it."

"You think you feel bad; I only needed one more

right answer to win!" Travis yells with childish behavior of his own. "I can't believe I had gotten so close, yet I failed." Both of them continue gazing at their statues with increasing outrage.

I think Gretchen is a little relieved to know that other people have failed the first challenge too. Maybe it gives her more courage, so for that I am thankful. Luckily, everyone is able to order whatever delectable dish they desire, no matter pass or fail.

It is a unanimous proclamation that the food is beyond perfect. Vitaly receives a delicious plate of spaghetti, while Travis inhales a juicy steak. No one could find any way to insult the brilliant Sphream chefs. As we all gaze at our statues, we can't help but be frightened and curious as to what is going to happen next; hopefully no sharks on the horizon.

After everybody has finished devouring their meals, the Jauntla once again materializes. She has a terrifying, yet hopeful tone to her voice.

"I'd advise you," she recites, "to be off to bed now. Your next challenge will be done with all five of you together. You have shown your initial strength individually, now it is time to see what you can do as a team. I wish all of you the best of luck." She then vanishes into the thin air, abandoning us in the booth.

"We can do this, guys," I immediately shout, slamming the table with my fist, trying to offer some encouragement for everyone. "There's no way we can lose if we all work together."

Despite my determined tone, there is surely a sense of discouragement in everyone. I desperately attempt to keep my head held high as we head off to the staircase, attempting to give everybody hope.

Reaching the top of the stairs, each of us paces

down the elaborate hallway to our respective hotel rooms. My eyes open wide at the discovery. My room has gone through a huge transformation. Last time, the bathroom was completely empty, aside from the toilet and shower. Now, it contains everything I would ever need, as if I had been living there my whole life.

From a toothbrush, toothpaste, shampoo, towels, etc., it has it all. Looking at the closet, I discover many jackets, pants, shorts, shirts, practically appearing by magic. Picking out the pajamas, I immediately change for bedtime. I am definitely lucky to be staying here; there's no doubt about that. As I tuck myself inside the comfy covers, I gaze at the wall imagining what in the world will happen tomorrow; as if I can ever even guess.

Sleeping, I can tell, is going to be very difficult.

Chapter 18
Demented

My mind and relaxation are enemies. Millions of thoughts twist and turn. Every memory floods through me. It all escalates to a shark devouring me whole. How can I possibly sleep after something like that?

I know I need to conserve all of my energy. I must get rest for the next Obstacle. So, I merely lie here like a statue. My eyes stare into the darkness of the night. My whole body shakes with adrenaline and nervous energy. This tiresome process goes on for what seems like one hundred years. Nothing seems to be happening nor improving. I alternate from my right to my left side. Sleeping always proves to be quite a challenge for me, never mind in a new place under these circumstances.

Suddenly, my heart jolts. A loud knock sounds at my door. As my eyes jerk open, I peek at the clock. On the table to the right of me, it clearly states two o'clock in the morning! *What is going on? Who in the world would be knocking at this time of night? Perhaps the next challenge has begun. It is certainly not morning.*

I haven't even gotten any sleep yet! This does not look very good for me. I force myself to get up. Wiping my eyes in annoyance, I hear the knocking getting louder. Whoever is there is obviously not a very patient person.

"Okay, okay!" I scream. My irritation grows exponentially. "I'm coming!" They are seriously getting on my nerves.

I stumble, dazed, over to the door. My trembling

hand rotates the doorknob. When it opens, I find someone unexpected. Vitaly grins with a carefree expression. Her demeanor is quite shocking. She looks like the happiest person in the world. Gigantic eyes peer into my soul. *What in the world is she doing outside my door at this time of night? Something must be seriously wrong; but then why does she look so happy?*

"Hey, Vitaly," I respond groggily. I'm still rubbing my eyes. "Are you okay? What's wrong?"

As I wait for an answer, she remains in the same position. The little kid says nothing at all. Her eyes never shift. It is as if I haven't even asked a question at all. This goes on for about ten seconds. I am starting to get really freaked out. *Is this some kind of weird Neptune tradition or something? To stare at people and smile at odd hours of the night?!* I repeat my question once more. The answer I receive startles me.

"We've been waiting, Alcott," she giggles with joy. There almost seems to be a touch of anger, as if I should have already known this.

"What?" I ask. *What could they possibly be waiting for?* If there was some meeting scheduled for this late at night I would have remembered. Vitaly behaves in a way that seriously frightens me.

"Are you deaf?" she wails, causing me to leap back. "We've been waiting; why are you taking so long?" Her smile remains unaltered, despite the outrage. The sight is nothing short of horrifying.

"What? I...I'm sorry...I have no idea what you are talking about. Has the next challenge begun or something?" Something is definitely not right here. Any fool can see that.

She says nothing again. The girl continues glaring with the unyielding grin. To stop this, I desperately attempt to charge back into my room.

"Just give me a second," I say to shield my confusion. "I'll get changed." As I prepare to shut the door, she juts her foot out. It blocks it in mid-close. She does so without an effort to look.

"No, you'll follow me now!" The cacophony is uncanny. She must have woken everyone in the building.

"Excuse me!?" I'm so appalled I can barely speak.

She then darts forward, slamming the door shut behind. This behavior leaves me flabbergasted. Little kid or not; I refuse to be treated this way. As I prepare to yell, I discover her already galloping down the hall.

If the next Obstacle is on its way, I reluctantly decide I don't want to miss out, despite this kid's insane behavior. So, I guess I have no choice. I stumble and follow her down the staircase to the lobby. Jaunting down the stairs, Vitaly appears quite tranquil. She occasionally peers back to make sure I'm there. The smile never ceases.

As we arrive in the lobby, I am shocked to discover Gretchen, Marya, and Travis standing there. They patiently watch as the two of us descend the stairs. The next thing I see makes my heart skip a beat. Each of them, to my horror, smiles the exact same way as Vitaly. All have the same exact expression. It's almost glued permanently to their faces. Part of me wants to just dart away while I still can, but the other part of me thinks that'll make it worse.

"Well, looks like someone finally decided to show up," Travis yells. The annoyed tone utterly contrasts his grin.

What is going on? Did I miss some memo? Why is everyone all creepy and rude all of a sudden? I continue striding down the stairs. Each pair of eyes remains glued upon my every move. I cannot even determine whether any of them pause to blink. This is really beginning to scare me.

Maybe I should run out the door and never come back.

Chapter 19
Baffled

"I'm sorry," I shout down to my Allies. Despite their ghastly attitudes, I hope to bring a bit of kindness to the situation. "Is it time for the next challenge?"

"Oh, it's already happening," Marya hollers. I'm astonished at the nonchalant tone. *It's already happening?* She speaks in a way that almost brags that I had not known about it. I don't understand the meaning for this insane behavior. *Aren't these people my friends?* I am certainly left completely in the dark.

"What?" I roar, taking a much swifter stride. "Nobody told me anything! What's the Obstacle?"

I suddenly detect faint footsteps. They are followed by a voice chanting something unknown. The footsteps lurk closer behind me. It doesn't take a moment to figure out the voice belongs to Gretchen. In an eerie whisper, she utters three words. They send chills up and down my spine.

"To kill you…"

I spin around instantly. Gretchen grasps an enormous axe. Blood already pours from the sharp blade.

"No!" I yell with all my might. She swings the monstrosity toward my face.

My eyes dart open. I hoist myself off the bed at full force. My heart pounds as I gaze around to discover I'm back in the hotel room; all of it was just a dream. I've never been so terrified in my life. Golden rays emanate from the window, indicating the sun is definitely up now. I am extremely thankful. Light pours into the room. I'm actually able to calm down a bit.

I'm still breathing harder than I can ever remember. Never before has a nightmare been so real and vivid. Just gripping my bed in uncontrollable fear, I stare at the ceiling. My mind again wanders in oblivion. After finally relaxing my nerves, I glance at the clock. It shows that morning has indeed arrived. I have never been so relieved to discover the night has ceased. Just when I am finally beginning to regain my sanity, another knock sounds at the door.

"No!" I yell at the top of my lungs. My body completely slithers off the bed. I slam onto the carpet.

"Alcott, are you okay in there?" a Sphream inquires. If it had eyebrows, it would be raising one. "The next challenge is about to begin. Please come down for breakfast, if you're ready."

My head bashed the floor pretty hard. Not hearing Vitaly's voice outside was a greater reward than ever; I would've lost my mind completely. Rubbing my head, I stand back up. I attempt a response.

"Yes, I'm sorry. I'm coming." I get dressed with the clothes in the closet. I'm still sweating. I need to pull myself together. *Just a dream*, I tell myself; *only a fragment of my imagination. That never even happened.* No matter how many times I tell myself that while brushing my teeth, I doubt I'll ever believe it.

Once I'm ready, I turn the door knob with hesitation.

"What was all that screaming?" the Sphream asks. It remains in delicate hover. "Is everything alright?"

"I'm sorry. It was just a nightmare."

"Well, it's your first night here," it reassures me with comfort. "I'm sure you're not alone. Nightmares can…" it continues, "seem pretty real. Just be sure to know when real life comes back."

"Thanks," I respond. "I'll try to…" *Much easier said than done; that's for darn sure.*

We head off down the hallway. I descend the staircase once again. The image of Vitaly smiling is glued into my head for quite some time. I need to have that memory removed as soon as possible. The statues remain the same as yesterday before I went to bed. Everyone has failed the first Obstacle.

"Is anyone else up yet?" I hunt for answers.

"No," the Sphream responds, "the rest of us are going to attend to them now."

It guides me to a booth as before. When another Sphream strides up for my order, I imagine a delicious meal. That relaxes my nerves. An answer pops into my brain; chocolate chip pancakes! Chocolate meshing with deep batter materializes in my mind. I can practically taste it right now.

I'm surely milking this place for all it's worth. A delectable breakfast is just what I need. I can get back to normal again.

With the Sphream leading them, I squint to see the others descend. They whisk down the stairs. From my view point, none are smiling with a creepy expression. Nobody seems to grasp an ax either. This makes me extremely happy. I watch all of them avoid peering at their statues. It is a bit embarrassing to see failure right above you.

"Hey guys!"

"Hey Alcott!" they all shout back. They commence a swifter gallop towards me.

"How'd you all sleep?"

"The first night was a little creepy," Gretchen answers my question, "but not bad." The rest ultimately agree.

87

"What about you?" Marya asks me.

"Pretty good," I lie. *No need to bring up to my new friends that I dreamt they all desire to murder me.* Somehow I believe that might bring morale down a tad. They all then sit next to me in the booth. We prepare to stuff our faces. Vitaly chooses to perch right beside me. I'm not going to lie, that makes me pretty uncomfortable. The whole dream was made up in my head. I, however, don't know if I can look at her the same way ever again.

"I'm ready for this next challenge," Vitaly states defiantly. "There's no way I'm going to be that stupid again. I'm ready for anything they throw at me." I haven't witnessed someone that determined in a long time. It's certainly encouraging to see that much oomph.

"Well, we're all in this one together; that's what the creepy gold god said," Gretchen recites. She gazes off at her statue. "There'd better not be planes."

Everyone gives the Sphream their order. We all have a spectacular breakfast together. Eventually, the last remnants of the nightmare leave my mind. Reality enters once more. *I really hope we can pass this next Obstacle. I don't want to watch Vitaly, Travis, Marya, and Gretchen lose again; I have grown far too attached to them.* Finishing the most buttery pancakes, syrup drips from my lower lip. Without warning, the Jauntla manifests a few tables away.

"Well, are we all ready for the second challenge?" she inquires. Her uplifting voice feels deceiving. "Not that you get a choice in the matter."

"Bring it on!" Vitaly screams, causing heads to turn.

The Jauntla smiles at that courage. "Determination can get you anywhere; wonderful attitude, Vitaly!"

Vitaly beams a dazzling grin right back at her. That's it; I'm never going to be able to look at her smile without freaking out. Everyone else immediately agrees. It's time for the Obstacle to begin.

The Jauntla announces with raised arms, "Please follow me outside."

We're all swiftly guided out of the hotel. I make my way across the courtyard. This hotel truly emanates majesty. Swirls of the deep orange and brown create a magical castle. All around the courtyard is elaborate shrubbery. Dazzling gardens lie as far as the eye can see. It seems like every color and species of flower is scattered around. The transition from sharp purple to bright blue mesmerizes the eyes.

As we all admire our temporary abode, the Jauntla directs us to another staircase. From what it looks like, this hotel floats in mid-air. Nothing is visible below or above but endless atmosphere. Clouds hover far above us. The extremely lengthy staircase leads up to hazy mist of some sort. As the Jauntla extends her arm, each of us begins the ascent. About halfway up, the hotel disappears from view. A desert of fog takes its place.

The top of the stairs comes into view. It appears just like the platform that transported us to our first challenges. I wonder if this is the same one. When everyone finally arrives on it, the staircase fades into the air. It loses all tangibility; naturally, a vanishing staircase.

"As I have affirmed," the Jauntla asserts, "all five of you will take on this next Obstacle together. You either all pass, or you all fail. There is no other outcome. Each of you should begin to prepare yourself. This test is not for the easily fazed."

Just as the first time, everything immediately fades to darkness. I have no time to contemplate. Blinking changes nothing, as the blackness shows no sign of departing. Though this has happened before, the fear has not lessened at all. I pray that this Obstacle isn't in an ocean. The voices begin the horrifying chant…"Alcott, Alcott, Alcott." Their increasing volume rattles my brain to no end. They seem petrified and upset, yet mournful. They seem to be seeking revenge on me in some way.

After far too long of this constant torture, I awake. Bright sunshine warms my cheeks. It feels extremely soothing. Beams shine on everything in sight. As I arise and take in my surroundings, I come across bright blue sky. I detect no hint of clouds anywhere. Around my feet, beautiful white sand lies all around. Grains delicately swish in the wind. There are many varieties of shells, boisterous and determined seagulls, and forceful waves slamming against the shore. No question about it; it's a marvelous beach. Based on my last challenge, I'm very thankful that I'm standing on land. I naturally shall avoid the ocean at all costs. So far, this challenge seems more like a reward than an Obstacle.

Glancing around at my Allies, Vitaly, Marya, Travis, and Gretchen are all taking in the wonderful surroundings as well. Everyone appears quite pleased with the current situation. Though, how could anybody not?

"Well, this is amazing!" Travis yells, gazing up at the sun. "Why do I feel like this isn't going to last?"

"Oh yeah," Gretchen gleams with positivity. "Let's just stay here forever." As everybody enjoys themselves, I take a gander back at Vitaly. My eyebrows lower to slants. Something is terribly wrong.

"Is she okay?" I ask, completely awestruck at the sight.

Everyone twists around to check what I'm ranting about. There Vitaly is, standing firmly in the sand. She gazes and points into the distance. Her eyes are open, but her mouth is wholly closed. After a few confusing seconds,

I realize Vitaly is completely frozen. She is a motionless statue. The child, or alien, appears to be in some sort of unbreakable trance.

"Vitaly!" Marya shouts. Her hand waves over her eyes. No answer; she is definitely not moving. A few more shakes and rattles only reaffirm that.

"What is she pointing at?" I implore. Her finger remains fixed off into the distance, unwavering.

As we gaze in that direction, we notice something appearing in the sky. What starts as a little spec grows large and luminous, just as the Jauntla had done upon the cliff. As it projects into view, I recognize another parchment. It folds and extends high up in the air. Perfectly aligning to where Vitaly is pointing, the paper clearly states:

'To solve this task, you have to find the deepest strength inside your mind. To render this challenge as complete, there lays a treasure you must seek. A map to this, underneath the sand, where your dear Vitaly now stands.'

Marya reads that aloud to us. We begin to interpret what it means.

"There must be some treasure map buried under her," Gretchen exclaims, index finger aimed directly at unyielding Vitaly. As we turn to look at her, she hasn't moved an inch. Her finger still points directly at the parchment in the sky. I guess she isn't coming out of that trance any time soon. So, moving up to her, I lift her up as delicately as I can. I transport her a few feet to the left of her spot. Marya kneels down amongst the sandy grains. She digs vigorously with her hands.

We all join in excavating. The sand becomes very moist. This doesn't pose us much of a challenge at all. After a few minutes, an object peeks out from the grains.

"It's a piece of paper," Travis shouts with

excitement. "Somebody read what it says."

I reach for it, and prepare to read it aloud. Based on the luxurious font and rhyming, it appears to be another message in a riddle. Gingerly unfolding it I read...

"'To awake Vitaly from this trance, one must be willing to take a dark chance. Follow the instructions on this scroll, and the location to the treasure will be told.'"

"What does that mean?" Gretchen asks with apprehension. She scratches her head in bewilderment.

"Maybe we have to follow these directions to wake her up," Travis replies. He appears baffled as well.

"Well," Marya shouts. "What else does it say?"

I attempt to interpret the rest...

"'Explore the wilderness of this island. Deep in this jungle, you will locate a large temple. Inside this temple, many puzzles shall manifest to test your memory and wisdom. Pass them all to get to the center. The way out will follow. Inside, you will be guided to another scroll with a password written on it. By reciting the password to Vitaly, she will awaken.'"

"That doesn't sound too bad," Gretchen replies. Her eyebrows swiftly rise. We just need to pass some trivia questions or something.

"'But, be warned,'" I continue in a grim tone. "'Fail a puzzle inside this temple, and you will transform to solid stone. If all four of you turn to stone, the Obstacle shall cease. This results in a failed challenge for everyone. Only one person is required to journey to the end. Once the word on the scroll is known and spoken aloud to young Vitaly, she will guide you to the treasure.'"

"Never mind," Gretchen flails her hands in the air. "Not so easy after all."

Chapter 20
Remember

"So, only one of us has to get through everything?" Marya quickly wonders with raised eyebrows as well. "Being turned to stone doesn't sound very fun."

"Yep," Travis answers. "Once we get the word, I guess we can wake her up. Apparently she knows some special answer that will lead us to the treasure; we have to get that magic word."

"Well," I yelp, flushed with anxiety. "Let's get started."

Bringing the scroll along, we rush into the enormous jungle. Abandoning the comforting sunshine and blissful beach is not something I'm ecstatic about. I guess there's nothing to be done about that. Almost immediately dark tree leaves close around us. They lock me inside their realm, blocking any ocean view; there goes that dream. Peering around for any sign of this ancient temple, I take the lead. We march into the unknown.

Screams and yelps of different animals overwhelm this place. From what my ears can tell, every living thing imaginable exists in this domain.

The cacophony jolts my brain, rendering it quite difficult to think. How we are ever going to find a temple in this gigantic jungle? Trees stretch up like skyscrapers. Branches envelop us in dense twilight. Millions of dirt paths jut out everywhere in sight. Glancing beneath my feet, I detect poison ivy lurking in far more places than I would have assumed.

Birds of all sizes and shades soar in the distance. They wholly appear to me as tranquil spirits flapping into the great unknown. Continuing the expedition, we're practically required to shout over all the noise. Marya remarks that she even detected a toucan flying amongst the trees. Nobody else can locate it, though.

Under our feet, tons of different insects roam the dirt. Billions of ants scatter their troops along in their conquest for dinner. Each scurries with utter intensity amongst fellow travelers. I'm probably crazy, but I swear that I notice a chimpanzee in the distance grasping a stick to capture them.

We've searched for what seems like hours. Precipitation descends without warning. Water droplets manifest almost out of thin air, swiftly plummeting. Not only rain, of course, lighting and thunder join the party. This makes for a very brutal storm indeed. It takes only minutes for dark clouds to overtake what remains of the sky.

"Oh no!" Travis wails, covering his head with his arm. "We better find this temple thing fast."

We all boisterously agree. Clamorous thunder booms in the distance with a lightning flash. Rain soaks all of us with no sign of subsiding. Branches dripping water onto me don't help the matter. It's not long before we are drenched, freezing, and miserable, all at the same time.

"Yeah," I add. "Everyone keep a sharp eye out!"

"I'm going to check over that hill!" Gretchen yells. She's smart; there is a pretty humongous hill up there. That probably is the ultimate place to get a good look around.

"Alright!" Marya yells back through a thunder roar. "Signal us if you see anything."

Gretchen darts up the hill. Her feet splash water and mud with each new step. We patiently watch her slide around. As we wait, irritation only increases.

"This rain better stop soon!" Travis yells reaffirming that. "How can we not find this temple?"

Once Gretchen arrives at the top, all of us gaze at her. As she appears to be searching around with her hand over her eyes, she stops and stares directly at once place. After a few seconds, she leaps up and down. Her finger points to the distance.

"Come up here!" she exclaims over the rushing storm.

I am nothing short of thrilled, desperately eager to escape this weather. There better be a temple on the other side of that hill. Starting up the hill, I find it extremely muddy and slippery. Climbing up is a lot harder than originally anticipated. Everyone's slipping and sliding all over the place. Despite the circumstances, I have to chuckle at everyone's struggles.

Marya wobbles uncontrollably about half way up, then falls on the ground flushed in mud. Dashing over, I quickly reach out my hand to her. Seeing me there, she grabs my hand. I haul her out of the muddy mess of ground. Her mud-drenched face is just too much for me. I can't help but snicker.

"Thanks Alcott," she shouts, even laughing a bit as well as spitting out dirt. "It's a little slippery up here."

"No problem. We're almost there."

Just then, lightning threateningly flashes right above. The pure strike of light remains visible in the sky for quite a few seconds, revealing the sheer danger of the circumstances. The three of us then trudge up with a burst of intensity.

When we all finally reach where Gretchen stands, everyone lays eyes on the discovery. A beautiful, seemingly four thousand year old monument stands at the bottom of the hill. Quite complex, most of the foundation is underground. There are deep, elegantly carved designs throughout the temple's pillars and walls; that's even visible from here. It is truly magnificent to gaze upon.

With no time to waste, we stampede down the muddy hill eager to reach our destination. Everyone slips and slides everywhere once again. No major wipe-outs occur this time. Lighting sparks accompanied by a new session of never-ending rain. As we reach the luxurious temple entrance, I can only hope Vitaly's lifeless body is doing okay.

We come across an eerie staircase descending into the deep underground. The few first steps show in the bit of light. They disappear into unrelenting darkness. There are no other passageways but this. All of the pillars and columns seem to just be there for design and show; the temple obviously only exists beneath those stairs. Atop of the entrance, there is another inscription. It accelerates my heartbeat.

'The Tunnel of Silence lies ahead, holding the secret to awake the dead. But if any speech is uttered inside, the speaker shall freeze to never arise.'

"Wait," I stammer a little frightened. "So, if anybody talks at all in there, we lose?"

"I guess so," Gretchen replies. "Who's ready for charades?" *That is certainly a new twist. We're not even able to talk to each other inside of this thing. What if something goes wrong? How are we supposed to warn anybody? Freezing forever never to arise does not sound like an enjoyable experience.*

"Well," Travis states. "I guess we have no choice. Everybody keep your mouths shut. Agreed?"

"Agreed," we all state in unison.

"Well, let's go." Travis moves off into the

blackness.

Descending the staircase, he fades into deep darkness. The guy becomes one with it. Gretchen, Marya, and I immediately follow. We're frightened of what horrors this structure may conceal. This is going to be awfully tricky with lack of light and speech. *How are we even going to solve these trivia things?* I guess there's no choice but to keep striding down the staircase, hopefully not abandoning my sanity along with the sunlight. When we finally arrive at the bottom, I detect an enormous dungeon. It's lit by numerous torches along the walls. At the end of the room, a crisp inscription contains another riddle.

'Hopefully, each of you have bonded through and through; because if not with Marya, distress must then ensue. Unless you wholly know your friend, this shall sadly be your end.'

That inscription hovers above what appears to be three doors. They stand four feet apart from each other. Each door has either an 'A,' 'B,' or 'C' carved above it. Apparently, these doors are going to be our answers to the trivia question. Based on the still wavering parchment, I'm assuming this will be a quiz on how well we know Marya.

The sharp reality jolts me. I know nothing about this girl! Could this be what the plane ride was for? That would certainly make sense. Marya had been extremely hostile and rude; she wouldn't tell us anything. Anger begins to rise inside my heart. If we lose this because of her attitude problem, I'm not going to be happy.

Immediately all of us glance back to locate Marya, but alas, there is no one there. Marya has vanished, just as we discover the question is about her. Where is she? We all know we can't shout her name or else we'll be turned to stone. Gretchen and Travis peer around in horror. It doesn't take long for me to figure out what is going on. Apparently, we don't get any time to study her, wherever they've taken the girl.

Just then, the doors under each letter open simultaneously. Another scroll manifests out of thin air. It explains the directions of what is expected of us.

'Three answers are given in doorway paths, two lead to your death, one to the next task.'

I guess two of the doors lead to nowhere. Only one takes us to the correct passage. Well, at least we have a one in three chance. *This can't be that difficult, can it? Bring on the question!* Then, both of the scrolls disappear into the abyss. A question is revealed, seemingly already carved into the decaying marble wall. It seems illegible in the darkness. So, I grab a torch off the wall and guide the flame to it. Now with bright fire up to it, the question is slowly unveiled.

'How old is Marya?' Gretchen and Travis trail close behind. They read the question as well. After I finish reading it, I glare at the three options carved into the stone.

A) 15
B) 16
C) 17

All of that is literally part of the foundation, as if that question had been crafted centuries ago. Through any of the three doorways, nothing is visible. Only darkness waits.

I surely have no idea. There's no mystery there. I barely even said two words to her. Looks like everything is on Gretchen and Travis's shoulders. Hopefully they know how old she is. That must have come up in conversation at some point.

Gretchen continues to point at the A door while

shaking her head. Apparently, she is sure fifteen is wrong. So, now the only options remaining are B or C. It could be either one, as I am useless to either of them at this point. Travis paces around the room for quite some time. We peer through both doors. I glance at Gretchen as she just continues to shake her head, meaning 'No,' at door A.

Both of us stare at Travis, when suddenly a light bulb goes off above his head. He halts in his tracks, then immediately heads straight toward the C 17. A grin spreads across his face. The guy must be sure of himself.

Immediately after he jaunts through, the other two doors slam shut. All entrance to both of them is blocked forever. Looks like we all have to go with the same answer, not that we would consider arguing that one. So, Gretchen and I follow Travis through the door into the eerie abyss. We are in complete darkness for quite a long time. Could this be the wrong passageway?

Maybe Travis is wrong and moments remain before each of us is frozen into stone. Just as doubts sink in, finally a delicate light gleams. A new room emerges ahead. Only this one appears to have a large scroll in it already. This delightful scroll proclaims…

'Correct.'

I couldn't be more ecstatic. I wipe off a lingering sweat bead from my forehead. We are more than lucky he remembered that one. I honestly have no idea what I would've chosen in retrospect. That scroll vanishes into thin air, abandoning us to the dark once more. Glancing around, I see only Gretchen and I have come out of the passageway. Gretchen's confused face proves my suspicions. Travis is definitely nowhere to be found.

Peering past the disappearing scroll, I discover Marya. She stands at the other end of this room! Halting myself, I am very cautious not to speak or else I'll turn to stone. She appears quite confused about what is going on, and frankly so am I. But there is no way to tell her what has just happened. I just offer an encouraging smile. Hopefully, this indicates we at least did something right. Another scroll then appears at the end of the room. My eyebrows rise with much intensity.

'Hopefully, each of you have bonded through and through; because if not with Travis, distress must then ensue. Unless you wholly know your friend, this shall sadly be your end.'

This replicates the earlier scroll, word for word. I'm nothing but positive now; that's why Travis has mysteriously vanished. Every time the question is about you, apparently you get taken somewhere else until it is over. Three doors again are present at the end, with the similar 'A,' 'B,' and 'C.'

Once more, the scroll reads…

'Three answers are given in doorway paths, two lead to your death, one to the next task.'

The scroll disappears revealing the new question. It is carved once again above the doorways. Still wielding my torch, I lift it up. Flames illuminate the question while Gretchen and Marya hover close by.

'Travis toils for his father, who tragically plummeted off a cliff into the rocks. But, what activity actually caused him to do so?'

A) Bike Riding
B) Roller Blading
C) Rock Climbing

These questions definitely show no mercy. No wonder that airplane ride had been so prolonged and tiresome. That's why we were all advised to get to know each other better. I just wish I paid closer attention to everybody's story. With this new-found question, I actually have a good idea it is A) Bike Riding, but I am not willing to fight for it.

This seems like a much simpler question. For that, I am grateful. Luckily, I'm not required to argue with charades. Marya and Gretchen both agree by pointing to the A as well. All three of us grin, whisking through the door. I'm feeling confident as the other two slam shut.

However, the corridor feels quite different to me this time. It appears much longer than before for some reason. Feeling all around me, I discover nobody is here except me. As I continue, I realize that I am totally alone. Gretchen, Marya, and Travis are nowhere to be found.

I have no choice but to trudge on to the corridor's end. For some reason, any indication of life itself ceases to exist. A light illuminates the dark space, as I suddenly emerge into a room mirroring the previous ones. This time, however, I stand alone. Based on the fact that I haven't died, and everyone's unanimous agreement, I doubt that we had chosen the wrong door. *So, why am I separated from the rest of my Allies?*

Perhaps the next question they have to solve is about me. That must be it! At least, that's my theory about the whole situation. Well, if that's true, guess I have nothing to do but wait for them. Hopefully, they can solve whatever question this dungeon will ask. Thinking about what it could be, my heartbeat accelerates. I hope I don't have a panic attack.

Did I tell them enough about myself on the airplane ride? What if I didn't elaborate on something important? Extreme paranoia jolts me, but I must calm myself. *Oh well, I guess it's too late to worry about that now. Whatever happens, happens; that's all there is to it.*

Pacing around like a mad man, I anticipate the arrival of my fellow Allies. After quite a long and tiresome time, nothing seems to be happening. Where could they possibly be? I think I see the hint of a shadow emerging through the doorway, but I realize I am nothing but delusional. Suddenly, the doorway ceases to exist. It leaves just the marble wall in its place. The sight makes me glare in extreme annoyance. That cannot be a good sign. Without any warning, another scroll manifests into the thin air.

'The rest have failed the question, each one of them must lose; so all their fates, Alcott, remain solely up to you.'

It requires a few seconds to comprehend, but alas it makes perfect sense. I don't want to believe the scroll's proclamation. There's no avoiding it now. My Allies have chosen the wrong pathway, and got my question wrong. Taking a sigh of rage, I contemplate what will happen next.

I chastise myself for not elaborating more about my life. Cursing my shyness and fear, I pull myself together as best as I can. Now, unless I complete this task, all of them are going to fail. Talk about pressure! Evidently, looks like everything now rests on my shivering shoulders.

The same scroll quickly appears just like all of the other ones had.

'Hopefully, each of you have bonded through and through; because if not with Gretchen, distress must then ensue. Unless you wholly know your friend, this shall sadly be your end.'

With the routine down, I lift my torch to the carved question once again.

'Gretchen fights to save her sister, deceased from attempting to rescue a squirrel. What was the child's name?'

A rocket launch of adrenaline shoots through me. I know this one! I don't know how I remember so vividly, but her name is definitely Sharia. I have never been so thankful that I paid attention in my life. Thank goodness this is something I actually have a clear picture of.

    A) Stephanie
    B) Samantha
    C) Sharia

Chapter 21
Delve

With much confidence, I stride through the third door with a C towering above it. The same darkness and freaky corridor follow. However, I have nothing but certainty building in me. The whole venture is a breeze. At the end of it, as expected, another room manifests. Each of these rooms completely copies the last, causing my mind to twirl in a slight haze. The new word inside brings waves of courage and positivity.

'Correct.'

Overjoyed is an understatement for my heart right now. Maybe I can actually do this after all. Relaxing with a few crisp breaths, I embark on figuring out the situation. Who is left to have a question about themselves? Alcott, Travis, Gretchen, and Marya are now all definitely complete. I know that much for sure.

There must only be one more question. The only Ally remaining is Vitaly. Everything copies all the other scrolls, except, yes, with Vitaly's name carved into the marble wall. However, in this room, something is surely peculiar. I can't decide whether to be ecstatic or paranoid upon first view. This time, instead of three doors, only two stand side by side in front of me. An 'A' door and a 'B' door tower over my shivering eyes. The torch's fire reveals the question.

'What country did Vitaly come from?'

A) Nepothria

B) Neptistone

Every ounce of hope and happiness abandons me. *Oh no, there is no possible way in the world I can remember that. Though I totally know the planet is Neptune, that does not help anything whatsoever.* The actual name of the country completely slips my mind. I peer at the new question with a blank expression. I'm desperate the answer will somehow magically pop into my head. *How can they possibly expect me to remember this?*

Dark smog in my soul reveals a horrible realization. This might be it for me and this Obstacle. I literally have no idea on this one at all. Both of the answers sound intelligent and correct. *How am I supposed to do this?* Pacing around the room, I rub the temples of my head praying for an answer. There is no way to determine how long this goes on for. All time blurs together in the torch's shimmering gleam. My whole life I have been told to go with my first instinct. Now, there isn't even one of those to go on.

After a long time, I arrive at a conclusion. This must be a fifty-fifty shot. No amount of contemplation will improve the situation. Without thinking too hard about it, I charge through the first door I saw, the A door.

The other slams shut into the stone, revealing my one and only pathway available. As now tradition, I whisk through the darkness. *There's definitely no turning back now. Here we go; about to freeze and turn into stone.* After a few seconds, my body does not feel rough. Letting out a sigh of relief only renders more fear. I detect a blue light shimmering in the distance. This has never happened before, which is nothing short of horrendous news.

Preparing for defeat, I lower my head. I grasp the little strength left to continue on. *Did I actually let them all down? Not only did I not reveal enough about myself for my question, I apparently didn't even pay attention well. Great job, Alcott. What will being frozen even feel like? Can I even tell?* The dazzling blue light widens and evolves, transforming into a new sight entirely.

In fact, the gleam appears to manifest into a new corridor. Putting aside all my delusions, I advance into a gigantic room before I even blink. This enormous place practically resembles the hotel lobby. I'm utterly flabbergasted. The towering ceiling bewilders me. Upon a golden scroll emerging from the air, a written inscription makes my soul leap in awe. In bright silver letters atop, the message reads…

'Correct.'

I stand speechless half-expecting some cruel joke. Breaking down right there, I collapse onto the floor. Shimmering tears remain a tangible sign of my shock. I honestly never dreamt I could make it to the end of this by myself. Gathering my strength for whatever may come next, I glance around this new room.

Everything, from the elaborate walls to the diamond floor tiles, is completely gold. No other color exists. Either that or my mind is hazy. Every candle, painting, table, and chair, shines and glistens. I'm literally entering buried treasure. An enormous chandelier dangles from the center. Lavishing gems catch my eye. Atop of this brilliant fixture, a giant word has been constructed throughout the jewels. There it is, I tell myself. That's what's going to wake up frozen Vitaly on the beach. The secret password is undoubtedly…UNLIMITED.

Another scroll shows itself to me, immediately sending me on my next mission.

'Repeat the magic word to Vitaly, and she will complete the end of the challenge. You've done well, survivor. Deliver the message, and she must accomplish the rest.'

Beyond the scroll and the beautiful chandelier, light protrudes from a miniature opening. It must be the way out of this temple. Finally being able to escape is wholly my biggest dream come true. UNLIMITED. I charge through the hole repeating that word to myself. UNLIMITED. I can't forget that. UNLIMITED. Exiting, I perceive the spectacular sights and smells of the sunny beach. With a few swift glances, I see the passageway has apparently come out of some very large tree. Jumping out of the tree hole, I stomp onto sand.

Sunshine blazes as the ocean glimmers with utter tranquility.

After being confined in the temple, my soul stands petrified in utter heaven. Gentle gusts flutter against my cheeks, causing a large grin to form. There is no time to take it all in though. Locating Vitaly has to be my one and only priority. Hopefully, she is still in the same spot as before, wherever that may be.

UNLIMITED. Dashing along the beach, I keep a sharp eye out for her in every direction. Wind crashes my face as the heavenly sun continues to sparkle. This is one of the best places I've ever been to, and I begin to contemplate life's mysteries despite the urgent situation. *Could this be what happens after you die? Beautiful beaches with sunlight gleam forever? That certainly sounds pretty awesome to me.* Getting my head back, I chastise myself for not focusing on the task at hand.

Long strides only bring about more heavy breaths. I charge across the sand with the sun becoming my mortal enemy. Sweat drips from my hair. The sting blazes my eyes. Desperately wiping it away, something appears in the distance up the beach. There, just as we left her in the distance, is Vitaly frozen in time. She remains in the same pose. Her finger desperately points to the scroll in the sky. UNLIMITED. UNLIMITED. UNLIMITED. Exhausted, I transfer all my strength into darting to the little kid.

Finally, with a few clumsy stumbles, I reach her petrified body. I hold my hands to my knees. I'm utterly exhausted.

"UNLIMITED!" I yell at her with every ounce of energy.

Immediately, the sound of the word breaks her trance. Her form practically implodes. Now with regained life and energy, Vitaly peers around with panic. She takes in her new surroundings. At the sight of me panting beside her, she acquires a giant grin of triumph.

"Alcott!" she wails, leaping up and down. "You did it! You passed it! I know what to do now. Is it only you? Did you finish it all by yourself?"

"Yes...I...I..." Everything begins to get hazy. The sun's blazing rays become far too much for my shaky body to handle. Losing myself entirely, all feeling in my legs disappears. The last sight I view is sunlight hovering amongst the crashing waves.

"Alcott!" I faintly hear Vitaly yell one last time. I fall victim to deep slumber. *What in the world is happening right now? Is this fainting, or sleeping?* I can't even tell anymore. I'm utterly gone.

***

Emerging back into consciousness, I jolt up to figure out what has occurred. Expecting to stand on burning sand, I now detect soft, comfortable blankets. No question about it, I'm back in my hotel room. I feel extremely rested and exuberant. In a few seconds, total anxiety replaces that. *What happened? Did Vitaly do what she was supposed to do? Did she find the treasure?* Darting up as fast as I can, I charge toward the door.

I rush down the hallway. My heart beats with anticipation. When I finally reach the bottom of the staircase, I am shocked to discover Gretchen, Travis, and Marya already down at the restaurant. I find them devouring their meals in the exact same booth as before. The idea of food distorts my mind into a world of deliciousness. Hungry is merely an understatement at this point. Shaking myself from hypnosis, I decipher their facial expressions. Each one of my Allies appears glum and depressed. They shovel food into their mouths.

"What happened?" I ask frantically. My fingers grasp an edge of the table with firm hands. "Did she do it? Did she get the treasure?"

Chapter 22
Strive

"Alcott!" Travis yelps with wide eyes. All three of them appear thrilled by the sight of me. "What happened with you? They won't tell us, they say it has to come from you."

"Did you get to the end of the temple?" Marya adds quickly, nearly dropping her fork.

"Yes!" I exclaim. "I got back to Vitaly with the secret word and she woke up! When I was in the temple, though, it said that the last part of the challenge would have to be done by her alone. Everything went hazy, I think I fainted or something. Then, I woke up here."

"That's amazing!" Gretchen screams.

"You actually finished it all by yourself?" Travis inquires, basically dumbfounded.

"Yeah," I say. "The last question was a complete guess, but luck must have been on my side for that. I guess it's all up to Vitaly now."

"I can't believe it, Alcott. Do you have any idea what she has to do to find whatever treasure it is?" Marya asks.

"No, it didn't say. I guess now the only thing we can do is hope for the best."

"I cannot believe we couldn't get your question right!" Travis wails in rage. "It was so simple, but we just couldn't do it."

"You told it to us specifically, Alcott, but none of us could remember the answer," Gretchen adds with a frown.

"What was the question about me?" I am surely eager to find out what it could possibly be.

"The question was," Marya glumly states, "what activity did you and Gari love to do the most? We were immediately all torn between video games, basketball, or tennis. All of them seemed right to me."

That is indeed a pretty difficult question. I know I told them it was video games at some point, but I barely elaborated on the fact at all. I guess that is my fault for not doing so. Video games were a pretty important part of our lives.

"So..." Gretchen continues with a mouthful of linguini, "we argued, silently of course, and finally decided we would go with basketball. It didn't really sound right to me, but I had no other inclination to go on."

"We traveled down the dark hallway," Travis adds. "A giant sign flashed 'incorrect,' and all senses seemed to vanish. Each of us appeared back in our hotel rooms. After the three of us met up, we discovered that you hadn't come back yet. A glimmer of hope arose that you might actually still be in the challenge. And you actually did it!"

"Thanks," I say, feeling proud of myself. "And its video games, for future reference."

"I knew it! I feel so stupid!" Gretchen shouts, dropping her fork to the plate in annoyance. "You definitely said that right to our faces in the plane."

Just then, a Sphream hovers over to our table. It seems to have an important message to deliver based on its increasing speed.

"Vitaly has arrived, she will be down shortly," it states immediately.

All of us are totally overcome with anticipation. Even with all the work we had to do, passing or failing is completely dependent on her. I can only hope that she succeeded in finding whatever treasure it was.

Faint footsteps echo from above. I leap up from the booth. With all of our eyes glued to the stairs, Vitaly strides down them. No bright light or dark mist hovers above the statues. It could go either way at this point. She heads toward us, and no denying it, with an enormous smile on her face. A gigantic light five times envelops the entire lobby. The extreme illumination is too much for our eyes. I raise my arm to cover them. After a few seconds, the bright light soars and shatters apart into five parchments, each taking a place over our statues. Each one reads the same thing.

'Challenge Number Two Passed.'

Chapter 23
Don't Make a Sound

I've never seen all of these people, nor even myself, so ecstatic before. Marya darts up and hugs Vitaly right away. Gretchen grins from ear to ear, as Travis peers at his statue. Everything seems to be going well for each of us at this point. Just then, the Jauntla magically appears right beside our table.

"Congratulations!" she wails with much intensity. "You've all done beautifully. Each one of you has passed the second Obstacle! Continue at this pace, and your goal will surely be achieved. You can truly reverse the cycle of death."

"Thank you so much!" I reply with a sharp grin. Everything is literally perfect. If all goes like this, I may actually save Gari's life, even if my own has to be over. Though these Obstacles are difficult, we just proved that we can do them. I honestly don't think I've ever been this proud of myself before.

"Vitaly," Travis inquires with a raised eyebrow. "What did you have to do in there?"

"Well," she stammers. "Right when we entered the challenge, a strange voice told me that I would be in a coma-thing the whole time. I would awake if one or all of you guys passed the temple trials, whatever those are. If that was to happen, I was to go back to that temple in the jungle, and dig under the largest pillar. It took a long time, but I finally got to a treasure chest. Now here I am."

So, that's where the treasure had been all along. It

rested underneath a pillar I stood inches away from at one point.

"Awesome!" I say, giving her an enormous hug myself. "I'm so proud of you."

"Thanks so much." She leaps up with a new burst of joy.

"Well, even with all this happiness, you must prepare for the next Obstacle to come. Your next challenge will be done individually," the Jauntla proclaims. "Pass three of the six, and you will win; fail four of the six, and life returns to normal. You are definitely exceeding expectations at this point. Good luck to each and every one of you."

With that conclusion of her speech, she disappears into nothingness. We are abandoned to an eerily silent restaurant.

Well, I think it's been a pretty good day. The next challenge won't begin for a while. So, we enjoy our time at the magnificent hotel. They do have video games lying there, and for that I am extremely thankful. Travis, Vitaly, and I play for hours on end. The thrill of crushing your opponent in battle never gets old. A few swear words get thrown around in the midst of competition I'm not too proud of.

The brawling and swift button-pushing remains fierce, very well reminding me of old times with Gari. Marya spends her free time away from us. I'm not too shocked about that. Perhaps one day we'll become friends.

She peruses literature throughout the establishment, while having in-depth conversations with the Sphreams. They aren't allowed to reveal very much about all of the hard-hitting questions she asks. However, they do have some pretty interesting conversations.

This downtime allows us to learn a lot more about

each other. Gretchen, for example, has had a life-long dream of becoming a pastry chef. She has always had a deep infatuation with baking. Throughout this hiatus, she personally spends a lot of time examining Sphream chefs in the kitchen. They teach her tons of different recipes. I surely appreciate that, as I'm always willing to be a dessert tester!

We later realize that, behind one locked door in the lobby, a spectacular swimming pool awaits! Diving into the water is like delving into a new world. The water helps everyone to relax and enjoy life, while getting great exercise in the process. Leaving this hotel is not something I am planning on doing anytime soon. If I keep winning, this could be my home for quite a while. That may be my motivation to win this thing alone, aside from saving a life of course.

After a while, I explore the beautiful garden once more. Though it is nighttime, the many lights scattered throughout the courtyard illuminate the exuberant flowers. There are so many varieties of plants everywhere, it is hard not to gaze in awe. Every color imaginable seems to be in there, as if a rainbow has transformed into plant form. Each contains a very unique and delightful smell too.

Peering ahead, I detect someone. I pace a few steps closer until I see Marya. Her shadowy form roams about sniffing various flowers.

"Hey," I wave to Marya, breaking the peaceful silence. She actually waves back with a grin. Wow, I certainly did not expect that response. That's more than I ever hoped for.

"What are you up to?" I ask.

"Oh," she turns toward the plants. "I'm just looking around."

"I still can't believe this is happening. It's all so

surreal," I state, rotating toward the vast hotel.

"Yeah." Her grin transitions to a deep frown. Perhaps I should get to the bottom of this.

"Is there something wrong? Why have you not talked to anyone lately?"

Ten seconds of utter silence follow. She casually kicks a pebble with her foot. I guess I'm not getting an answer.

Suddenly, her eyes look into mine.

"I've just been thinking about this man I killed."

My heartbeat stops as my eyes widen. The statement astonishes me; I have no idea how to respond to that. I open my mouth to attempt, but no words come out. Thankfully, she continues.

"Yeah, I wasn't the most responsible kid. Let's just say I had a very large amount of drink. I chose to drive home anyway. Guess I didn't think about anyone but myself."

I continue to stay completely silent. No words at all are mustered.

"Well, long story short, I crashed into another car. The guy's dead because of me. I couldn't even comprehend what just happened; I was so startled. Some policeman offered me the book, *'Altering Fate'*. How he got a hold of that thing I'll never know. Why I actually tried the insanity I'll never know. But, I'm here. I'm going to save him if I can."

Her story is horrifying. It's difficult for me to put myself in her shoes. I utter the only words of comfort I can.

"That's very brave of you, Marya. I know you can save him."

"I hope so," she says, delicately touching one of the flowers. "I'm ready to give everything I've got. Are you prepared to battle another monster like the shark?"

Oh man, I thought. In all the tranquility, I forgot how horrific that had been. How that could have slipped my mind I'll never know. I wouldn't possibly have to fight anything like that again, would I?

"Ready as I'll ever be," is the only thing I can mutter. Great, fear now jolts my heart once again.

"I still can't believe you did that," she adds, plucking a green petal. "Even fathoming being alone in an ocean causes chills to run up and down my spine."

"Well, let's just say," I gaze up at the sky, "I'll be glad if I never see another shark again."

We both have to laugh, despite the dark circumstances.

Marya then states, "Fighting a great white shark…a temple of silence…an undersea exploration…what could they possibly throw at us next?"

"Well," I say, "I have no idea what else it could be. It seems, though, we should be ready for anything out there. There's definitely no mercy in these Obstacles."

My peaceful demeanor transforms to apprehension. The two of us gaze off into the darkness. I suddenly hear the pitter-patter of footsteps coming from the hotel. Turning around, I discover Gretchen has come out to join us.

"Hey guys," she shouts, with a skip. "How's it going out here?"

"Great." Marya waves a hand of welcome. "How about you? Still learning in the kitchen?" It's awesome to see Marya's mood uplifting.

"Yep," she responds instantly. "I figured out how to cook a lot of new foods! Won't be much use if I pass this thing and die though, will it?"

Everyone had to smile despite the deadly undertone of the statement. That's definitely what you call dark humor.

"What do you think happens when you die?" Gretchen asks, not shying away from the scariest question of them all. "I always imagined going to a beautiful castle forever in sunlight. What about you guys?"

I don't know what to say, but that sounds pretty awesome to me. However, that for some reason also seems a bit boring, if you can understand my mindset. I really don't want the competition and fight of life to ever end, you know?

"I never really dwelt on it that much," I reply amongst my deep contemplation. "I work at a hospital, so there's always new life coming in and out right away. You never really think about it."

"What's it like being a doctor?" she asks. "I heard the schooling is pretty tough."

"Yeah, there's lots of studying, but I'd take it over a shark any day." They both grin as I continue... "It's really fun, though. It's good to be needed, you know? I love walking in to have somebody smile at my arrival. It just dawns on me, if I hadn't worked there, I never would have even gotten that book."

Hearing another sound, I swiftly glance toward the door. Just then a Sphream arrives to greet us all. Floating up to us along the pathway of flowers, it whispers...

"Hello Marya, Gretchen, and Alcott. I'd advise you to get some rest for your next challenge. This one's going to be done individually again, remember? Vitaly and Travis have already returned to their rooms."

"Alright," Marya replies with a yawn. "I'm ready to sleep."

"I need to pass this one," Gretchen states with defiance. "I can't fail another one, or I'll have only one failure left."

"You can do it, Gretchen." I rest a hand on her

118

shoulder. "We've got one win under our belts already."

With that the three of us head in up the stairs. We disperse to our respective hotel rooms. I still have a few nightmares after falling asleep, but nothing as serious as the first night. At least, nothing that literally feels real. Or if there are, I forget about them before I wake up. *I guess nightmares aren't that bad when you don't remember them. However, I suppose I usually do. Let's just say if I ever see Vitaly knocking at my door at two in the morning, I will not be answering.*

"Rise and shine!" a voice wails from the hallway.

It doesn't take long to figure out it is the Sphream that shouts. It beckons, awaking me from my slumber. I rise, stretch, and rub my eyes preparing for a new day. *This is new; I'm not used to it being my alarm for the morning. Oh well, guess I better get ready.*

"Prepare yourself for Obstacle #3! Remember, this one will, like the first, be done on your own."

I'm ready now. I'm pumped to take on anything. Perhaps dueling a shark will fill you with that confidence and adrenaline. I'm almost excited as to what's going to happen. Well, let's get this show on the road.

We do the same thing as the day before, stride down to the booth at the restaurant. There is definitely no question as to what I am getting...chocolate chip pancakes. No day could be a failure started with chocolate chip pancakes. It's science. Looks like I had a positive influence on Travis and Gretchen, because they order the same thing after watching me devour them.

Wiping chocolate from my lips, I reminisce about the last individual challenges. Vitaly and Travis were given trivia from a story, Gretchen had to be a fighter pilot, Marya journeyed on a deep treasure hunt, and I fought a giant sea monster. There are definitely unlimited Obstacles in this reverse death cycle thing. Nobody here can deny that.

"You think," Vitaly inquires while chewing, "we'll have to do each other's challenges? Like...I mean... everyone's get switched around or something?"

"I don't think so," I say, thinking that would be too simple. "Although, if you guys would like to fight a shark, go right ahead."

Everyone laughs. However, I sense a little fear inside each of them. That brings the tension and nervousness down a lot, at least for me anyway. *This really is a great group of people. I guess if we all succeed, I'll be glad to leave this life along with them.*

Suddenly, interrupting my thoughts, the Jauntla appears by our booth.

Chapter 24
Abyss

"Hello again!" she exclaims. "Are you all ready for Challenge Number Three? You all have fought marvelously so far, from battling sharks to solving puzzles in dark temples. Many of you have surpassed the highest expectations. Remember, this Obstacle must be attempted by you alone. No depending on someone else to do all the work. The burden will be wholly yours. Please, if you would now follow me."

Just as before, we are guided out into the flowery courtyard toward the gigantic staircase. Multiplying plants appear even brighter with the shimmering sun. Looking at them gives me a calming feeling. They are like little fans cheering me on. Nervousness once again sinks in.

Guess this is going to be the routine for a while. We all continue to leap up the stairs until the hotel disappears amongst deep smog. This is certainly horrifying. Last time we knew we were all going in together. This task requires much more bravery from everyone, knowing that all we have to count on is our own self.

Again, we arrive on the platform. Almost immediately as we do so, the Jauntla vanishes. Without even a goodbye, the five of us are left alone. As now expected, the darkness envelops me and everything around. Vitaly, Travis, Marya, and Gretchen disappear entirely.

"Alcott, Alcott, Alcott," the voices whisper, shout, and wail in unison. Even though I know this part is coming, the constant creepy chanting never fails to terrify.

"Alcott, Alcott, Alcott." Either the voices desire to kill me, or beg for my help. The combination of that at extremely high volume is just a bit much for me to handle.

Thankfully, it quickly begins to subside and fades into nothingness. When the eerie noise finally ceases, I find myself remaining in entire darkness. *Does that mean the Obstacle has begun?* I feel around myself, discovering I am in some type of enclosed space. Immediately, claustrophobia sinks in. As I am trying to figure a way out of wherever I am, a dark voice whispers in my ear.

"Shhhhhh…Alcott…Shhhh…don't make a sound." The raspy voice contains an urgent tone. It's as if it's even frightening itself.

Instantly petrified, I have no idea what to do. I immediately pull my hands back and prepare for it to say something else.

"You are in a giant mansion, Alcott; it is very late at night; very, very late indeed. You are the only living person in the mansion, but you are definitely not alone."

What is that supposed to mean? Ghosts or something? At the least the great white shark thing I can actually kill. What in the world am I going to do now?

"Every door and window is now locked from the inside. There is no escape, Alcott; no escape whatsoever. In this deathly mansion, you will hear many spirits conversing. Some speak to themselves, and some to others. A few just yammer on for no reason whatsoever. However, these demons will be invisible to your living eyes. One of these unseen spirits shall speak of the location of a key inside."

"You must find this spirit," it continues with a sharp cough. I get the impression time grows thin. "Listen to what it has to say. Head to the location of the key. Once the key is located, use it on any door, escape, and you have won the Obstacle."

I inhale a deep breath, praying I'm not completely insane. Apparently I have to search around and listen to a bunch of ghosts. One of them is supposed to be talking about a key. I have to retrieve this key, unlock a door, and walk out. Despite the whole haunted ghost thing, this doesn't seem that complicated.

"But be careful, Alcott," the voice wheezes. "None of these spirits know that you have entered their domain. If any of them find out that you are here, you will be transported back to this cabinet. The Obstacle begins again."

Oh, this certainly adds difficulty. *I have to hide from them too? How am I going to listen and keep myself secret at the same time?* This is going to be much harder than I thought.

"You have until morning to complete this task." The whisper fades into softer decibels. "If the sun rises with you inside, you shall fail. Begin now!"

I pause, awaiting the slightest hint of more instruction. After a few moments, though, I decide the strange whispering voice is finished. Anxiety manifests inside my heart. I must shove it down. Confidence is required to battle through this.

I take a few seconds to pull myself together and plan a course of action. First things first, I must figure out what the heck I am inside of. Gently shoving my left hand forward, I feel part of the enclosed structure moves. Creaking it open, I find myself inside a very dark room. It is extremely tiny. Little light gets in at all. I crawl out in haste, realizing I have been inside a cabinet of some sort. From the material and color, it has been more oddly crafted than any piece of ancient furniture I have ever seen.

My surroundings indicate nothing too significant. It

has an attic type of feel. Before I make any attempt at moving, I peer toward the end of the room. There looks to be a hole on the ground where a little light emanates from. Tip-toeing as quietly as I possibly can, I reach the hole. It leads down to the next floor. *Yep, I'm definitely in the attic. What a wonderful place to begin.* I drop down on all fours to acquire a better view of where this actually leads to. A ladder hangs about five feet down. *That must be where I need to--*

Just then, I hear a faint scream. The wail twists my heart with a sharp jolt. It could either be a moan, or a massive cry for help. Utterly frozen, I lean my head in a bit closer to get a better sound. The obnoxious voice becomes far more boisterous. I fear, whoever it is, may be coming this way. As the volume increases, I realize that is the inevitable truth.

Petrified to death, I crawl away from the hole. I pray I'm inaudible. The voice's volume and urgency dramatically increases, frightening me enough to make me return to the rusty cabinet. I slam the door shut. Whoever this spirit is, it is definitely heading up to this room.

Attempting to breathe softly, I hunker down on my knees. *What did that voice say at the start of this thing? I'm not supposed to let anything or anyone know that I am here.* The voice gains rage and decibels as the ladder creaks with a foot in place. There is nothing interpretable in the moan whatsoever. Constant yelps of pure agony continue without end.

Whoever this is enters the attic, and the abominable moaning suddenly ceases. Breathing through my nose is certainly no longer an option. I just inhale with a wide open mouth, and cover my knees in my face. *Go away.* After about ten seconds, the spirit seems to determine there's nothing here. It initiates its descent back down the ladder.

The wailing has literally vanished as eerie silence takes its place. After a few minutes, I know for sure that it is gone.

That was way too close! This Obstacle is going to be hell, perhaps literally. I must evacuate this room for good. Careful not to make the tiniest squeak, I leave the cabinet. Once again, I crawl on all fours to the hole.

Taking my first step on the ladder, I am grateful it does not squeak. Based on the deep blackness underneath, it does not look like anywhere in this house will be much brighter than the attic.

Finally reaching the foot of the ladder, I leap onto the floor. My eyes dart back and forth. No sign of spirits is revealed. *Where am I supposed to search, or listen, first? One of them is supposed to be talking about the location of some key. Who knows where to find them?* Getting caught in the process also remains a prevalent issue.

The first room sits to the right of me. Peering inside, I can even tell in the blackness it's the washroom. Since the door is already open, I decide to go inside. I need to assess my options from a somewhat more stable location. From what I can determine, it looks like any other bathroom I've ever seen. This is despite the freaky, ancient feel to it. As I examine the wooden cupboards, I gasp. Another voice wails from outside.

The sonorous tone rises, becoming much more powerful with each second. Whoever this is, it strides down the hall humming a deep, blissful melody. My heart rapidly beats again. I wonder what I should do. Having no idea where to dash or hide, I conclude my best course of action is to dive into the empty bath tub. What other choice do I have?

Lying down as cautiously as possible, I pray I'm unnoticeable. I should be as long as nobody decides to look in here. If I make no noise whatsoever, I may be safe. The cheerful singing comes pretty close to me now. This spirit whisks at a swifter pace. I could not have leaped into this tub at a better time. To my horror, I hear an abrupt first step into the washroom. *Of course, they must enter the bathroom now, at the most inopportune moment.* There is no way to calm my fear.

With the art I've seemingly mastered, breathing totally through my mouth I make no sound. Thankfully, the creaking ceases right as it hits the sink. A faucet squeaks. As rushing water fills the sink, the spirit hums its little ditty with much more gusto.

"Dum de dum, de de dum," it belts out while scrubbing. "I'm ready to enter a peaceful slumber. This night has been magical." As the spirit maintains the light conversation with itself, I continue remaining still.

This ghost's voice actually sounds tender and wholesome. Thinking I am safe for the time being, I relax a bit. The next thing I hear renders the hair on the back of my neck to stand on end.

"Right after a nice bath, of course," the spirit blissfully states. At that horrifying proclamation, I hear creaking approaching closer and closer to my current location. My heart sinks. Oh no, this is it. I'm definitely going to be seen.

"Whoops, need to get a towel," the spirit shouts with a swift rotation. "Dum de de, dum de…"

Based on the shut door, I assume it has exited. Darting out of the tub as fast as I can, I tip-toe to the door.

But my darkest fear manifests, and all of my hope departs. The door knob turns and creaks, as its goal has been reached. My eyes dart open in pure panic at the realization. I have to hide on the other side of the now opening door. I barely get there in time before the spirit reenters. I stand behind the door. It doesn't take long for me to figure out what its next move will be; closing the door. If it succeeds in accomplishing this, I will be found out for sure. Out of sheer panic, I grasp the handle, hauling the door the opposite way.

"What in the world...this stupid door!" the spirit yelps, obviously aggravated. "Too old and creaky to even close properly...How am I supposed to take a proper bath in this household? I guess I better get Tom to come shut it."

My legs shiver in complete shock. *I never believed that would work. My pulling the door back caused it to believe the door was actually stuck.* Thankfully this ghost is not the sharpest tool in the shed. As footsteps slowly fade down the stairs, I don't hesitate for a moment. My time in this bathroom is surely over. I refuse to remain here any longer. Dashing out, my eyes peer around for any other place to hide before they come back. Continuing down the hallway with vigilance, I discover various bedrooms on both sides.

Based on the previous ghost's statement, bathrooms will probably be best to avoid if ghosts are heading off to sleep soon. So, I head toward the staircase. There's no proper way to do this without being detected. Therefore, I'm just going to attempt it the best way I can.

Surprisingly, however, nothing seems to notice my hunched body descend the stairs. For the moment, I'm pretty sure I am safe. There are no nearby voices. The reason for this instantly becomes clear. From a very large living room beyond the bottom of the stairs, I hear various voices shouting and laughing. They aren't boisterous or choleric, but actually quite joyful. It appears as if some game may actually be going on.

"Well, would you look at that," says an excited spirit.

"Oh, Mary," says another giggling ghost, "you've

obviously cheated. You couldn't possibly have won that quickly."

"Someone's a sore loser, aren't they?" the apparent winner responds.

During this conversation, I finally reach the bottom of the stairs. I slither behind a wall. At the last jest by the winner, the whole table erupts into unanimous laughter. From what I can tell, about five or six spirits are playing a card game of some sort. Tilting my head to where the voices emerge, I detect a table with cards floating in the air by themselves. No one exists there to hold them.

The sight baffles and intrigues me. I guess I won't be able to see these ghosts at all, yet I can view the inanimate objects they control. In the midst of all this, I hear another pair of footsteps stampeding down the staircase. Gotta move, and fast. Crawling on all fours, I locate a perfect hiding place behind an enormous cabinet. Squeezing through, I just may be in the clear.

Now, I can concentrate fully on listening to these spirits. With the large number of voices, one of them must have some knowledge about a key. At this point, I hear the bathroom ghost. It yells at someone in the next room.

"Tom! Please fix your confounded door up there. It's stuck on something and won't shut!"

Chapter 25
Alone

"What? Stuck on what? I'll go check it out," this Tom, apparently, answers in confusion.

Both of their footsteps indicate they stride toward the staircase. I can't see them either. Creaks and voices are the only way I can tell location and intentions. Now that those two are out of the way, I turn my attention back to the card game.

"So, have you heard about these intruders?" a new voice inquires in a sly tone.

"Oh, yes," another responds. "Everyone's been talking about them. I don't know what they are going to do about that whole situation. It frankly terrifies me to death."

Intruders? That sounds very similar to what that voice in the cabinet said I am doing in their abode. *They can't be speaking about me, can they?*

"Well, I heard that in the dead of night," a ghastly voice states, "they sneak into your household, and steal everything they can find."

"Yes, it's true!" another responds. I hear a fist slam against the table. "The last one they caught thieved just a few houses down from here!"

"What did they do with him again?"

"Let's just say it wasn't a pretty sight."

Oh no. Somehow I think I fit the qualifications for this description. The last statement fills me with complete terror. *What's going to happen if they find me?*

"Do you think one of them would come into this

house?"

"Well, enough of this depressing talk," an elderly spirit proclaims, changing the horrific subject. "Let's play another round."

"Sounds great to me!"

They all commence playing their game. Cards levitate in the air. The sight of them jolting up in fives frankly terrifies me. I don't know what these intruder people do, but apparently these ghosts aren't fond of them. This is starting to freak me out a little bit. I feel like I haven't made remote progress yet. Just then, footsteps creak from upstairs.

"That old hag is crazy!" the voice screams. "The door isn't stuck at all! She's losing her marbles, not that she ever had any."

Everyone at the tables laughs at the proclamation.

"Hey Tom! We are just talking about these intruders everyone's going on about. What are your thoughts on the matter?"

"Oh, I've heard about them," Tom's haunting tone is rough. "If I ever see one strolling in my house, it'll be the last thing they ever do."

"Leave it to Tom to get all morbid."

After that, Tom exits the room. He returns to his original location. I hunker down behind the cabinet, as moving is not on my favorite-things-to-do list. What better hiding place could there possibly be? But after a while of spying on these card players, I realize none of them has anything of value to say. Or at least, they are not saying it. Since Tom is the one who apparently owns this establishment, my best bet would be to follow him. If anyone knows where this so-called key is, it would be Tom.

So, I slide out from behind the cabinet. I go over the stairs to where Tom was. As I peer into the elegant study,

Tom peruses some literature in contentment. I naturally assume this, based on the book floating in the air. A page turns by itself. I'm certainly not going to get anything out of him like this. Contemplating what to do, I hear another voice from the card table shout.

"Who would like some refreshments?"

"Sounds great!"

"Okay, I'll be right back."

They must be going to the kitchen. I assume that's where the drinks are kept. That's just peachy. To my horror, I realize the kitchen is directly next to us. If I walk in there, I'm dead! Yet it is the only place I can go. I must get as far away from the refrigerator as possible. I dive under a table close to the back and wait.

Sure enough a spirit comes into the kitchen. The refrigerator juts open by itself. After drinks float out in mid-air, they move closer to my general direction, increasing my heart rate. To my terror, she sets the beverages on the table above me with a big clunk.

Based on all the noise, I think she's organizing them all onto a tray. This tray clinks as she raises it up, making it float in the air. Just at that moment, I lose all hope as a can falls off the tray. Aluminum slams onto the floor a foot in front of me. The giant bang actually causes me to gasp. I cover my eyes. It isn't long before a giant yelp in my face: "INTRUDER!"

The deadly volume startles me. I have no choice but to scream at the top of my lungs.

"INTRUDER! INTRUDER! INTRUDER!" the voice yells. Intensity increases each time she wails.

I dive out from under the table and desperately attempt to escape. There is no use now, my cover has been blown. When I reach the other room, the cards all immediately drop onto the table. All the other spirits see me

131

as well. My deathly screams only increase with a simultaneous chant.

"INTRUDER! INTRUDER! INTRUDER!"

The voices accumulate. I stand frozen in the middle of the room. I can't even tell if my own wailing or theirs has more volume. Peering around, I grasp the nearest stool to me. I know I can't conquer ghosts with this implement, but I don't know what else to do.

Now the spirits circle me, proving there is surely no escape now. I hurl the stool into the abyss ahead of me. Maybe the object will cause some damage. Alas, it travels right through as if nothing is there at all. Just as the stool crashes against the wall, I begin to faint. A blunt object bashes my forehead.

***

Returning to consciousness, I leap up in panic. I discover I'm back in the same attic cabinet. This is just as the original voice said would happen. I'm still pretty woozy, but I have to get myself back. Exactly as last time, the wailing ghost jerks up through the hole. Again, it returns back down as if nothing happened.

I wait for the spirit to depart before I make any move. Climbing out of the cabinet, I once again whisk toward the hole, gravitating down the ladder. There is no way I'm dealing with the wailing or bathroom ghosts again. As I head toward the stairs, it dawns on me. Perhaps I may have bypassed the bedrooms too quickly. I'm pretty sure they are deserted, based on everyone playing cards downstairs.

Purely out of my curiosity, I tip-toe into one right beside the ladder. I discover a magnificent master bedroom. Dazzling maroon sheets envelop the bed. It appears extremely organized with nothing out of place. Whoever sleeps here certainly has an obsession with order. Suddenly I detect footsteps. The same annoying voice hums as before; definitely the bathroom ghost. I will not be making that mistake again, that's for sure. So, I dive under the bed for the time being.

"Dum de de, dum dee dum," it sings in utter tranquility once more.

It decides to take a bath as before. Of course, it narrates its own intentions. Repeating the same circumstances, it forgets the towel. Only when it returns with one floating in mid-air, the door does indeed close. No intruder hides there to stop it. As the sound of the tub filling with water enters my ears, I abandon this bedroom. I dash into another.

With my premature haste to get downstairs, I can't believe I missed this before. The queen-sized bed's sheets bulge up and down, as if someone sleeps beneath them. As I look, I determine the bump in the bed is quite miniature indeed. That definitely assures me a child rests under there. At the moment of this discovery, footsteps charge up the stairs.

So, naturally, I crawl under the bed. I cannot wake whoever this is. Shoving my entire body under, from what I can tell, has been successful, as no child shrieks. I am grateful that I did this. The footsteps now enter the room I am in now! I hear a jolt from the child above me, causing me to lightly gasp as well.

"You scared me, mom!" I hear from directly above. Obviously the child that was lost in slumber just a moment ago.

"Oh I'm sorry, baby," the adult spirit whispers, striding in with caution. "I just wanted to check on you."

"I'm sleeping fine!" the child yelps. "Now I'm

scared. I thought you were an intruder or something!"

"No intruder is going to get you," she says, gently sitting on the bed with the kid. "Not while I'm around."

"Well, now I'm really going to have nightmares. Thanks a lot! I hear these intruders are getting closer to our house. What if they steal all our treasures or something?"

"Oh baby," the mother replies with a gentle demeanor. "All our treasures are safe and sound. You know no one can unlock anything. All the keys are packed away in the cellar."

My eyes shoot wide open at the last statement. There it is; there's the ghost that's supposed to talk about a key. I actually found her. I could not have been more ecstatic at that moment. This cellar becomes my next destination. How I am going to get there unseen, however, remains a mystery.

"Yeah," the child replies with a sigh. "I guess so."

"Alright, I'm going to let you sleep now. Good night!"

"Wait, mom!" the child yells. "Can you check under the bed just in case?"

Oh, no.

"Of course, dear." The covers gently lift, leaving nothing left at all to conceal me.

"See, honey, no...INTRUDER! INTRUDER! INTR…"

The whole situation causes me to actually laugh. Usually kids are told nothing lurks under the bed. Yet, now I actually am one of those monsters. Again, I immediately black out as darkness overtakes my vision. She definitely smashed me in the head with something blunt.

***

There's no questioning it, I'm back to the cabinet again. But the mission was a complete success. I have exciting new-found information. The keys are all kept in the cellar. Where that is and how I am to get there I do not know, but I finally have a destination. Since I now am aware of everybody's routines, I carefully avoid the invisible spirits, the wailing woman, the bathroom ghost, along with the child and mother, in such a way as to skillfully return to the cabinet by the poker table. That is definitely the best hiding place ever. At least, it is one that hasn't resulted in my head getting crushed.

Again all the card players ramble on. They speak about intruders and the horrible things they, so me, do. Only this time, she does get refreshments successfully to the table, without stopping to kill me. They continue speaking of the goings on of the day; nothing of any importance to me, as I had already figured out. Slyly slipping away from that room, I alter my course. I head into a deserted, side corridor.

Luckily, there is silence. This is good. No spirits roam about. After attempting a few different pathways, I discover a tiny stairway. It extends into the dark abyss. If there is any path to the cellar, this must certainly be it.

Grabbing the nearest candle from a hallway table, I summon all my courage. I descend to the scary unknown. So far, no ghosts lurk. Eerie silence envelops me. That seems quite odd to me, as this should be the primary realm of spirit dwellers. But, oh well. I continue downward to find, from what I can tell with a candle's illuminating flame, an enormous cellar.

It is quite dusty. I wave the light around, discovering every new relic. Each appears more ancient than the last. I'd rather not stay down here any longer than I'm required to.

Exploring this gigantic basement, I find nothing of value other than some old photographs of people that used to, or probably still, occupy this house. None of them appear happy in their pictures. I search up and down many shelves. Nothing seems to indicate any sign of keys.

Then, I detect a very dusty black box. It lies somewhat hidden on a low shelf to the left of me. The box doesn't look very important, but I suppose I should try everything. Setting the candle down upon the top of the cabinet, I grab the box. I bring it up to the light.

Chapter 26
There

With minimal effort, the latch lifts allowing me to pull the top cover off. The discovery of what's inside, as if the heavens sent it themselves, causes an unyielding grin. It contains a collection of rusty keys! Adrenaline floods my veins. I rummage through its contents.

One key certainly stands out from the rest. Amongst the old, miniature keys, an enormous one hides. As it glimmers and gleams in the candle light, I know there is no question as to which one I'm supposed to get. I grasp the dazzling key in my hand and immediately dash back to the stairs, leaving the burning candle behind. *This could all be almost over! All I have to do now is reach a door, unlock it, and prance out to victory. Things are finally turning around.* As I reach the first step however, another noise shatters my dreams…

It's the wailing ghost! *Oh no! Why is this happening now?* I certainly can't leave the basement now; that would be getting caught on my own accord! As nervousness floods my heart, I jerk my body across the stairs, thankfully causing no obvious noise. Grasping the burning candle, I blow it out with the softest air stream I can muster. I hunker down by the side of the steps with the unlit candle. I can only pray it will leave. But, no, the rough wailing only continues louder, until the spirit halts directly in front of the cellar. This cannot be happening. My heart, again, beats far too rapidly as I attempt to blend in with the dark.

The spirit screeches as it decides to descend the basement stairs. When it reaches the bottom, the wailing suddenly ceases. This cannot be a good sign. At this point I realize the complete horror of my situation; I forgot to close the box to the keys! In my haste to put them back and dart out of the mansion, I left it out in the open. How could I have been so stupid?! The horrifying silence breaks with footsteps slamming the floor. Covering my mouth with my hand, I attempt to breathe without making any noise. I am literally staring into nothing but complete blackness at this point. Has it noticed the opened key box? If so, it certainly isn't making much of a--

"Wauaauahhhhhh!!" the spirit shrieks at the top of its lungs, practically inches away from my face. The extreme shock forces me to scream with all my might in return. Despite this being a ghost and my first experience, my instincts tell me to hurl my candle at the invisible foe. Alas, this is to no avail. The candle merely passes right through with a crash against the wall. Many footsteps descend the stairs with candle light emerging. In no time at all, I'm totally illuminated. Fire sprawls out in all directions.

"INTRUDER, INTRUDER, INTRUD...!" I dash up the basement stairs, despite my obvious location revealed to seemingly everyone. Sadly, my world quickly turns to black and darkness. I fade away into limbo...

***

When I finally open my eyes, I jolt up expecting to head down to the basement once more. This time however, the rough cabinet floor is not there. The absence of it fills me with deadly doubts. I can still do this can't I? This can't be over yet! As much as I would like to deny it, I make the realization that I do not arise in the dark attic cabinet again.

Big comfy sheets and the warm hotel room reveal the inevitable; I now reside in my hotel room. Have I actually failed the Obstacle? Of course I have, the directions were clearly to escape, and I did not do so. I have never been more upset with myself in my entire life. I was so close to leaving the mansion and yet couldn't even reach the door. How could I have possibly not succeeded? My suspicions are confirmed when the Sphream knocks at my door. Deep depression engulfs me as I stumble over.

"Alcott, I'm terribly sorry," it whispers with compassion. "You came so close."

Its depressive tone nearly matches the feeling in my heart.

"Thanks," I stammer, offering a transparent smile. It's impossible fighting the tears from coming when I say that. There is no way that should have happened. Everything was going so well. I had the key in my hand, for goodness sake. Again I'm led down the stairwell, except with a far worse attitude than ever before. In no time at all, it seems, the black mist manifests over my statue, abolishing any hope left in my soul.

'Challenge Number Three Failed.'

Chapter 27
Concern

"Alcott, I'm not allowed to give opinions," the Sphream slurs, peering from side to side. It almost acts as if it's committing a felony by speaking to me. "You have gotten the closest anyone ever has before with the challenge. Nobody has ever actually retrieved the key before. I just want you to know that."

"Thank you," I reply with raised eyebrows. My mood vastly improves. "That makes me feel better." Apparently, no one else did well in that challenge. It will still, however, nag at me forever that I came so close for nothing. That sparkling key and mansion shall haunt my dreams forever.

This time, I am surprised to discover I'm the last to arrive. Everyone else's statues have signs hovering over them. Each of them except one states the same exact thing…

'Challenge Number Three Failed.'

Marya's sign however states...

'Challenge Number Three Passed.'

Everyone failed the third challenge except for Marya. I cannot believe it.

"Hey Alcott!" Gretchen shouts. She already senses my dark mood as I approach the restaurant. "Don't mind that stupid parchment; I'm sure you did great."

I offer a fake smile and glare back at my statue. My fiery eyes flare with rage. I don't know what has come over me, but I'm filled to the brim with depression. *It just seems like I let myself down. Thinking that way, I know, is nothing but pointless. I just can't seem to locate a way out.*

"I just need a little time to myself," I stammer to my Allies. Not even remote eye contact is made. After that, I stride off toward the pool area on the other side of the lobby. Plumping down in one of the pull-out chairs, I gaze at the still water. Chlorine overwhelms my senses. It is quite relaxing in here. Suddenly a door opens behind me. Glancing back that direction, not really caring whoever it could be, I see Gretchen emerging.

"Alcott!" she joyfully yells, skipping over to my chair. "It's okay. Everyone except Marya failed. Remember if it wasn't for you, we would have failed the second one for sure!"

"Thank you," I say, feeling embarrassed. "I'm sorry; I'm just being a baby. You have no idea how close I was to completing that Obstacle, though. There is no way I should have lost that."

"Remember my first challenge. I certainly wasn't the type of fighter pilot you'd send into war."

"Oh, I'm sure you did fine," I grin with doubt. "You're really smart."

"So, what did you have to do anyway?" Gretchen inquires with those wide eyes.

So, I recap the whole tale of wailing ghosts, haunted mansions, and a dusty box of keys. She appears more intrigued with every new detail. It's awesome actually having someone care that much. Every time I stop to ask Gretchen about her Obstacle, she shrugs me off, urging me to finish mine first. Gretchen bites her nails in anticipation throughout my retelling. I reminisce retrieving the key, lurking under the bed, and sneaking behind the cabinet. After I finally conclude my tale, Gretchen shouts with flailing arms.

"That's not fair! You were so close!" The fact that she's so animated bewilders me. I can't even tell who is more upset.

"Yeah," I respond, losing myself once again in the shimmering pool. "I guess it took too long to figure out where the box of keys was even at. Maybe if I had noticed the child sleeping the first time…oh never mind, Gretchen. Enough about mine; now tell me about yours!"

"Oh well," she speaks with nonchalance. "I just transformed into a tuna fish."

"Excuse me?" She can't be serious.

"Yeah, I woke up underwater immediately after the platform. I had gills, fins, and the whole shebang. A voice whispered I had to survive for a certain amount of time."

"Well," I stammer. It's difficult to get a picture of what she's talking about. "That sounds pretty rough. What did you have to hide fro--?"

"Pelicans," she instantly states. Horror gleams in her eyes. "So many pelicans; I'm never going to look at one the same way again." There is sheer terror in her voice, but for some reason, that last comment just breaks me. I can't control myself. I erupt into laughter that just cannot be stopped. Despite her horrible experience, Gretchen emits a quick chuckle. It's not long before she snickers uncontrollably as well.

Marya, Vitaly, and Travis abruptly stride in. They find both of us hysterical.

"I'm...so sorry…just the way you said that," I stammer, wiping tears from my eyes. "What did the rest of you have to do?"

So, we all discuss each vast and difficult experience. Everyone unanimously agrees mine is the creepiest. However, I didn't even pass the dang thing. I find myself growing more attached to these people. I've got pretty darn good Allies, that's for sure. After I'm feeling better, everyone disperses through the hotel. The next hiatus has begun.

I decide to head back once more and peer at the towering statues. It's certainly interesting how lifelike they stand. In perfect shining gold, it appears each has taken millenniums to be crafted. We each have a sophisticated, defiant pose. I feel like a superhero prepared to save the world. It's still completely insane to me that all of this is even happening. The idea of waking up at some point still seems highly possible.

There I am planted with unwavering pride. One pass and two failures hover above my golden head. Everyone is allowed only three failures in the Obstacles. I must pass two more of these next three. My eyes move over to Marya. All of us are in the same boat except her. She's passed two! Perhaps we all underestimated the high school kid.

I must maintain all focus on the next challenge, despite my here and there attention span. There is no time to dwell upon any negative thoughts; I've got a little kid counting on me. It's time to stop being a baby and bulk up. I've brawled with ghosts and great white sharks. What else could they possibly hurl at me?

Hearing the swift patter of footsteps behind me, I sense the Jauntla approaching. She instantly breaks the silence.

"Oh, Alcott!" she pronounces, constantly smiling as ever. "I just wanted to speak with you. Do not be discouraged that you did not pass that last one. Remember, as long as you complete two of the next three, all will be well. That Obstacle's difficulty, in my opinion, well...oh never mind...just never get down on yourself."

"Thank you very much! That really means a lot."

It's awesome to receive such positive encouragement; though I am still enraged that all I had to do was dash outside the freaking building. Still, I did discover the hidden key. All in all, I'm pretty proud of what I accomplished in there.

After some light chit-chat, the Jauntla bids me farewell. She strides towards the lobby. Her long robe slides along the ground.

**

Suddenly, I hear the crash of stampeding from the upstairs hallway. It doesn't take long for me to determine that it's Gretchen. She darts directly to my location at full speed. Her frantic eyes reveal a dark panic rising in her soul.

"Alcott!" she wails. The woman finally reaches me. "Have you seen Marya anywhere? I was going to congratulate her on beating so many of these Obstacles thingies. I've been looking all over the hotel. She seems to have just vanished. Where in the world could she have possibly gone?"

"No," I respond instantly. Her intensity startles me. *Where has Marya gone? I suppose I haven't seen her for quite a while. I just assumed she was off speaking to Sphreams like before.* "The last time I saw her was with you guys, by the pool. Where did she head after that?"

"I know she went upstairs for a little bit." Gretchen glances toward the staircase. "I just thought she went to nap or something. When I knocked on the door, I got no answer. So, I barged in to find nothing but a bed…a perfectly made bed."

I'd be lying if I said that wasn't peculiar. Where could she have possibly gone? The hotel floats in mid-air, so her options are surely limited. Maybe she chose to explore the garden or something. My mind floats back to her statue. Two passes hover above. A realization suddenly dawns on me.

"Marya's won two Obstacles; maybe they're giving her a special reward or something."

"Oh," said Gretchen, raising her eyebrows. Her breathing calms down. "You're right, Alcott. She does only need one more to actually pass, doesn't she?"

"Yeah." I attempt to portray confidence underneath my apprehension. "I guess so. I just hope she's alright. You think she would've said something though; it's been like four hours."

"It seems pretty fishy to me." Her eyes squint toward the floor.

Just then, Travis jaunts up to the two of us. "Hey guys," he extends a friendly wave. "What are y'all talking about?"

"We can't seem to find Marya." I explain the situation. "Do you have any idea where she could be?"

"Nope," he states nonchalantly. He appears not to care less. "I'm sure the Jauntla and Sphreams are taking care of her."

"Well, shouldn't we find out?" Gretchen pleads in a high-pitched tone. "I mean what if she's hurt or--"

"Stop it, Gretchen!" Travis unexpectedly yelps. The screech echoes throughout the lobby. "I'm sure the Sphreams have everything under control. They would never let anything happen to her. What if they heard you talking bad about them? What if they take away your chance to save Sharia?!"

With that unexpected outburst, he storms off. Feet pound against marble flooring.

Gretchen stands there in utter bewilderment, as do I.

His outrage is nothing short of shocking. "What was that?! Why is he so angry all of a sudden?!" Gretchen yells to me, as if I possibly have any explanation to that insane behavior.

I certainly have no idea what came over Travis. Are the challenges getting too much for him? I'm surely aware it's stressful, but why in the world would that happen? The odd thing is that he had such a tranquil demeanor until Gretchen spoke. The mere mention of Marya seemed to distort him into hatred.

I've been here the whole time, yet I feel I've missed out on something important.

"I have no idea." I briskly rub my forehead. "He must just be stressed out or something. Now about Marya, I am beginning to get a little worried." A mystery certainly brews. I intend to get to the bottom of it.

"How about we go check the garden?" I ask Gretchen, trying to uplift her mood. That is the only other place I can think of anyway.

"I was there not too long ago." Her skepticism is tangible. "But I suppose it couldn't hurt."

Gretchen and I go outside, vigilantly searching for our friend. The same breathtaking plants engulf the entire courtyard. Each petal dances with a delicate gust's caress. Despite the soul-clutching beauty, a dark eeriness lurks beneath. No Marya anywhere. Where in the world could our Ally have gone?

"Let's check the back of the hotel," Gretchen sparks, wasting no more time to enjoy the scenery.

"Alright," I yell back. Just as Gretchen disappears into the hotel, I detect stirring in the shadows. Cupping my hand above my eyes, it's immediately apparent a Sphream hovers.

"Excuse me?" I stride toward it. There is just a

rustle of slight movement. Could it have been waiting there the whole time?

"Gretchen," it exposes itself into the sunlight. "Where are you off to?" My heart jerks at the shock of the tone. It's no surprise the Sphream is not pleased.

"Oh..." Gretchen says. "I was looking for one of you guys. Do you have any idea where Marya is? None of us can find her anywhere!"

"That information is classified, Gretchen," the Sphream whispers. "She...will reveal that when the time is right."

"I'd just really like to know if she's okay," Gretchen pleads. Her eyes peer into its soul with pure sympathy. "You can't tell me anything at all?"

Chapter 28
Wrong

"Gretchen," the Sphream lashes words like exploding dynamite. "If I could tell you anything, I would without a doubt. Please go back inside."

With that the Sphream vanishes into thin air, imitating the god woman's mysterious talent.

Its behavior is extremely peculiar. The outburst was certainly terrifying. If they did reward Marya, you would think she would be back after four hours; or maybe have the decency to tell us about it. Without warning, a morbid thought manifests deep in the corridors of my mind. It pains me to ponder this. Maybe Marya winning these Obstacles isn't necessarily a good thing. These challenges do seem astronomically hard. Perhaps altering the course of fate isn't as glamorous as originally thought. What if she isn't being given an "award" at all? I haven't any idea where these dark ideas emerge from, but they surely, for some reason, take hold in my mind. Once that kind of thing starts with me, it's not easily halted.

I decide to wait a little bit longer before making these suspicions known to the others. I certainly don't want to risk Gari's life over some stupid fears. What would the Jauntla think if I believed she did something horrible to Marya? I'm sure I'm just overly paranoid. She could kick me out of the whole Obstacles! No; for Gari's sake, I'll keep my mouth shut. I'll just have to assume the best for as long as I can.

Gretchen, from what I can tell, seems to have made

this decision as well. She drops the subject of Marya entirely. However, wavering eyes reveal it wholly prominent in her mind.

Based on the Sphream's orders, I decide it best to get our minds onto a happier subject. So, we dash off to the video games. Vitaly arrives too. I feel no need to worry her about the situation. The three of us have the time of our lives, brawling, bashing, and snickering to no end. As I'm grinning from ear to ear, a sharp frown suddenly takes its place. The golden clock above reveals two more hours have passed. Marya is still nowhere to be found.

The Jauntla manifests herself out of thin air.

"Hello there, Allies."

Everybody jolts at her arrival; Gretchen even lets out a massive gasp. Though I try not to portray animosity, she's not exactly the most trustworthy person. Immediately rising up from the game, Gretchen glares right into the center of the Jauntla's eyes.

"Where's Marya?" Gretchen queries with aggression. Her utter confidence is nothing short of mesmerizing. All I can do is stare in awe. What's going to happen next? "Did she go somewhere or something?"

"I regret to inform you all, that Marya…is not doing very well. These Obstacles have taken a toll on her. I warned her of taking this venture at the beginning, she certainly knew the risks."

I then chime in, "Can we go see her? Maybe we can cheer her up."

Almost immediately the Jauntla snaps, "NO! She's in critical condition, didn't you hear me? She needs rest; not pestering from you."

The extreme volume renders my jaw to drop. Why am I being chastised for caring about my Ally? Gretchen's eyebrows lower to slants. Her hatred is transparent, and she's okay with that. None of us have ever seen this woman get that way. Vitaly passively stares at her feet, hoping the tension will soon cease.

"Now," the Jauntla continues with glee. The moment before had basically never taken place. "I suggest you all get ready for your next challenge. Good night."

Each of us strolls up the stairwell to our respective rooms. None of us whisper a word to each other. We all know what is going on in each other's minds. They, those in charge of this place, are definitely shielding something. We're not supposed to know about it. Gari's life is the only thing keeping me from marching right up and finding out. Despite the confusing circumstances, I must keep him as top priority. Even with drastic mood swings, I'm going to have to trust this Jauntla. I have to behave, despite part of me desiring to bash her in the face. I know Vitaly, Gretchen, and hopefully Travis remain on my side. Despite them being my Allies, I feel more alone now than ever.

However, I'm not willing to let this matter go for the night. As everyone enters their rooms, I sneak down the hall. A Sphream roams. It appears to be checking that everyone made it into their rooms. Why does this make me feel like I'm in kindergarten?

"Excuse me," I delicately whisper. "Do you have any idea what's going on with Marya? I just really need to know."

"I'm sorry, Alcott, I cannot reveal any information at the present time," it replies, thankfully showing more compassion than the one outside. "The Jauntla has told you all she can for the time being."

"I just want to know if she's oka--"

"I can't!" he snaps out of nowhere. Empathy is entirely abandoned. "Alcott, if I tell you anything, you have no idea the trouble I will be in. Please go to bed this instant."

Being yelled at a third time is just a bit much today. Again, I feel like a baby, but that's how I'm being treated! I wobble back to my hotel room. Part of me hopes I never come out again. Wiping my forehead, I concentrate on pulling myself together.

Something is definitely wrong here. No Sphream has ever been anything but extremely generous. I almost doubted if they actually had emotion. When you start asking questions about things people don't want you to, it doesn't take long to get verbally attacked. That question triggers something, though. My suspicions around Marya only grow. But, as I can do nothing about the situation, I close my eyelids and enter the abyss of slumber. Yes, I'm aware sleeping will be a challenge once again.

Around two in the morning, the horrendous voices wail in my head. "Alcott, Alcott, Alcott," they chant in unison. Practically tradition now, I leap out of bed with a scream gasping for air. Pacing around the room for a little bit, I try to get my head back on straight. *I'm so sick of nightmares every freaking night!*

I need rest for this next Obstacle. Summoning the courage to crawl back under the covers, I drift back off to sleep. Despite the initial peace, it doesn't take long at all before…"INTRUDER, INTRUDER, INTRUDER!" blasts through my head. I go through the same horrible process again.

That mansion will surely never leave my nightmares. I thought the shark was the worst it could get.

It's now totally evident I will be getting no shut eye. I plump down on the edge of my bed swinging my legs over the edge. Deciding my next course of action, I think about something that would relax me. Then, a light bulb illuminates above my head. Why, video games of course!

Tip-toeing out of my room, I head out into the bright hallway, causing me to squint instantly. I honestly don't give a crap if I get in trouble for leaving or not.

Descending the long staircase, I immediately dart to the video game set in the lobby. Something needs to get my subconscious off whatever it dwells upon when I'm asleep. I play for a little bit. Things actually calm down. All nightmares abandon my brain as I immerse in game-play. Just as all seems to be okay…

"Help! He…" wails from the shadows.

Stopping dead in my tracks, I shut off the television. My wide open eyes peer into the darkness, praying my mind is playing tricks on me. Only eerie silence follows. I desperately listen for any sign of the sound again. *What in the world was that?! Was it real? I must be in another nightmare again, that's all there is to it.* Whatever the voice was, it was too distant to comprehend the source.

I freeze and listen intently for the yelp again. All I hear is dead silence of a deserted hotel. Despite initial fear, curiosity forces me to explore. *I can't just pretend that didn't happen, can I? After all, this is just a nightmare so it doesn't matter anyway.*

So, I migrate over to the empty restaurant. Various tables remain perfectly set as always, preparing for an onslaught of customers, though only us five ever eat here. Slowly peeking around each table, I detect no sign of any living soul. I definitely imagined it; wouldn't be the first time my subconscious triumphed.

***

Bright rays of sunlight pour into the dim lobby. I've never been so ecstatic that night has ended. No sleep; but at least there's sunlight. I'm not alone with my awful thoughts. As the morning begins, I continue hunting around the restaurant. I peer under every table. I know that voice came from here! My mind hasn't exactly been in the best place lately, though. Picking up footsteps from above, my eyes dart up to discover Vitaly, Gretchen, and Travis jaunting down the stairs.

"Alcott," Travis inquires with raised eyebrows. "What are you doing down here?"

"I couldn't sleep; too many nightmares." I'm obviously embarrassed. I guess I didn't have to add the nightmare part.

"What are you doing in the restaurant? Getting breakfast already?" Vitaly adds with the same confused tone.

"No, I thought I heard someone yell from this direction, but, oh, I don't know," I reply, realizing I probably sound crazy.

This time, however, I would bet my life something was there. There's no way I would've made that up in this awake state. My heart knows I heard a voice, even if my brain won't admit to it just yet.

"Good morning," the Jauntla proclaims. Her appearance, of course, scares me half to death. She has a knack for appearing out of thin air; we're all beginning to accept that. She crouches directly adjacent to Vitaly. Who knows how long she has been lurking?

"Wonderful to see you all up and about! There's a bit of a surprise for your next Obstacle. Now seems like an appropriate time to tell you. You will be fighting the challenge…in pairs."

Intense adrenaline shoots up my veins. *We get partners? Awesome! That sounds like a spectacular idea!* It's certainly comforting knowing I have a friend with me this time around. The last group challenge was quite successful, so I'm thrilled.

"Marya will, sadly, not be joining you," she continues, glancing at the ground as if avoiding eye contact. "Her time in the Obstacles, I regret to inform you, is over."

I'm enveloped with terror and confusion. *My friend is never coming back, and I'm just hearing about it now? What?! How can she just be gone? No less, gone forever? What is going on here?!*

"Her injuries from the Obstacles, I regret to tell you, are far too severe," she states, avoiding my eyes. "Since it is far too dangerous for her to continue, we have erased her memory and returned her to her normal life."

Oh no, she really is gone. Just like that. Hatred wells up within me at an uncontrollable rate.

"So, wait, we're really never going to see her again?" Gretchen glares in disgust.

"No," the Jauntla reaffirms. "Marya must now exist purely in your memories. I'm terribly sorry, but now we must focus on the matter at hand. There is no time to dawdle; on to the Obstacle. Your partners have already been selected for today. Gretchen, you will be paired with Alcott, and Travis, you are with Vitaly."

We stand too stunned at the news of Marya to comprehend what's going on. She seemed to be in tip-top shape when I saw her last by the pool. How could she have possibly gone from that to such serious condition? It makes no sense whatsoever. What bugs me the most is that she just nonchalantly announces it; like it's no big deal. Marya was nothing of significance. Vitaly's eyes portray the same horror. She definitely feels the same as the rest of us.

I guess, for now, all my focus must remain on this Obstacle. My fears and doubts about this place have surely not subsided, but I need to win this; getting so close in the haunted mansion was far too much for me to bear. Everyone seems content with the partner decisions. I would have been fine with any of these people as a partner, frankly; though Gretchen is great.

"There is one more thing, as well," the Jauntla adds. Another twinkle dances in her eye. "When you get onto the platform, you will be allowed to choose your own Obstacle."

Everyone immediately smiles at that statement. I guess all of us have gotten accustomed to being thrown into insane situations. We never really thought about choosing our own fate.

"There are three challenges available; naturally, by three spiraling portals resting side by side...you will find them upon the large platform above the hotel, as usual. When you and your partner have agreed upon one and only one, you both must carefully step into the portal. You will then be transported to your Obstacle."

Alright, that sounds much better than being thrust into the terrifying unknown. I am anxious to discover what the selections will be; hopefully, no haunted houses or sea monsters on the menu. I'm sure Gretchen would say the same about planes and missiles.

We are, once again, guided to the towering stairwell through the magnificent garden out front. It seems awfully bizarre with only four people this time. It is like our fellow soldier has been shot down. We did not even get to send her off. Based on the Obstacles, however, there is no time for grieving; only for courage. So, I suck it up and force one leg in front of the other.

The platform surfaces as always, except something is quite unique this time. As she proclaimed, there are indeed three magical portals glowing. Each one contains a spiraling mesh of white and purple chasing each other into oblivion. The sight practically hypnotizes me. I lose my concentration for a few seconds. As each of us treads a little closer, scrolls materialize on top of each of the portals.

"Sword Fighting," "Swimming," and "Climbing," Vitaly recites in a projecting voice.

Those are the three challenges. Each sign hangs above its designated portal. Sword fighting, climbing, and swimming are the options. As for me, I'm dandy with any of them. Although, swimming certainly strikes a dark fear, as you can probably imagine. The sheer vulnerability of not knowing what lurks in overpowering waters is petrifying. Who knows what they will put in that challenge? Surely, though, that can be said for all of them.

Chapter 29
Battling

"What do you think, Gretchen?" I beg for any guidance in the matter.

"Sword Fighting," Gretchen immediately responds. I jolt back. She didn't even have to think about it. The words flow out of her mouth before I even finish the question.

"Really," I ask taken aback. "Why?"

"Well," she rotates toward me. "The fact that swimming and climbing are portrayed so innocently makes me believe that there will be much more trouble. At least sword fighting is straightforward. I don't know, what do you think?"

"Sounds good to me," I reply. I can offer no better ideas.

"Alright, let's hope those two don't want it as well." Gretchen circles back towards Vitaly and Travis, in the midst of a discussion.

Oh, I hadn't considered that. Would there be an issue if Vitaly and Travis chose the same Obstacle? The Jauntla hadn't gone into detail about that. Luckily, no problems arise as Travis marches up.

"We've decided climbing would be best for us. Both of us have experience in that area, so I think that's the best option. Is that okay with the two of you?"

"Yep," Gretchen grins at the mutual agreement. "We both are ready to sword fight, anyway."

"Are you sure?" Vitaly wonders with gigantic eyes.

"That sounds pretty difficult. Who knows who you will have to face?"

"Well, I'm certainly not swimming through tidal waves, sharks, and who knows what else," I briskly respond.

"Yeah," Vitaly responds. "We both can agree on staying away from water. Your great white shark tale set that in stone. Well, good luck you guys. I guess we're off."

Both of them cautiously step into the portal. Their forms disappear into thin air. Off they go to climb whatever monstrosity the Obstacle could contain. What could that possibly mean? Mountains? Skyscrapers? I certainly am not jealous of either of them at the moment. Heights certainly shift me into a state of panic as well.

Frankly, sword fighting doesn't sound much better. Will we duel super ancient warriors, or something like that? I guess we'll find out soon enough.

Mirroring Vitaly and Travis, we stride into the portal. Everything in sight instantly vanishes as ritual dictates.

"Alcott, Alcott, Alcott," the chastising voices yelp into my brain. After the fourth time, they don't really bother me too much. Again, each becomes more aggravated with each scream. Darkness finally disappears. My eyes dart open, eager to determine where the portal has transported us.

I instantly feel my body slam against the rugged ground. No special perks in the Obstacles, that's for sure. Gretchen grunts as she smacks the terrain as well. Taking in my new surroundings, I realize I now lie inside a vast mountain range. Sun rays flash through cobalt blue sky in one quick glimpse. Upon rotation, I detect towering cliffs completely enclosing us.

"This looks interesting," Gretchen states. We raise

ourselves off the ground. The rocky ground is certainly not a comfortable place. I wipe off grains of dirt clinging to my shirt.

"Yeah," I stammer. High scenery mesmerizes me. In the distance, a giant stadium rests amongst the many cliffs. Inside this arena, a little speck appears to be darting about. Striding a few steps closer to the monstrosity, we see a solitary figure practicing sword techniques. Swift and sudden stabs and jabs give me the impression this person knows their stuff. Could this be our mentor?

"Who do you think that is up there?" I ask, wondering if Gretchen has the same suspicion.

"I don't know." Gretchen peers that way. "Hopefully we don't have to fight him; he looks pretty good."

"Yeah," the thought of dueling this apparent little master frightens me. Both of us march toward the magnificent circular arena, prepared for the worst. The tiny old man demonstrates various sword moves. He shouts karate terms into the crisp mountain air. A lengthy beard flails in the wind, almost overtaking his entire body. The old man wears a sophisticated dark robe with well woven sandals on his feet. As we finally arrive at the arena, he begins to speak.

"Gretchen...Alcott..." his voice echoes throughout the cliffs. "I have been patiently awaiting you. You both have selected sword fighting, correct? I shall do the best I can to instill in you the deep knowledge of demolishing your opponent. Are you both ready to begin?"

We take a swift glance at each other. "I guess so," is the mutual conclusion.

"Well, then," he states, aiming his sword up to the sky with a wail. "Let us begin!"

Out of thin air, it seems, two swords magically

manifest in front of Gretchen and me. The blades hover in mid-air, patiently waiting to be grasped. The two appear to be twins. They exhibit few if any differences at all from each other.

As I grab hold of the one in front of me, a sense of immense power pulses through my veins. The sensation almost frightens me. It's like there's a warrior lurking inside me I was unaware of. As Gretchen and I get used to handling our new implements, the old man speaks once more.

"First off!" he yells at full volume. Nothing is held back. "What is most important in sword fights?"

Gretchen takes a guess, "Uh…strength?"

"NO!" the old man screams in frustration. "Balance! Lose balance for one second, and then you lose your head." My eyes open wide at that remark; this guy is hard core.

"Alcott," he spins his head towards me. "How do you have proper balance?"

"Ummm…" I stammer, preparing for more yelling. "I don't know…good position?"

"Good!" he wails, leaping up and down like a child at a theme park. "Position is the key to balance. Remember to always keep your blade in a moveable place. NEVER put your feet too close to each other, EVER!" This guy's beginning to scare me a bit.

"The next important thing to remember," the old man continues with new-found bursts of energy, "is to always be on guard. Lose concentration for even a second and what do you lose, Gretchen?"

"Your…head?"

"Yes!" he screams. "Who wants to lose their head? NOBODY, that's who!"

As he says that, his eyes enlarge to beach balls. The

man dashes around in a circle. This guy seems to be completely crazy, and it takes all my willpower to not laugh. But, I have to concentrate and remain tenacious.

"Now," he motions with his sword. "Alcott stand here, and Gretchen over there."

Both of us whisk to the designated spots, causing us to face each other directly. The elderly swordsman then instructs us on various techniques and brawling skills. We learn what to do, and not, with our feet. Adjusting the sword in battle proves difficult.

Tilting the sword even an inch the wrong way can bring immediate death. Holding it steady between the eyes allows for clever maneuvering.

After a few more lessons, he states without warning, "Your training, as limited as it may have been, is now complete. You must begin the Obstacle immediately. Alcott, you shall duel Thwart for the first round. Wait here and he will appear. Gretchen, you will be dueling Maltye. I will guide you to the second arena just beyond that pass."

Gretchen rests her hand on my shoulder as the old man departs. "You can do this, Alcott," she states with a smile. "I know you; you're stronger than anyone they can throw at you." That's the nicest thing anyone has ever said to me. Be that as it may, I just can't believe it.

"You too," I respond with gusto. My shaky tone surely makes fear transparent. The old swordsman guides Gretchen away through the passage between the mountains, abandoning me to await my challenger.

Chapter 30
The First Round

Thwart is my opponent. What a friendly name indeed. Despite attempting to portray confidence, terror envelops me. Strength depletes quickly. This definitely isn't any video game. My heart skips a beat as the bottom section of the mountain rumbles. It begins to separate into two rock slabs. Upon further squinting, I see a doorway opening. A dark figure marches out. The soldier strides up to the arena with a sharp glare directed right at me. He jaunts up with increasing rage, wholly evident in lowering eyebrows.

His attire is black, with flashes of silver gleaming in the sun. In one hand, he grasps a blade similar to my own. No armor or protection for either of us it seems.

"Alcott," he defiantly proclaims, "I am your first opponent. If you defeat me, move on to your next match through the mountain from whence I came. If you should lose, you fail the Obstacle. Good luck!"

I nod my head to show my understanding. Inside I feel an accelerating heartbeat. His swift twirls with the blade indicate he's truly a master. How in the world am I going to beat him? Courage is what I require the most, yet it's what I lack entirely. Every step he takes closer only reaffirms that. I wish I could detect some fear in his eyes, but I find nothing. He strides to the arena's center where Gretchen had stood. I somehow maneuver my shaky legs to the designated area.

With that, he prepares his stance for battle. I mirror

the action. Here we go.

He gently sidesteps to the left, feet never losing balance. Constant motion is retained. Our eye contact never breaks as we rotate in a circle. Making the first move is certainly not something I am willing to attempt. *One mistake and I could lose…my head.* So, I mirror everything he does. I pray I can somehow deflect an onslaught.

Without any warning, my opponent screeches "Ahhhh!" diving right for my legs.

Leaping just in time, the sword misses my feet by inches. Figuring this may be my only opportunity, I head straight for his bent torso. Sadly, as expected, he retreats just in time. My attack is blocked. Both of us return to our original positions, viciously circling. He can demolish me, and he's not afraid to show it. *How am I possibly going to defeat someone like this?*

Visions of video games flash through my brain. I attempt to remember the different tactics my character performed. Life was certainly easier when just swinging a controller. *What did the old swordsman keep repeating? Balance is most important.* I never keep my feet too close to each other with each new step. The game taught me swift jabs prevail. Long stabs leave you vulnerable.

Not willing to go through another lunge at my feet, I dart forward to stab him. He naturally foresees this. He casts my sword off like an insect. Pulling back, he rotates again for a counter slash. I parry it with ease.

We return to our original positions. Sweat drenches my hair and stings my eyes to no end. The pain is difficult to bear, but I can't lose concentration. Even one blink could be the difference between victory and defeat.

Throughout the next few minutes, each of us thrusts, stabs, and slashes with no contact. Plenty of counter attacks are attempted, but none successful. This match could go on into oblivion.

I can sense impatience by his flickering eyes. I predict he may take a big chance, as neither of us can last forever.

Suddenly, he charges at full speed wailing in rage. The blade is heading straight towards my neck. Assessing all my options, I duck to the floor. I somehow manage to get low enough, barely evading the slash. In the millisecond of doing so, my opponent is vulnerable. I boot his legs as hard as I can with my lingering foot. The kick works perfectly, as he yelps in agony, losing all balance. He slams against the floor with a thump, leaving an exposed body. With no time to waste, I shove my sword directly into his chest.

"Ahhhh!" he screams, dropping his sword as mine pierces. The echoes of horror flood through the mountains along each gust of wind. Could I have actually won? As the sword fully enters his body, his molecules morph with the air. It isn't long before he has faded completely. The only thing left is his sword resting on the arena floor.

I inhale enormous gulps of oxygen, trying to take in what happened. Did I actually defeat him?

The door in the mountains suddenly emanates a bright hue. It rumbles like an earthquake into a deep rupture. The door once again opens, revealing a tangible sign of pure victory. *That is it. Against all odds, I actually won the first round.* I can only pray Gretchen was that lucky.

Summoning my fortitude, I wipe off remaining sweat from my brow. I whisk through the new-found passageway. Through the darkness, I enter a petite, dimly lit dungeon. There is, from what I can make out by few sun rays, another doorway. It lies beyond several boulders. The new pathway appears far more intimidating. If my assumption is correct, the second warrior waits through there. Suddenly, a voice whispers in my ear. I gasp into the blackness.

"Alcott," it wheezes. "Congratulations, you have defeated your first opponent." The voice sounds pessimistic, as if I could never accomplish that again. "Gretchen, I'm sorry to tell you, has failed."

The news jolts my heart. I can't even take it in straight off. *My friend has actually lost! That's her third failure! How can she still possibly succeed in these Obstacles now?* Gretchen's chances are now certainly slim to none. The disappointment manifesting within me erupts into utter rage.

There's no way anybody will take me down now. A puissant flame explodes inside my soul. An earthquake shifts the boulders ahead. New beams of sunlight shine into the room rendering me to squint. I'm waiting for no permission; I whisk out into the mountain air, ready to eliminate anyone that dares to challenge me. Re-entering brightness only increases my passion. I catch a glimpse of another dark figure grasping a blade up above, mirroring Thwart. My next challenger, it seems, already stands in the next arena.

He appears extremely ferocious. Beady eyes glare at me with each step forward I take. The soldier's expression remains firm as the mountain behind him. Again, portraying fear is not on my to-do list. I've taken down one warrior; I can easily break one again.

"Welcome, Alcott," he states. "I am your second opponent. Defeat me and you will have one final boss to face. Lose, and, as I'm sure you now know, you will fail. Are you ready?"

"Yes," I state with a glare back. My blade rises to killing position. "I'm ready."

He takes a preparatory stance in the center. I instantly imitate. Instead of cowering like last time, I immediately charge on the offensive. Using all my stamina, I create the illusion that I will attack his head. I secretly swing low toward his feet. As predicted, he is far too savvy for that. By my transparent eyes, he blasts through that charade. He slashes to his feet and parries.

Upon doing so, he lifts his foot and kicks me square in the face. The blow pummels me to the floor. Wind is knocked out of me. My head throbs viciously while I wail in agony. His face emanates utter determination. Flashes of Gari fill my mind, and I force myself to find courage. There is no way I am going down like this. I'm too good for that, and so is Gari.

He raises his foot once more, ready to annihilate me. Rolling and leaping up, I barely avoid the attempt at stomping my body in. I take another chance to directly stab him. Once again, he is too clever for my lunge.

The man then appears as if he will take a swipe at my legs. However, his eyes portray it differently. This discovery ignites a fire within me. I know exactly what his strategy is, but I surely can't let him know that. Faking a block to my legs, I jerk my blade. I parry the onslaught with ease.

That takes him by surprise, I can tell. Maybe I'm better at this than I thought. Deciding to pounce at this adrenaline, I kick him in the stomach with every bit of power I can muster. He lets out a choleric yelp. The man stumbles back a few paces, but not enough to cause any damage. This unleashes the hell manifesting in his heart.

He dives at me in full-out frenzy. A fiery sword lunges at my head, surely taking no prisoners. Despite being shoved across the arena, our swords clash in an uproar. I need a miracle now. I should have never let him take the offensive.

I'm cornered at the end of the arena. He stampedes. Just then, an idea pops into my brain. Though it may not sound promising, I have no other strategy up my sleeve. Ducking his last stab, I dash around the circular arena, somehow escaping his grasp. Despite my extreme doubt, it actually works. I hover in the clear once again. His eyes emanate sheer outrage, and if I'm not mistaken, a grain of weakness. There is no way that I will let this opportunity pass me by.

Sprinting as a tiger toward an antelope, I prepare to win. I swing with all my might. The blade has a mind of its own; ready to draw blood. Though he successfully parries many attacks, I possess a trick up my sleeve.

Throughout the battle, I've noticed most fake shots have been thwarted by eye movements. So, I think it's time for eyes to be deceiving once more. I close in, imitating his previous strategy. This time, however, I do something unexpected. Focusing straight above his eyes, I make it appear I shall slice his head.

Chapter 31
Duel

He jolts his sword up to stop me. At that exact second, I secretly slice at his legs. Though challenging without looking, I know I've succeeded. As my blade penetrates skin, my challenger shrieks louder than ever before. I peer downward proving the fact I already know; I conquered my second opponent. His sword plummets to the ground, slamming against the bloody floor.

Mirroring Thwart, he vanishes into mountain gusts. The screams echo off each mountaintop.

I can actually do this.

That duel overtook my stamina, making me crash to the floor. I take a few deep breaths. Sweat scorches my eyes, causing even more discomfort. Immense sun rays only accelerate my stomach's urge to vomit. Thankfully, I could fend that off during the fight.

Again, more sweat drenches my eyes, followed by a new outburst of stinging. I close my eyes, attempting to contemplate how this happened. There are few moments when I have ever been wholly proud of myself, and this is definitely one of those. I accomplished what I never thought I could. Nothing feels more rewarding than that. Gazing off into the mountain range, I let out a grin.

Just then, the mountain fissures with intensity. Once again, it emanates a bright green light, contrasting the shady boulders. A rumbling roars out. Two shifts separate revealing my next passageway. Well, this is it. According to this man, the final boss lurks beyond that pass. If these two are that experienced, what could this next duel possibly contain? Casting the jitters away from my heart, I rouse myself, bloody blade in hand. I march through the dark opening.

This icy room appears as murky as the last. As I prepare myself for whatever demon emerges, the next voice floods me with bliss.

"Alcott!" it erupts from the dark abyss. The exuberant voice undoubtedly comes from Gretchen. I couldn't have been more excited to have my friend again.

"Alcott!" She leaps up and down like a puppy. "You won, you did it! You beat them both! I'm so happy for you." I can't see her in the dark, but an incoming hug reveals her presence.

"Thank you so much," I reply, overjoyed at her return. "What are you doing here? Didn't you lose? Shouldn't you be back at the hotel?" Just then a voice wheezes into my ear.

"Alcott," it whispers in the lowest but still audible decibel. "Congratulations, once again, you have defeated your second opponent; truly magnificent work indeed. You will find your partner inside this enclosure, though she has already been defeated. Because you have made it to the final boss, she may assist you in facing it."

That news instantly thrills me. It did strike me as odd we weren't fighting together; we are partners after all. How can I ever lose with Gretchen alongside me? Despite my blithe attitude, the voice carries dark apprehension. When speaking of the final boss, 'it' is the title given. 'It' implies this thing isn't human, leaving me pretty freaked out. It could be my imagination, but the eerie tone probably means our chances are slim. After making it this far, I'm fully aware these thoughts bring nothing but hardship. Gretchen then replaces all despair with enthusiasm.

"I'm so happy for you! I don't care if I've already lost this challenge, we're beating this thing. I guess it's too late for Sharia, but I'm ready to fight for someone else. Gari's got two heroes now. Let's go!"

Tears well in my eyes. Her time at the Obstacles may draw to a close, yet she's willing to give everything for me.

"Alright," I shout with an unyielding smile in darkness. "Let's go!" Rumbling follows, revealing an enormous doorway. Sun rays fill the room. I squint and hold both hands, even the one grasping the sword, over my eyes. Utter brightness is not enjoyable after extreme blackness. We both cautiously advance into the sunlight.

Everything shifts into a different dimension. Every dirt path, boulder, and mountain ceases to exist. Swift whirlwinds of the mountains have vanished, leaving us to a completely unknown world. In one blink, it seems, everything is gone.

"What the heck is this?!" Gretchen shouts. Eyes dart all about. I can't possibly think of an answer to that question myself. Deep, murky fog covers everything, imprisoning us in an endless sea of smog. It's impossible to identify anything. By using our voices, we can locate each other and finally find a little comfort. What can this possibly be? Are we going to have to fight something in this mess? Confidence fades fast.

"What should we do?" Gretchen yells. She acts as if some monster will pop out at any second.

"I…" I stammer to myself. "I guess we should start walking somewhere...whatever this boss is, I'd rather not be ambushed when we can't see anything."

"Yeah," she grasps my forearm for comfort. "It wouldn't really be a fair fight at this point."

"Let's stick close together," I wheeze through the

fog.

"Well," Gretchen states with an eye roll, "we're certainly not splitting up."

So, we delve into the unknown universe of smog. It's hopeless to determine anything from the time of day to where I'm stepping next. Oceans of smoke consume my last ounce of fortitude. After a few minutes voyaging into nowhere, sanity slips away.

"Why won't this end!?" I shriek into the void.

Gretchen's eyes glisten with a ghostly terror. "Look over there," she yelps. "I think I see something."

We dash in the direction she pointed hoping to escape this hell. As we continue, something definitely manifests in the distance. It almost shimmers like a body of water. Fog suddenly clears. This rouses an intense feeling of relief. Finally reaching this new green water, I realize we have stridden into a mucky swamp.

A lustrous forest surrounds the water. It clutches it with vines. Peering into the grime, I contemplate the evil lurking beneath. Gretchen's lowered eyebrows portray deep apprehension as well.

"What do you think the boss is going to be?" I pray for a happier second opinion.

"Well," she whispers. "If this is a swamp, it could be anything from an alligator to--" She gasps, too petrified to finish the sentence.

"What?!"

"Bzzzzz," bombards my eardrums.

"Mosquito," I state, knowing the annoyance of these pests.

"Well, it is a swamp, Alcott; there's going to be mosquitoes," Gretchen sparks back. She keeps a locked glare at the muck. "Now, what in the world are we going to fight?!" She now hyperventilates, losing all composure.

"Gretchen," I pronounce in a soothing tone, "come on…" Just then, the drone becomes quite loud. I rotate around, searching for the source of the clamor. The hum has gotten so immense it sounds like a jet taking off.

Almost on an instant, the sharp buzz ceases. We're abandoned to eerie silence.

Gretchen freezes into a disturbed statue.

"Alcott…" she hushes. Mist overtakes.

The buzzing roars directly in front of us! In the sheer pandemonium we drop our swords. They splash into the mud. What glides out of the immense fog is certainly not the boss we had expected. This monstrosity shocks me so much, I can do nothing but gasp. A colossal mosquito rockets out of the abyss at a devilish velocity.

Chapter 32
Courage

The demonic insect rushes to our location. It's practically the size of a minivan. Hovering above the murky grime, it adjusts its stance into killing position. Both of us lift off the dirt. We lunge for the fallen weapons. A giant bloodsucking snout strikes a dark fear into me. It patiently flies in the smog, longing to taste blood. That is the monstrosity we are going to have to destroy; no doubt about it. How to accomplish that is an unanswerable question.

Both of us now stand, swords at the ready, as the mosquito toys with its new-found dinner. It practically laughs as its helpless victims prepare for the struggle. Pushing that mindset aside, I lower my eyebrows. I grasp the hilt even tighter.

The monster dive bombs.

Gretchen screams in horror. It flies at me with full force, smashing my head. My sword is hurled away.

I slam against the ground. The wind almost gets knocked out of me again. Staring up at the demonic creature from ground level, I discover its aggression has not subsided. It turns back for me. Mosquitoes do truly look evil, no less an enormous one ready to kill me. *How am I ever going to do this?*

It charges for my helpless body, prepared to devour. Without sufficient time to get up, I manage to roll away. The beast is inches from trapping me. My heart beats with a rapid and unyielding intensity. Over to my left side, I discover a weighty stone amongst the weeds. It is roughly the size of my fist. I put all my strength into reaching across the mud. As I grasp the rock between my fingers, I summon the energy to stand.

Terror follows. I realize the mosquito has altered its target. It boldly barrels into Gretchen. She attempts to slice it with the blade to no avail. Without much effort, the mosquito knocks the sword out of her hand. To my horror, as I finally get up, I see the mosquito pinning her down. It prepares to pierce her.

"Ahhhhhhhh!" Gretchen screams at the top of her lungs. In sheer panic, I catapult my rock toward the mosquito. Just as it is about to stick its bloodsucker into her, the stone crashes into the millions of hellish eyes.

Gretchen wails as loud as she can now, mortified to death. Directly on impact, the mosquito leaps off Gretchen. It's in utter pain. This allows her time to dash and retrieve her sword. I may have saved Gretchen, but the mosquito certainly is not the happiest with me. Though it is difficult to tell, I detect the remaining little eyes glaring with contempt.

It flies at me at full speed, but this time, I am ready. My sword is already in fighting position as it barrels towards me. I attempt to slice the snout, but alas my blade misses. It slices off a giant front leg instead. It isn't what I was aiming for, but I'll surely take it. Mosquitoes' legs are quite long, gangling appendages. Without the front ones especially, sucking blood will be challenging. I'm certain that the mosquito has figured this out by now.

With its now missing limb, the monster abandons interest in Gretchen. It focuses all of its attention on me. Frankly, I would be pretty upset too if someone cut off one of my legs, but I had no choice in the matter. It wants revenge. It wants me gone. Without any warning, it soars behind me.

I'm caught completely off guard. From my back, it shoves my body toward the swampy water with full force. I never had expected it to be this strong. I cannot put up a fight as it pushes me closer. The unrelenting swamp draws near. My sword is quickly knocked out of my hands. It flies back onto the muddy dirt before I can protest.

Gretchen darts as fast as she can. Her blade is swung at the beast to rescue me; but it is far too late. With all the force and strength it contains, I am surely at its mercy now. Both of us head toward the watery area. I flail and struggle as much as I possibly can. Kicking and punching are my only attacks available. Nothing seems to budge. It seems much more vigorous than originally anticipated. To my and Gretchen's horror, it bulldozes me into the deep murky swamp.

The muddy water engulfs my eyes. I plunge into the deep. The sensation is incredibly gross. Panic fills me to my very core. Swimming and yelling through masses of bubbles, I force myself to head to the surface. Thankfully, all my strength hasn't left me. I can swim there without ultimate hardship.

Gulping in breaths of air, I take in the looming situation. The giant mosquito and Gretchen are woefully in mid-battle. It continually dive bombs her. With each new onslaught, she swings her blade in an attempt to kill. When she glimpses my return to the surface, I hear her yell.

"Alcott! Alcott!" she screams. "Swim out! Get out of there now!"

Exhausted, I start paddling back to the edge of the dirty water. Extreme fatigue begins to set in. I almost reach the edge. Just then, the most horrible thing that could ever happen occurs. If ever there is a time in life when I would completely lose hope, it is now.

I try to think of Gari, to know what I am fighting for. However, when enough is enough, you just don't know what to do. Every ounce of courage and strength seems to pour out of me at that moment. Something clutches my leg, and quickly drags me back under.

Without even a small warning to breathe, I catch the glimpse of a giant snake. It hauls my body to the depths. Whether it is constricting me or swallowing me, I have to say I can't even tell. All I know is that the surface of the swampy water is way out of reach. I punch, thrash, yelp, and attack with all my might. However, there is no way my legs are breaking free. It's not that I give up at this point; my mind just wanders into a delusional state.

That may not make sense, but it just soars to every memory. Everything, and literally everything, appears to be unimaginable and surreal. I just can't find a discernible way to believe that what is happening really is.

That's it; time for this dream to stop. I'm ready to wake up. It's fun imagining fighting giant sharks and sneaking around haunted houses, but reality must manifest once again. It's now time for me to disembark this crazy fantasy. Part of me knew this was a dream the whole time anyway; I guess I just never believed it. Now it's time to wake up in my real bed, with Gari and Antuna. I must accept the fact that Gari is going to have to pass away. The surface begins to seem almost nonexistent. Contraction around my leg gets even tighter.

Suddenly, a giant splash bursts off the top of the water. I'm shaken from my elaborate daydream. A figure emerges traveling downward to my current location. This dream state vanishes. Squinting toward it, I frantically realize Gretchen has dived into the water. In her hand, she possesses her merciless blade. The woman continues swimming downward to me and the snake. As she passes by me, she doesn't even make eye contact, darting straight past, right up next to the snake. Looking downward in amazement, I see Gretchen clawing, slicing, and swinging. After a few quick scratches with her hand and slices with the sword, she removes an eye from the beast.

The lack of air has almost done me in. Sharp constriction begins to subside. In seemingly seconds, my legs are free allowing me to paddle. I dart to the top of the water faster than ever. Barely before I would've drowned, I make it to the surface. These gulps of air are the most precious and needed in my entire life. The harsh reality sets in. *I should be dead right now. That actually happened. That was real. That really happened. This is really happening now.*

The mosquito, of course, waits patiently on the land. It hovers beside the water in its devilish stance. There is no time to dawdle pondering about that now; Gretchen's still down there! I immediately dive down after replenishing my air supply.

It doesn't take long to discover the hopelessness of the situation. To my horror, the snake that had caught me had not been the only one. At least three of the giant creatures slither now. Each of them completely constricts Gretchen. Her weapon is nowhere to be found. Swimming and paddling down as fast I can, Gretchen's face comes into view. My mind jolts with sheer abhorrence.

This person has just saved my life, only to be destroyed by three monsters herself. There has never been a deeper incentive or determination in me than now. I shove as much water as I can behind me. I pray that I can reach Gretchen in time.

Three snakes or one hundred snakes; I'm not going down without a war. As I continue to swim closer to her face, I detect something shocking. Instead of complete terror in the previously inconsolable Gretchen, she looks tranquil and calm. She appears to be at peace.

Three snakes attempt to devour her from the bottom up. She desperately mouths one word under water. Her eyes peer toward the surface. Despite the horrible conditions of my eyes and everything else, there is no doubt whatsoever. This one word tells me what I have to do.

"GO!"

After one more look, I glide through the mucky water. I abandon her to be devoured. Letting her get taken by these monsters is the hardest thing I have ever had to do. Complete depression invades me. I glimpse the body of the snake cover her eyes from my view. Despite tears in my eyes begging to fall as I reach the surface, something harshly sparks in me at that moment. For some reason, no more fear resides inside me. All of it completely vanishes. There is no doubt in my mind about what I am going to do. I can't explain why, but this mosquito will perish. *I am going to kill it. This is a true statement. It is going to happen. Losing is neither a possibility nor even an option.*

Paddling swiftly, I am desperate to reach the land. Thankfully, this time I reach the grass. I pull myself up before anything grabs me. The mosquito is quite aware that I have arrived. It makes no movement in response; not even an attempt to adjust its wings or legs. In a few moments, the reason why becomes clear. My sword lies directly under its belly; it surely knows what it's doing. I have no manner of attack. What a smart bug it is.

Just then, it dawns on me. I am not wholly out of weapons yet. When it went for Gretchen earlier, I bashed it with a stone. Thankfully, peering around, I find a rock just a little larger than that one had been. The mosquito shifts back a little bit as I do so, aware of the pain I can now inflict. It definitely does not like these rocks. That encourages me very much, indeed.

I wave the rock around threateningly. I hover it from side to side, somewhat as you do with a pet looking at a treat. However, this is certainly no reward. The mosquito portrays much apprehension. It reverses while slowly lifting itself off the ground. The buzz then returns as it flies about a couple of inches up. I continue to fake a few throwing motions to scare it. My strategy works! The beast delicately hovers backward leaving my sword wide open. Suddenly, it realizes that it has left my weapon unguarded.

Despite how close I am with the rock, it soars back to its original location. It stands over the blade. Hoping to catch it off guard, I stride closer and hurl the rock directly at its eyes.

It makes direct impact. The stone slams into its face. Knowing I already damaged most of its eyes, it certainly is not happy at that moment. It swerves around in a crazed and unpredictable manner, proving that I have driven the monster insane. In an extreme state of terror, it flies down, over, and around, fully destroyed without eyesight.

As the mosquito enters this state of terror, my sword is left out once more. Realizing this may be my only chance, I dart up and grab it as quickly as I can. I raise the blade directly in the fighting position as I had been in before the monster arrived. For some reason, the beast can tell where I am. It halts immediately in mid-flight. I don't know what it is, maybe some chemical or heat sensation, because its eyes are destroyed; but it surely figures out my location.

It then repeats a tactic performed before. The beast flies directly behind attempting to shove me. I am not stupid; it's definitely trying to push me into the "snake swamp water" again.

Chapter 33
Stamina

Not today, my friend. Again I am surprised by its strength. The threatening water gets closer. There is no way I am going in there again.

This time, to the monster's chagrin, I keep a firm grasp on my sword. I raise the weapon vertically, pointed toward the sky. Once in that position, I lift my hands and arms completely above my head. This stabs the beast right through the head. Though I cannot see what has occurred, I know in my heart my plot has succeeded. Buzzing begins to subside as it crashes to the dirty mud.

I turn to face the monster. With all my might, I lift the sword out of its head and slash right through the snout. This time, I certainly do not miss. The mosquito is definitely doomed at this point. It lies down in submission to my victory. Breathing heavily and keeping my blade at the ready, I patiently wait to view what will happen next.

The gigantic mosquito transfigures into a shimmering white illumination. Every ounce and limb disappears into the magnificent white energy. This light hovers for a few seconds, as if taken in by the newly departing creature. It is truly a spectacular sight to see. After a few more seconds, the magical energy fades into nothingness. It takes any remnants of the mosquito into the abyss along with it.

Chapter 34
Deception

Darkness overwhelms my soul. The whole world around me vanishes. It implodes into an unknown black universe. Whether I am fainting, sleeping, dying, or dreaming is completely impossible to identify. Suddenly, I recognize myself lying on pleasant and cozy sheets.

I realize I am back in my hotel room. This time, however, I feel no need to rush downstairs to discover the new proclaiming script above my statue. I just lazily lie in awe. It's hard to comprehend everything that just occurred. What would Gari and Antuna think if I told them what I had just done?

Thoughts of Gretchen immediately flash through my head. She went through the sheer pain of drowning and being choked by snakes, all for me. That is something I'm never going to get over. I really hope I would be willing to do that if someone needed me; Gretchen is really one of a kind. Deciding it's now about time to head down, I rouse myself off the bed.

I stride toward the door. This time, however, no Sphream waits to greet me. The absence is very peculiar, seeing it happened directly after every other Obstacle. As I travel down the staircase, I sense Vitaly and Travis at the bottom. They both look ecstatic to see me.

"Alcott!" Travis yells. "I'm so sorry, but don't worry about it. The important thing is that you did your best."

"Yeah," Vitaly adds. "Sword fighting looked way

too tough anyway, at least you gave it everything you had."

What are they talking about? I definitely won that Obstacle. I destroyed two warriors and a gigantic, horrifying beast. Gretchen certainly didn't drown for nothing.

"What are you guys…?" Just then the room turns to darkness. A white light shines, calming my confusion. Rising once again above my statue, it hovers and transforms into a beautiful parchment. Thankfully, despite those two's odd comments, it blatantly states that I have passed the Obstacle. Extreme relief floods me at that. *What are Travis and Vitaly talking about? There is no way I have done all that work and not won.*

Glancing at Gretchen's, I see that she has failed. Despite everything she did for me with the boss in the water, she receives no credit whatsoever for it. That is pretty maddening to look at. Still, she did that for me. I conquered the mosquito; I am pretty proud of that.

"I passed it, you guys," I gleam from ear to ear. I don't feel guilty, because based on their joyful look, I'm assuming they did well themselves. "Why would you think I didn't?"

Vitaly and Travis stare at the parchment in bewilderment. There is complete surprise, and I swear I detect a little disappointment in each of their faces. I thought we were friends; how can they not be happy for my victory?

Travis circles around, altering his tone entirely. He grins again, "Alcott! You actually passed the Obstacle?! Good for you!"

Vitaly also abandons her fluster and shouts, "That's amazing!" It is great that they are happy for me now. It is, however, a little upsetting they would just assume I would lose without a doubt.

"How was the rock climbing?" I ask, trying to change the subject.

"It was completely awful!" Vitaly waves her arms in frustration. "We both did our best, but neither of us won. I'm kind of glad, though."

"That's okay," Travis continues. "Knowing we fought hard is all that we needed. You don't always have to win."

"I'm so sorry." I'm a bit taken back by their nonchalant attitude. "I'm sure you both did great though. Where is Gretchen now? I certainly wouldn't have won without her."

"She's resting," Vitaly states. "The challenge took a lot out of her."

Just then, the Jauntla manifests out of nowhere, as usual. She has never greeted me after a challenge this quickly before.

"Congratulations Alcott!" the Jauntla exclaims. "You have done beautifully!" Of course she is yelling this right in front of the other two; making me feel terrible. I just grin at her and stare back at the ground. Vitaly and Travis stumble away, almost in shame it seems.

Gretchen should have passed. I know I'm repeating myself, but she is the reason I was not digested alive. I bring up everything that occurred in the swamp with Gretchen, but the Jauntla does not even seem to care. She completely brushes off the subject and congratulates me more.

She moves her face closer. "No one has ever passed that challenge before, either. But you did. Yes, you did. Defying all odds, you defeated the monster. Very smart and brave you are, Alcott, indeed."

"Thank you, but, again, I couldn't have survived at all without--"

Completely interrupting that statement, she shouts, "You have no idea how special you are. The Sphreams and I have prepared a little celebration for you. It shall be spectacular, indeed. You surely deserve it."

Celebration? Despite the extreme positivity in her expression, something doesn't feel right about this. Her expression appears way too positive and cheerful. I know I shouldn't be thinking so, but something lurks beneath those eyes.

"Oh no, that's okay," I attempt to evade this. "I've been through so much, I'd just like to rest for a little bit."

"No, Alcott, don't be silly; you'll follow me now. I don't mean be to be rude," she exclaims, "but we've all worked very hard on this. It is not something you would like to decline." I can't remember the last time anybody was that rude to me, ordering me to follow. Being bossed around is not something I will ever tolerate. But then Gari crosses my mind. I fear upsetting her in any way.

"Alright," I state. I know I'm just being stupid. Declining this celebration would be extremely rude. "I'm sorry; it's just the exhaustion talking. I'd love to see what it is."

"Wonderful." Her hands clasp together. Appearing much more settled, she whisks back toward the restaurant area. The Jauntla guides me across many booths and tables. Finally maneuvering past them, she motions for me to follow her into the kitchen. This is where I viewed the Sphreams preparing the meals.

"Don't tell anyone this," she whispers, peering left and right cautiously, "but there is a secret room kept beneath the kitchen. We call it the Celebration Room. You have indeed earned your stay, Alcott."

She proceeds to grab one of the dusty cookbooks above the counter. This book, I discover, is nothing but a fake. It is literally attached to the wall by a lever. At this motion, the floor begins to shake. The rumble is almost as the mountains had done between duels. My eyes stare in perplexity. Tiles separate under the floor, revealing a passageway through a dark hole.

I am not very excited to see what skulks down there. *What kind of reward could this possibly be?* Suddenly, four or five Sphreams briskly float into the kitchen. I raise my hand as a wave. They do not utter one word.

"Hello," I say nervously. I'm relieved to not be alone with her anymore. "Is this the celebration room thing?" The Sphreams make no attempt at even acknowledging my question. They carefully and deliberately assemble around me, forming a small circle. They surround me in every direction. No one says a thing.

"What's going on?!" I'm getting a bit concerned. "What are they doing?" No answer from the Jauntla or any of them. She just stares at me with the same wide-eyed look of excitement. Her blissful eyes indicate there is nothing in the world to fear.

In literally an instant, that mindset and expression completely alters. Outrage swells in her eyes. Tears cascade down her cheeks.

"This should not have happened, this should not have happened, this should not have happened…" she yammers to herself. Her fist slams against the table with each repetition. A sudden jolt and immense pain jams the back of my head. All my senses evaporate into shadows.

Chapter 35
The Celebration Room

Awaking to consciousness once again, I bolt up. I must figure out what happened. I feel as if I am inside a very small cellar. Though mostly enveloped in darkness, some light sneaks in from the top of the rafters; enough to get a feel of what goes on around me.

Attempting to move my arms, I make an alarming and terrifying discovery; I am tied up with a very large rope. Not only that, there is a large piece of duct tape covering my mouth. My eyes open wide. I attempt to scream. This is to no avail. Tears swiftly descend my cheeks at the confusion of the situation. Whatever is going on, I am utterly powerless and helpless.

Suddenly, I hear another voice attempt to whisper. It wheezes from across the room. The sheer shock of the figure startles me. I jerk to my side. At the realization of who it is, my heart leaps with anticipation. A high school girl rests on the other side of the room. It is Marya!

She appears to be in the exact same horrible position I find myself. Duct tape is harshly placed over the mouth. A rough rope wraps her. It is the greatest relief in the world knowing that I am not alone. She portrays every sign of having that same exact feeling. Breathing heavily, the sight of me calms her down.

I am inches away from passing out. Marya tries to say something from the confines of the duct tape, but it's mumbling gibberish. I am a little too terrified to communicate at the moment.

Suddenly, the top of the ceiling widens a bit. A hole emerges above. Angelic light pours into the room. From the view of it, I know this is the hole the Jauntla created by moving the cook book lever. Memories flood back through me at an alarming rate. *Could this be the Celebration Room the Jauntla spoke so highly of?*

It is at that moment that pieces of this horrific puzzle fit together. *When had Marya mysteriously disappeared? It was the minute she heard that she won her second Obstacle. Nobody had seen her after that news was revealed.*

Conquering the giant mosquito is passing my second! This is what must happen after two Obstacles are passed. There can be no other explanation. Why, though?! What could this possibly mean? Is it a punishment for doing well in the challenges? Many questions assemble in my brain.

The Jauntla descends a ladder into our chamber. As she lands on the floor, she reaches for a particular book in a very large, ancient bookcase. It rests a few feet away from my feet. Just as she does so, the hole up top instantaneously closes. All returns to the unknown darkness as before. She then flicks a switch, turning the lights on. The luminosity is way too much. My eyes shut in an instant. Her eerie voice glides off her demonic tongue.

"I assure the both of you that it was never supposed to come to this. You both have surely defied our expectations indeed," she proclaims. A sense of regret travels in her voice. "I see the both of you are confused. Let me explain. This whole thing…has been nothing but a sham."

What?! Both of us are in a state of extreme shock. My whole world is turned upside down once more. *What could she possibly be talking about? This is all made up? A sham? Ascending the ropes above the ocean, shooting arrows into the shark, answering trivia inside the temple, the questions, sword fighting a demonic bug, the terrifying ghosts: all of it for nothing!?*

"Fate is not at all changeable." Her shoe bangs the floor in defiance. "That's why they call it fate, my dears. You never had the power to change any of that, despite what that book may have said."

How in the world can this be happening? I worked and toiled so hard and so long just to be chastised and deceived? Looking at Marya, the same hatred resides inside her heart as well. I can't disagree with the girl. Rage devours my heart and sense of morality.

"The whole point of these Obstacles is," she continues, "to offer a bit of comfort for you all, so that you can feel like you truly fought for the one you lost; even though you would inevitably lose. The tests were certainly passable, but extremely unlikely. You two just had to be extremely unlikely, didn't you?"

"So, to sum this up, you two are too strong for your own good. Everybody is supposed to only attempt, maybe even pass one, to feel like they accomplished something. After that though, everyone inevitably fails everything. They go back to their everyday lives with the closure of knowing that they at least tried to change their loved one's fate."

So, I guess this whole thing is made up. I am nothing more than a little puppet. They were pulling the strings the whole time. I was never going to save Gari after all, nor did I ever have a chance. Realizing this, uncontrollable dark anger wells up.

"You each needed just one more win. By the strength of your skills at this point, you probably would have done it. That cannot happen. Let me repeat myself...

that cannot happen. It would defy the laws of the universe, and chaos will undoubtedly ensue. Sadly, now that you know this much about the current predicament…it leaves us no other choice. Both of you have to be exterminated immediately."

Her words can barely be contemplated. *Exterminated?! This god tells us that everything we've been working toward is all a hoax. Now we're going to be murdered; like bugs.*

What happens next I can't exactly say. Is it out of pure passion, or pure madness? That last statement is just enough to push me over the edge, I shift my position upward. My legs rotate enough to make a leap. 'God' or not, I have to try. Inching closer with the ounce of balance I have, I prepare for what I am about to do, concealing any notion of doing so.

In an instant, I jump and circle in just the correct motion. My foot boots both of her legs wholly out from under her. It all happens far too suddenly for her to realize what is happening. She lets out a yelp. The woman tumbles backwards onto the cold, hard floor. This 'god' is definitely out cold leading me to wonder; she doesn't seem like much of a god at all.

Rolling over in my direction, Marya appears stunned. Perhaps she is horrified at what I have just done. However, I certainly sense a bit of glee in those eyes. Despite that outburst, I have literally no idea what is going to happen next. In retrospect, maybe karate kicking the one 'god-like' person in charge of this place isn't the best idea.

This hotel appears to be floating. It solitarily hovers way up in the sky. How in the world am I to escape from something like that? There is, though, no time to ponder all that at the present time. *Now, I have to focus. Duct tape needs to come off.* Biting through seems far too time consuming. So, I decide to use my toes to grab it. It requires quite a bit of effort, flexibility and determination, but the duct tape finally peels off. I hurl the sticky mess across the basement.

Taking a few deep breaths, I regain my sanity. I turn over to Marya. Both of us now begin trying to stand up, as best as we can. The tight rope is surely unyielding.

While this is happening, Marya keeps making a peculiar motion. Her eyes extend back and forth to the top of a cabinet. She obviously is trying to signal me something. It doesn't take a mind-reader to figure it out. I thrust my body over. Cement floor slams my limbs.

Glancing up, I know what Marya wants. A knife rests above the wooden structure. With my hands tied, it isn't possible to reach. I barrel my body into the cabinet. After a few attempts, the knife slides toward the edge. My strategy is working. One more slam concludes it. The knife plummets toward the floor. It hits with a clink.

Upon better inspection, I discover it to be a miniature pocket knife. So, with it between my toes, I endeavor to open it up. On my first attempt, the blade emerges from its case; when suddenly, my foot slips. The knife slices delicate skin between my toes. I close my eyes and grit my teeth. Blood oozes onto the ground.

This, I know, is neither the time nor place to be weak. This has to be done. After venturing again with my toes, the knife finally opens correctly. I retain a firm grasp on it. Bringing my foot up to my stomach area is far more manageable.

So, after executing that, I attempt to slash the sturdy rope. It encompasses my torso. A tiresome process ensues. Eventually, enough rope has been severed allowing my free hand to take over. Things moves much smoother and I'm able to free myself from restraints completely. Thankfully, the inanimate god has not moved. She remains in her place on the ground. *Maybe I killed her? How could a 'god' get knocked out that easily?* Getting my mind back, I convince myself there is no time whatsoever to dawdle.

Crawling over to Marya, I embark on slicing the ropes. I cut with the same swift precision after removing her duct tape. This task is much easier to do in my standing position.

"Thank you, Alcott." She rubs her jaw. Her eyes glare at the 'god'. "What are we going to do now? Looks like she's out for a while, but I'd rather not stay down here to find out."

Both of us immediately look toward the top of the room. I attempt to estimate a location for the hole. The Jauntla pulled one of the books to close it, so, I suggest the both of us initiate yanking out books. Walking is a little difficult after being tied up for so long. This is especially the case for Marya. She has been imprisoned in this chamber a lot longer than me.

Our shaky bodies eventually make it there. We commence grabbing random books in hopes that one of them may unlock the passageway. It takes about five minutes. Tons of tossed literature rests all over the place. Eventually, Marya yanks a book that will not budge; it's attached to the bookcase. Bingo. As she does so, the trap door opens directly on cue.

Marya and I then ascend the rusty ladder. We escape our grim enclosure for good. As I reach the top, I find myself inside the kitchen again as expected. Marya crawls out as well. The room is completely deserted, other than the both of us. *What are we possibly supposed to do now? We just found out that everything we have been working for has been a lie. I may have just killed the person responsible. Would a trial consider it self-defense? She did say she was going to exterminate me. Am I going to go to prison forever? Are there trials or any courts of law in this...universe? Is this real life? Am I really in a hotel competing for Gari? When is this dream going to end?!* Just as in the disgusting swamp being forced under the deep, I freak out. My entire perception of reality evaporates.

Everything fully bombards me at once. I feel completely woozy. Differentiating reality from imagination is nearly impossible now; considering the composition of either is in vain. In this extreme chaos, I swiftly sit down at a table. My head smacks down into my hands. *Please wake up, I tell myself. Please, I can't do this anymore. There is no way that I really just killed somebody.*

"Alcott! Alcott!" Marya whispers as loudly as she can without being heard. "You need to pull yourself to together now. I can't do this without you."

After a few deep breaths, I begin to calm down. I force myself to assess the current situation. *Dream or not, I have knocked the Jauntla out. Marya is definitely talking to me. Worrying is going to get me nowhere now. Acquiring some sort of fortitude is my course of action.* Immediately getting up, I whimper.

"I'm sorry, I just had a moment...what do you think we should do?"

"I have no idea, but I assume these Sphreams will not be too happy to find out what happened to their... leader," she responds cautiously. Her eyes dart around for someone to jump out. "I guess the only thing we can do now is find the others. Whether we die or not, they deserve to know the truth about what is really going on here."

"You're right," I briskly respond, somewhat regaining my sanity. "They need to know."

Before we depart the kitchen, I decide it best to

acquire some sort of weapon, just in case. To my dismay all the knives seem to be locked away. None of the drawers are accessible. There is, however, a frying pan left out in the open. It rests on the counter; guess it'll have to do. After grasping the heavy implement, Marya and I immediately move out. We emerge into the restaurant. The many elaborate pre-set booths and tables are still completely deserted. Unrelenting darkness encompasses the place.

It appears that nobody has discovered us. The chaos in the underground chamber must have been unnoticed. At least, nobody shows themselves directly. We evade any sign of detection while sneaking to the lobby area. Five statue replicas remain at large. None of them have been altered in any way, despite the fact that Marya and I are now meant to be 'exterminated,' because both of us have been too successful. The sight of the statues haunts me. A sharp sense of loathing creeps into me. My glamorous double poses with two victories above his head, all for nothing but delusion.

Suddenly, Marya gasps. I hear footsteps across the side of the lobby. The figure somewhat materializes in the blackness. It hovers by the staircase, waiting, patiently it seems. Who in the world can it be? I literally have no idea. Ghastly suspicion and apprehension jolts my heartbeat. From the looks of its immobility, I figure the odds of it being a friend are slim to none.

Chapter 36
Darkness

"Who are you?!" Marya shouts. Our secret is surely blown; there is no need to worry about getting caught. The shadowy figure rests in its same stationary position. It shows no acknowledgment of Marya's question. Lobby lights begin to slowly come to life, eliminating the dark unknown.

After a while, the entire lobby is illuminated. It is not morning yet. Blackness outside the windows still remains, but something has turned on the lights. The true nature of the dark figure emerges. It does not take a magnifying glass to see. The dark shadow is Travis. Relief floods through me. I let out a sigh as we dash up to our friend.

"Travis!" Marya and I yell. It is such a surprise to find him there; I just assumed he would be drifting off to sleep. However, what is more intriguing is the look upon his face. His expression portrays misery, or even signs of hatred. Travis appears to be giving us the same look a parent would scold a child with. Something is certainly not right here.

"Travis," Marya continues. We finally reach him. "This whole thing is a sham! It's completely made up, you have to--"

His eyebrows lower to slits. Travis punches Marya square in the face, causing her to crash down at least a yard away. Blood gushes along her forehead. The immense impact was certainly powerful. I stare in complete bewilderment upon the horror he has just committed. *There is no possible way this happened; Travis is our friend.* Fury swells up inside of me.

"What is wrong with you!?" I scream at the top of my lungs. As I rush towards Travis, he quickly steps forward. The man smashes me directly in the gut. I'm knocked down to the floor as well. I lose grip of my frying pan. It flies across the room, banging into the floor. A cacophonous clang erupts.

Getting up as quickly as I can, despite my now weaponless state, I charge toward him. He tries to jab me again. I manage to evade it, stepping to the side. My fist bashes him straight in the face. Slamming him hard enough, the man tumbles down the stairs. Blood cascades from his new bright red wound.

What is going on? What has come over him? Why does he want to attack us? These thoughts all race through my head. Travis summons the strength to lift himself from the stairwell. The look of anger has now evolved into extreme abhorrence. I don't think it would be wrong to assume he definitely wants me dead.

He stumbles towards me. I back away cautiously hoping to stop this madness.

"What is going on? Why are you doing this?" I shout in utter confusion.

"You just had to be perfect, didn't you, Alcott? Had to surpass everybody and do the impossible..." he wails at the top of his lungs. He rushes directly at me. He cocks back his arm to punch me with full force. Agility is with me as I elude the shot. Preparing myself for battle, I circle and kick him straight in the stomach.

He groans in pain. Just as I do so, he forcefully slams my chest with his fist, bringing me to shout the same annoyance. Both of us duel in sheer agony. No animosity subsides.

"Now..." he defiantly states... "I will end you."

I quickly dash for my fallen frying pan. It lies a few feet away from me. As he detects my intention, he cautiously removes his shoe. The man hurls it toward my face at full speed. Before I can even attempt to stop it, the projectile bashes into me. I retreat a few steps. Wooziness envelops my mind. I determine my next course of action.

Luckily, no part of me appears to be severely damaged from the skirmish. As my eyes dart up, I see Travis charging. He has retrieved my frying pan and raises it to killing a position. Here I am, weaponless and alone. I'm about to be destroyed.

Alert as possible, I duck in time to evade the swing of the pan. After doing so, I kick his shin with all my energy. This forces him to stumble back, holding his leg in agony. Sadly, he still clutches the valuable frying pan, the only weapon available. *It never feels good to see anybody in pain, no less that I caused. I had no other choice.*

At that moment, I decide my best move. That is to make a dash for the kitchen area. He hasn't begun to follow me yet. Travis rubs his damaged leg. Irritation grows by the second. When I arrive back in the room past the now lit up restaurant, I search all around for any potential weapons. The frying pan had been the only one I had seen before. Nothing has changed since a few minutes ago, as everything remains undoubtedly locked. Quickly, I begin to check all of the drawers once more.

I hold on to sheer hope one of them will pop open. That mindset proves futile. None budge, just as before.

Luckily, something manifests in my mind that hadn't the previous time. Thank goodness it has, as his footsteps stride deliberately closer from the restaurant. Success! A new drawer shielded by the cabinet's shadows is not locked! Pulling it open, many varieties of sharp and deadly knives come into sight. Clutching the biggest one, practically measuring a foot in length, I circle around. Travis darts into the kitchen with a glare of contempt. Now carrying a useful weapon, I feel far more powerful. The situation is surely now in my favor.

Fear overtakes his eyes. He notices the shimmering blade, causing him to dart away from the kitchen. He runs at full speed while I give chase.

"I don't want to hurt you!" I scream. I gulp giant breaths with each new step. "Why are you doing this?!" All of this I shout, chasing him through the restaurant. We begin to enter the lobby once more. No answer or recognition from him, as he begins running toward the staircase. Once he arrives, he directly rotates to face me. I halt a couple yards away with my knife pointed in his direction. He then hurls the frying pan, out of nowhere, directly at my head.

This time, however, I am able to remove myself from the path of the oncoming projectile, unlike the shoe before. I do somehow pull my face out of the way, but the rest of my body is not so lucky. It crashes into my arm at with an alarming force, causing massive pain to well up. To my horror, the knife is smashed out of my grasp, now swiftly sliding across the smooth lobby tiles.

Both of us are now weaponless and unprotected. This has been made a fair fight once again. The sheer dominance and power the knife gave me ultimately escapes my mind. We lock eyes with deadly glares.

"You have done too well at these Obstacles, Alcott," he breaks eerie silence. "Your skills have been greatly underestimated by us all, and for that you must pay. She will find you when she learns of your escape…and she will kill you…if I can't accomplish the deed myself."

As he is in the middle of this dark proclamation, I catch a quick glimpse of someone. This figure delicately descends the stairwell. My peripheral vision hazily reveals it is Gretchen! In the millisecond I view her figure, I believe she possesses some implement in her right hand. Gretchen nods at me carefully. She tip-toes toward Travis without making a sound.

Gazing straight into Travis' eyes, I pretend that I didn't see anything. It appears to have worked. He makes no motion to look backwards. My stalling has succeeded long enough as she charges at him with all her might. The woman stabs him from the back through the heart. He shouts louder than I have ever heard in my life. Utter agony overpowers him. Blood flows out from his chest, and he topples over to the floor. Oceans of blood gush all around him. Travis lays there inanimately; eyes completely open and staring into space. There is no question about it, Travis has undoubtedly been killed.

I topple onto the ground on all fours gasping for sweet air. I blankly stare at the ground. I am trying to take in all this information in contemplation for my next move. *Travis had stated the exact same thing the Jauntla did; I had exceeded expectations in the Obstacles.*

'I must be destroyed.' He still was unaware of what I had done to the Jauntla, however. That is known to me because he said that she would kill me when she found out I had escaped. She definitely lies stiff as a board in the basement. Suddenly, it dawns on me…she may not be dead.

"Alcott!" Gretchen screams in panic. The woman dashes down the stairs to meet me. "What's going on?! Why was he attacking you?! Why did you disappear last night?"

Answering all these questions is going to prove difficult in my exhausted state. Despite my condition, I do the best I can.

"Whole thing…is…" I stutter between deep breaths, "a… sham…" I let out a few pretty deep coughs, definitely spurting blood out. "All…made…up…me and Marya… passed too many tests…" I wheeze immensely as tears descend. "So, the Jauntla wanted us dead…we were locked in a cellar…but we escaped…I knocked her out… and then Travis attacked us. He was saying the same things she said…"

Gretchen then, trying to process the new information, starts to lift me up off the ground. With her gracious assistance, we both stumble over to Marya. She lies unconscious on the floor. At least, that's what I'm praying in my heart is so.

"Marya!" I wheeze as best as I can. More hacks are let out.

"Marya," Gretchen leans down to the girl, "Come on, Marya, stay with us." There is no response whatsoever. She leans her head onto her chest, viewing no visible inflation. "I don't think she's breathing!"

I have never been happier to be in the profession I am in.

"Gretchen, you have to…put your hand on her chest…and your other hand…on top of that…" More rough, bloody coughs emerge from me. "Make sure your arms…are…straight…press down about two inches and don't stop until…I tell you…" I'm definitely in pretty rough shape myself; that fight demolished me.

Gretchen performs as I instruct, placing her hands in the correct position. She begins the compressions. Being too weak at the moment, all I can do is watch. I hope that my friend is still alive. Helplessly praying with all my heart is my only course of action. Gretchen continues the various resuscitating techniques with her ultimate focus. Out of nowhere, something amazing occurs. The chest movements do not lie; Marya's breathing! After a little while, eyes delicately flicker open rendering a tear to fall down my cheek.

It requires a little bit more work from Gretchen, and my instruction. We finally get her up okay. I immediately hug her when the opportunity arises, ecstatic as I didn't think she would survive that blow.

"What was that all about?" she inquires. The young girl rubs her head in sheer bafflement. "What did I ever do to that guy? What in the world?"

"Well," Gretchen prepares to tell the whole story, "apparently, Travis wants you guys dead for passing the Obstacles."

"What?" Marya looks horrified. "First the Jauntla and now him? He seems like such a nice person."

My eye catches a glimpse of the dead body lying at the bottom of the stairs. The knife pierces his chest with a sea of blood around.

"Where did you get the knife anyway?" I ask Gretchen.

"From cooking with the Sphreams," she responds, looking back at Travis. "I decided to take an extra one with me, in case of emergencies. Looks like it's a very good thing I did."

I certainly attest to that. All of this new information burst out at once. We must assess the severity of our current situation. There is still no sign of the Sphreams, and no remote strategy of how to escape.

"What do you think we should do?" I ask both of them, praying for any simple solution. "Well," Marya replies, "I think it would be best to get out of this hotel. Nothing good seems to come from staying here."

"What about Vitaly?" Gretchen quickly asks. Her

high-pitched tone indicates utter horror. Amongst all the sheer chaos, I completely forgot about Vitaly. She must still be up in her room sleeping. But then a haunting thought hits the dark places of my mind. *Can we trust her?*

Chapter 37
Vitaly

"Well," I respond trying to figure this mess out. "If Travis was on the Jauntla's side, what makes you think we can trust Vitaly?"

"I," Gretchen continues, "guess we can't. I suggest we just get out of here for now. I'm sure causing the kid to join our rebellion would be far worse than letting her remain innocent."

"I have to agree," Marya affirms Gretchen's statement. "Being attacked once is enough for me." She continues wiping her face onto a bloody cloth.

The Jauntla's terrifying voice replays in my mind. "You will have to be exterminated." *All this time we were pawns. These people would actually murder us. Again, exterminated is emphasized. It puts us exactly as insects in their minds. Vitaly could be up there hiding under the covers alone right now, scared to death. There is no way I'm going to let her go through this torture. Granted we have no way of trusting her, but if she is real, and she passed another challenge…Vitaly would most likely die, and I'm not going to let that happen.*

"I'm sorry, I just can't do that," I state with defiance. "What if she passes another challenge? We passed two, and they were about to destroy us. I could never forgive myself if that happened to her."

Extreme guilt overtakes their faces. Marya, I'm sure, is picturing the celebration room again. She's well aware what could happen to the child. Her stay there had been far longer than my own.

"You're right, Alcott," Marya replies with confidence. "I don't know what I was thinking. Let's go get her."

"There's no need for all of us; Gretchen, you watch over Marya," I say. "Go explore the outside of the hotel. See if you can find any sign of a way out of here. I'll head up and get her."

My condition has gotten much better. I am able to dash up the stairs while the two of them head out into the dark courtyard. *There is no way Vitaly could be a spy. We have been through too much together. Could that have all been a lie? I tend to dwell upon dark thoughts, so I must force myself to cast it aside. I'm rescuing her.*

As I approach the top of the stairs, I hope with every fiber of my being no Sphreams lurk. It's probably the stupidest thing to charge up unguarded. Still, my conscience won't let me rest until I know she's okay.

Vitaly's room is at the end of the elaborate hallway. From my initial view, there is no Sphream in sight. *Where could they all have gone? Where have they gone every night anyway?* Many questions with unknown answers flood my brain. Nobody can be trusted anymore. As I finally arrive at her room and reach the door knob, I find it unlocked.

That is very peculiar. We are advised to lock our doors every night, for some reason. I always have, why has she not locked hers? I rotate the knob gently. My shaky hand barely gets a firm grip. The door creaks open.

The room is extremely dark. Of course, the light switch is unresponsive. In the distance, I sense the blanket rising up and down. This surely indicates a person sleeping inside. Tip-toeing up to the bed, I peer underneath the covers. Just as I expected, little Vitaly's lost in slumber. I

Obstacles

have never seen anybody look more innocent. Chastising myself for doubting her, I shake her. Her eyes slowly open.

"Vitaly," I whisper with urgency. "Get up! This is very important." Her body delicately rises up from her daze. She appears extremely worn out, and the sight of me scares her to death.

"Alco...Alcott?" she becomes frantic. "What... what are you doing?! Where did you go? Why did you leave us all of sudden?!"

"I don't have time to explain now," I calmly state. "We just have to get out of here immediately."

"Why?" she inquires with wide eyes. "What's going on?"

"This whole thing is a sham; it's not real, I'll explain later," I say. "These people aren't good, Vitaly, we have to go right now; come on!"

"Okay." She adheres to my order despite her confusion. "Can I go get my stuff?"

"You brought stuff?" I ask a bit taken back. "I wasn't allowed to bring anything."

She makes no attempt at answering my question. Her shadow whisks into the bathroom. I stand there in the silent darkness for quite a while. No one emerges from the bathroom. What in the world could she possibly be getting? This is ridiculous. We have to go now!

"Vitaly, come on!" I call in the softest possible way across the room. Still no verbal answer, but I detect a hazy figure exit the bathroom. She then proceeds to stand in front of the hallway door. No words are spoken. She skips there joyfully, as if nothing is wrong in the world at all.

"What are you doing?" I wail, extremely irritated at this behavior. There is utter silence as a response. Vitaly then charges towards my location. This kid is scaring me to death. It doesn't take long to realize the horror of what is going on; little Vitaly clutches a knife in her hand.

"How dare you hurt our god?" she yells at the top of her lungs. Every chance of secrecy is demolished. "How dare you pass the impassable? You will not be getting out of here peacefully, Alcott, I can assure you. Travis hasn't finished you off, so I guess it's up to me."

Frozen with horror is an understatement for me. I feel wholly idiotic and betrayed. Suddenly, a few things start to make sense in my mind. *No wonder Travis and Vitaly were paired together in that last challenge. They probably didn't go on a challenge at all! Both of their tests had always seemed rather peculiar and similar.* Everything begins to click. Especially the baffled faces when I had conquered the sword fighting Obstacle. *Both of them expected me to have failed. I knew something was up; why did I not see it before? I'm so stupid!*

As the little child approaches, knife at the ready, I only have one option left. Darting to the window as fast as I can, I desperately attempt to shove it open. My efforts don't seem to be working. Her speed increases.

"Alcott..." she sings, laughing creepily to herself. "Is someone scared, Alcott?"

Thankfully, luck returns to my side. A burst of adrenaline helps me dislodge the window and slide it open. Swinging my body over the ledge, I successfully climb onto the slanted roof.

"Ahhhhh!" Vitaly yelps in extreme contempt.

I have just brawled with Travis for quite some time; I am in no mood or condition to battle again.

Before Vitaly can reach me, I dart across the inclined roof. It is somewhat slanted but nearly horizontal. My feet can retain a steady friction. Rushing past various windows, I turn the corner sharply. Just as I do so, I hear screams and threats of Vitaly climbing out. She escapes much quicker than I had anticipated. Getting away from this alien seems like much more of a challenge.

There is certainly no time to open any of these windows before she can get to me. My only option is to keep running until a miracle arrives. As I continue along, the miracle actually manifests. There is an open window a few yards away!

Jogging to it, I dive in and shut it. Hopefully my dive through the window was undetected. Peering at my new surroundings, I find this room pitch black as well; however, this time that's exactly what I need. If luck rests with me, maybe she will dart past and miss me. Sitting in the corner, I patiently wait. I pray my predator will be fooled.

After a few minutes, the sound of her feet rushing along reaches me. I hold my breath entirely. To my luck, my strategy works. Vitaly charges past unaware of my new hiding spot. Finally, able to relax for a bit, I am safe for the time being.

I keep on looking around. I must determine what this new place is. I have never been in or known about any other rooms of this hotel. Who knows what they contain? The size and length are completely unknown as all I view is the window and darkness. Suddenly…

Chapter 38
Dash

"Alcott," a familiar voice whispers. It is recognizable anywhere; it emanates from a Sphream. The Sphreams had previously knocked me out in the kitchen. At least, that's what I assumed had occurred. After that encounter, I am not thrilled to be stuck in the unknown with one of them. *Oh no; I'm doomed. They have discovered me.* Just as all hope is lost…

"Alcott, don't worry, we're on your side…" continuing the dark tone. What? Complete shock and bemusement flood my mind. I know for sure that these things surrounded me in the kitchen. One of them definitely knocked me out before I arose in the Celebration Room. So, naturally I have doubts at this statement.

"You knocked her out, but sadly, you have not killed her," another adds. None are visible to me. Only raspy voices indicate location. "She will be back…oh she will be back…You must enter the Portal."

She will be back?! They're obviously talking about this Jauntla. Oh no, where is she going to be? And what in the world is this portal thing?

"The Portal?" I quickly ask. "Where is that? What's going on? Why do I have to kill her?"

"Behind the hotel…you will be taken…to her… you, Gretchen, and Marya will have to battle her once and for all…we will assist you in any way we can…" another wails. The eerie undertone suggests this will be an impossible feat.

I cannot understand what they are saying. *How in the world am I supposed to battle a god?* It is a bit calming to know that these things are on my side; at least, that's what they say.

"Thank you," I whisper, paranoid about Vitaly. The whole scenario is surreal. "How do I escape? Vitaly just chased me in here with a knife! You still haven't told me why all this is happening?"

"You passed too many tests, Alcott…too many tests. She will stop at nothing to kill you and erase your existence now," another Sphream responds. "We were going to give this to you later, but, since you have discovered our hideout…"

Just then, a beautiful light shimmers, disrupting the unyielding blackness. Some implement shines completely white, hovering with enormous power. Looking at this new object closely, I discover that it is a flail, containing a handle and chain, and a deadly enormous spiked ball attached to the end of it. You attack by swinging the ball around. It destroys ferociously, making it truly a magnificent weapon.

"This flail…" the Sphreams speak in unison, "is no ordinary flail; its true power cannot be used without each and every one of our assistance. We will arrive when the time is right, if you can survive that long, that is. Until then, you will be on your own."

"This isn't like an Obstacle; if you lose this…. you die forever" That statement sends shivers up my spine.

"We can use our power," the scary voice again states, "to transport you to the Portal, behind the hotel. Gretchen has taken Marya there now and is beginning to head back in for you. There is no time, Alcott; you'll have to go now!"

"O…kay," I stammer, trying to prepare myself. *Is*

this really going to happen? How are we going to take down the Jauntla? It does make me feel better knowing that the Sphreams will help in any way they can. But, with me already worn out from fighting Travis, this doesn't seem nearly possible. Nonetheless, Marya's not in the best condition. However, I didn't survive this long dwelling upon negative thoughts. I have to be strong, no matter what happens in the end.

Just then, a luminous, blue light hovers across the room. The Sphreams become visible for a millisecond. The abrupt flash reveals seven in the miniature enclosure. As the blue light glows with much more energy, my eyes are blinded. Before I can determine what is even happening, I am transported back outside.

Chapter 39
Final Battle

From the view, I quickly determine I am at the back of the hotel, completely contrasting the front. Having never explored it before, it is truly a dazzling sight. Endless silver benches and chairs surround a spectacular fountain. The center statue resembles the Jauntla. Water spurts from her mouth to return to the large basin, just to start the cycle again.

The water rushes upwards in a majestic manner. Lights outside reveal full reverence. There are also many flowers, as there had been in the front courtyard. These are much more petite and delicate, ranging from spiraling pink to orange oval. Gazing at it all for a long period of time would definitely cause you to be dizzy. Darting past the giant structure, I find Gretchen and Marya hunched over by the benches.

"Alcott!" Gretchen shouts at my presence. "You just appeared out of thin air! What happened? When did you get that...thing?!"

I quickly answer, breaking the fountain's hypnosis. "The Sphreams gave it to me and teleported me here, after Vitaly tried to kill me..."

"Oh no," Marya says. "So that means, she is also--"

"Yeah."

"Well, thinking back, it does make a lot of sense," Gretchen states. "So the Sphreams are on our side? Did they mention what this big vortex thing is?"

Behind the fountain, a magical spectacle manifests

in my vision. Spiraling round and round are two waves of blue and purple shades. Each of them follow the other endlessly into limbo, forming the magnificent portal spoken of.

"Yes…" I look at the magic. "The Jauntla awaits us. We're going to have to battle her, once and for all; the Sphreams said they will assist in any way they can."

"What?!" Gretchen exclaims in horror. "We have to actually fight her? How are we possibly going to do that? It's not like you two aren't exhausted or anyth--" Gretchen is then cut off by harsh screaming in the distance.

"Alcott! Gretchen! Marya! I will find you, and I will kill each and every one of you!"

The voice definitely belongs to Vitaly; and, to our dismay, she lurks outside the hotel. She is certainly approaching. No mercy at all in her childlike body. We have no choice about our next course of action. There is no time to lose, and all of us are well aware of that.

So, without another word, each of us cautiously steps through the portal. We disappear from this place forever. The inevitable darkness awaits.

The world around me loses itself in a vortex of nothingness. I can neither view nor remotely understand anything anymore. *Am I falling, sleeping, vibrantly dreaming, fainting, literally dying, or all of the above?* Nothing makes sense.

Expecting to hear voices shouting my name, I prepare myself to keep some sanity. Strangely enough, no voices arrive this time. There exists only unrelenting abyss and tranquility…and my never-ending thoughts. *This seems to have been going on for a very long time; could be a few seconds, or maybe years, perhaps even forever.* Just as my mind wanders into oblivion, something happens.

"Alcott!" Marya yells with gusto. "Get up!" My

eyes dart open in awe of the next realization. I awake inside a gigantic stadium.

Billions of seats surround me arranged in varieties of rows and locations. As I rise from the durable, marble flooring, the many walls tower over all dominately. Upon the end of every section, a large pillar stands. A deadly spiked diamond rests upon the summit of each. This definitely sparks fear into all our hearts. Darkness of space is clearly visible in the night sky. An enormous purple planet glares down above the stadium. My eyes can only gaze in awe at the spectacle. The celestial body hovers so close to us, I feel as if I could reach out and grasp it.

I find Gretchen examining my newly received weapon.

"This is pretty hard-core, Alcott. Those Sphreams must really mean business."

"Yeah," I respond. Pointy spikes protrude from around the sphere. "I just hope I don't take my own head off when I swing it."

"That wouldn't be very good," Marya adds. "This place is completely magnificent! I'm so ready to fight; being tied up for as long as I was is certainly not a grudge I'm willing to let go." She almost seems excited to battle.

"I still can't believe all the work we did was completely for nothing," Gretchen's eyebrows lower to a demonic level. "Everything…all for nothing." Complete frustration engulfs her at that comment. "I'm ready too; let's go."

"Alright," I readily agree. Glancing around the immense stadium, I detect no sign of a soul anywhere. We continue walking toward the center. I must look confident as the spiked ball swings behind me.

Suddenly, out of thin air, the Jauntla appears at the far end of the stadium. She faces the opposite direction to all of us. She immediately begins chanting some spell to herself. None of us can understand the dialect. The chanting then becomes more boisterous with a much harsher tone. It isn't long before she swiftly rotates without warning, the chant evolving into a direct shout to us all.

"What I am doing is good! The Obstacles were a spectacular and productive strategy! Until the two of you decided to screw it all up by doing the impossible… Everyone that had attempted this before had lost, as it is supposed to be. You can't change fate, only a fool would think that. You are meant to lose knowing that you had closure fighting for the one you lost. But, you…just couldn't do that. Now, all of you know far too much, and must be erased from existence forever.

"The world and life will be as if you hadn't ever been there; it's fate, after all. This action cannot be done, however, without a fair fight. So, each of you may receive these weapons, and these creatures. That's as fair as a fight with me you will ever get. Now, let us begin."

Immediately at the conclusion of her proclamation, six enormous winged creatures appear in front of us; an assortment of vicious weapons lies adjacent. They are no doubt some species of pelican. Gigantic bills protrude from their faces. Fierce wings prepare to soar. Slender necks lead up to beady eyes.

These eyes, however, are certainly not typical for the birds. The two dots are completely shimmering white. They resemble a cross between demons and angels.

The weapons laid out are truly marvelous indeed; ranging from elaborate bows and arrows, to varieties of swords, knives, shields, and various implements. As each of us admires our new selection of weapons, I glare at the god once again. The last time I had seen her was when I was convinced I murdered her; it's tearing me up inside knowing she's watching me now.

So, apparently she intends to wipe all of us from existence. Poor Gretchen got sucked into this too because of us. Thankfully, she said this would have to be a fair brawl. However, I severely doubt fair means the same to her as it does to us. Fate or not; I'm not going to let this happen. It's time to fight.

Just then, the Jauntla begins to levitate. Her body hovers off the ground. Swerving left to right, her torso is penetrated by a luminous yellow energy. This light is so bright it spreads throughout the entire stadium. I'm blinded completely. As light pours throughout, I am reduced to dropping my flail to the ground. My eyes must be covered or else I'm sure they'll burst. Luckily after a few moments, it starts to die down.

Retrieving my flail from the dirt, I glare at her again. Her golden form grows larger at a rapid and dangerous pace. Towering over the three of us, she literally evolves into a gigantic skyscraper; rendering all of our jaws to drop. I can barely see the top of her now. How in the world can the three of us defeat this monstrosity? Instantly, the immense illumination disappears. It's as if it never existed in the first place. She then emanates a bloody red hue, an almost holographic image. It appears as if she is evolving.

As the shape of this creature finally takes hold, we gaze in amazement. There is no question about it; this god has transformed into a gigantic bat. She flaps devilishly in the sky. A sharp screech pierces the night. The enormous uproar makes my ears throb.

***

With no time to waste, Gretchen and Marya charge

over to the weapons. They admire the many killing machines. Both of them examine all of them, figuring out which would work best.

As I see them ruffling through all the swords, I dart straight over to the shields. I already grasp my flail. So, now all I have to worry about is protection. There are certainly many shields about, though it seems quite difficult to tell which is best. Gretchen and Marya seem to have chosen weapons without issue.

Marya selects the deadly bow and arrow, while Gretchen wields an enormous sword. As I ruffle amongst the shields, I determine the one I already found suits me the best. It appears very sturdy; hopefully it will help me evade this demon. The Jauntla flaps quickly in the dark sky, giving us time, it seems, to choose what we wish. Hopefully that time doesn't run out soon. I walk over to the mesmerizing pelicans.

Each looks truly heroic. I can't spot any differences between them as I stride nearby. As I do so, each one of the six begins to bow their head toward the ground. Lengthy wings extend at arrival. That is, as I can assume, an invitation to ride whoever I choose. Without knowing any way to judge, I pick the closest bird. Lunging my body over, I attempt to climb it. Once I swing my leg over it, the pelican offers a swift glare. Its menacing white eyes petrify me. I can't determine whether I'm a welcome rider or a trespasser.

My remaining Allies select their avian soldiers as well. All of us now sit on our pelicans. The extra birds then begin to rise. They soar off into the distance, perhaps relieved they don't have to battle. Without warning, the Jauntla does something incredible and horrifying.

She lets out the loudest screech I have ever heard. The noise demolishes everyone's ears, including the dark pelicans. The Jauntla then descends swiftly to our level, anticipating a melee to the death.

The pelicans give each other a swift glance, as if to relay a message of some sort. At that, wings simultaneously flap. We're immediately airborne. The sensation shocks me. I wrap my arms around the beast for balance.

Rising a bit, the Jauntla spins herself in a circle toward the lower end of the stadium. Rotating with extreme speed, she envelops the stadium in overpowering whirlwinds.

Immense gales sway the pelicans' flight. My body's almost thrown completely off. Thankfully, I keep a firm hold. Each pelican begins to flap with frantic acceleration. We all rise high into the stadium. The next sight fills me with horror.

Along each gust of wind, purple flames burst. An overpowering heat engulfs half of the arena. The fire soars along the wind practically flying itself. Without the birds, we would be fried. The Jauntla even has to take a moment to rest after the attack. Had we stayed down there a moment longer, we would have for sure been killed.

"What is it doing?!" Marya wails with wide eyes.

"Some flame wind thing; good thing we got out of there." Gretchen shares the same terror.

"How do you suppose we fight this thing?" I inquire, hoping for any kind of worthy advice.

No response from either of them. Not that they would have had time anyway, as the Jauntla regains her strength instantly. The beast soars up at a ferocious speed. Each pelican detects the god, letting out a simultaneous squawk. At the sight of the oncoming bat, each darts away from the stadium. They fly much better than I expected. Glancing back, I see the monster giving chase.

I desperately attempt to balance myself. I have no

idea where the pelicans' destination is, if there is one at all. Perhaps the Jauntla just drove them into frenzy? Either way, we're utterly dependent. I have to put complete faith in them. We continue flying into the dark abyss. The Jauntla certainly has no trouble keeping up.

"Alcott!" I hear a voice yell, scaring me half to death. "You have to stand up. She will hurl something powerful. You must fight it back!"

Where is this coming from?! Frantically peering all around, I see no sign of anyone. *Did I just make that up in my head?* My eyes then glance downward. The voice begins to speak again. I discover it coming from my pelican! Through telepathy, it must be delving into my mind.

"Hurry! You have no time to lose," the pelican shouts. A beady eye rotates to me. "Don't worry about balance, my feathers will hold you. Go!"

For some reason, my pelican is the only one to speak. Gretchen immediately yells, "What did your bird say? We have to stand up?"

Balancing and communicating prove difficult. I attempt to stand up, but my shaky legs send me right back onto my stomach.

I then shout back. "Yes, she's going to--"

"Alcott!" my pelican yelps.

A giant sphere of flames barrels into my torso. The purple ball appears as large as a basketball. My body is slammed off the pelican. Before I even figure out what's going on, I am plummeting towards the ground.

Chapter 40
Delving into the Unknown

I am now completely in mid-air. My fingers grasp the flail as gravity drags me down. At my departure, my pelican lets out a roaring squawk. Gretchen's pelican immediately nosedives to my falling body. It flies at a record pace. Luckily, it had been flying at a lower level than where I had originally been.

My body continues hurtling toward the ground. The planet in the sky shrinks with every second. Sharp pains bash my stomach. Closing my eyes, I prepare to slam against the ground in inevitable demise. Suddenly, I hear a squawk directly below me. My eyes dart open. The next sight I see is certainly not something I ever expected. Gretchen and her pelican are about to break my fall!

Without much warning, my body smacks Gretchen. I almost knock the sword completely out of her hand.

"Alcott!" Gretchen yells with a whimper. I have obviously knocked the wind out of her. "Please don't fall again."

Though I was seconds from death, I have to smile at that comment. Lying on top of Gretchen, I hold on for dear life. It takes all my strength to not slide off into the darkness once again.

"I'll try not to," I respond.

Peering up above me, I see bursts of light. The Jauntla's flaming fireballs have surely not subsided. Marya deflects them standing upon her pelican. Arrows fling from her bow at a rapid pace. She seems to have mastered this technique quite well. The Jauntla grows impatient. As I stare at the spectacle, this new pelican screeches. It charges towards Marya. Falling off seems like a close reality I do not want to repeat. My original pelican now descends, aware of my presence. It shows a look of panic. Maybe it believed I was dead.

My pelican seems to nod in a way to Gretchen's. It acrobatically swerves a few feet under it. In a very impressive gesture, Gretchen's pelican spirals completely around. This action releases me onto the bird's back. Landing back on with a thump, I offer a smile to Gretchen.

"Falling is unacceptable," is the first thing my pelican speaks. It's not the happiest with me at the moment. "That will most likely not happen again. Dying here is really dying. Stand up now!"

"Sorry," I stammer, taken aback by its rough attitude.

With much more agility than last time, I get up. My feet attempt to locate a hold amongst the features. This doesn't prove an issue as I am firmly locked in. My pelican then starts its ascent to where Gretchen and Marya are. Both successfully parry the monster's fire.

The Jauntla wails a clamorous screech. She is filled with outrage at her failed projectiles. Her eyes dart around. Suddenly, they lock on to something in the distance. She flaps at the swiftest speed she can muster. The monster heads off to that unknown location in the night. We finally reach the height of Marya and Gretchen once more. Both of them look extremely exhausted at their efforts.

"You have made her angry," my pelican pronounces. "She needs time to recharge. She has headed to the Icy Mountains; we must attack now."

The other two pelicans swiftly nod. My pelican is obviously the alpha of the group. We then trail the Jauntla to these so-called mountains. The pure name of the location strikes an eerie fear into my mind. Breaking my brain from the trance, I contemplate my falling. I am very disappointed in how I handled myself on the pelican. I cannot believe I wasn't more agile and focused. One more mistake could very well be the last one I ever make.

"How are you guys so good at blocking the fireballs?" I shout across the sky. It doesn't seem to make sense to me how skilled they are in this unpredictable situation. It makes me feel a bit inferior too.

"Pure luck," Marya states. "Our weapons are a bit easier to handle; yours is going to take a bit of practice." The flail does seem pretty complicated. Using it has proven difficult. Marya has a point. Each spike protruding from the enormous metal sphere has death written all over. I definitely should have practiced a little more.

"Yeah," Gretchen adds. She switches her sword to the opposite hand for a better grip. "Work with the flail a little more before we get to the island; you can do it!"

"Okay," I whimper with close to no confidence at all.

"It takes skill, but don't be discouraged; you have to have complete determination," my pelican reassures me.

So, all three of us head toward the Icy Mountain. The giant planet shimmers in space. Though my Allies comfortably lie down on their birds, I stand directly on top of mine. Finding my foothold, I make a note of where provides the best balance. Raising the flail in the air, the chain rocks back and forth. A deadly sphere swings like a pendulum. For quite some time, I concentrate on spinning and circling. This must be done in the proper manner without killing anybody around me; or me for that matter. This does require much skill and practice to do it with ease.

I certainly have no intention of going through

another episode like the one before. The more I master the weapon, the more it appears horrifying. Dying from this little beauty doesn't sound very pleasant at all. It does scare me how one little mistake can take me out. It looks like my fear of death has not nearly subsided. However, I have to be constantly determined. My demise can arrive in an instant.

After a little while, a new land starts to come into sight. I squint and adjust my head. Moving a bit forward, I catch a glimpse of a mountainous structure. Immense darkness covers most of it. However, a few spots remain visible. As the three of us fly toward this new land, I take deep breaths. Another battle is about to commence.

"Now is the weakest she will be for a while," the pelican whimpers. "You must strike now, for this opportunity may never arise again."

My pelican continues to be the one in charge. The other two quickly nod in submission, putting up no counter arguments whatsoever.

Gretchen then answers my pelican's statement. "How are we supposed to do that?"

Based on the fireball spin in the stadium, none of us are urging to take her head on. That task appears nothing short of a death wish.

"I don't know," it plainly states. Its eerie tone shields no apprehension. "But you have to try."

Silence follows that last statement. My heart races with anticipation. *What is going to happen if we don't prevail?* I'm well aware my days of waking up in a hotel room are over. Flashbacks of the Jauntla demolish my head. So many memories occurred throughout the Obstacles. *She had seemed so welcoming and compassionate. Of course, before the giant bat thing happened. How could someone like that immediately turn into wanting to exterminate me from existence?!*

What could that have possibly meant? Where would you go? Pass on forever into oblivion?! No matter what it meant, I am not willing to find out. Conquering all those Obstacles for nothing; and then being chastised for winning? That's it; she is going down.

Glancing around the new location, it becomes clear we have finally arrived at the snowy mountain. Along with the unrelenting blindness of night, the mountains tower over us. The pelicans seem to have somewhat of an illuminating power. A light delicately emanates throughout their bodies. This glow makes the area slightly more visible. I can look through the land.

As we are soaring inland, my pelican yelps with urgency…"Shhhh, don't make a sound!" Everyone completely stops in their tracks. The only sound is the soft flapping of wings.

Gretchen then delicately extends her index finger. This indicates something in the distance. She motions us to fly over as our pelicans obey. As I peer into the dark, I discover there is definitely something shiny over there; the question is what in the world could it be? The sparkles twinkle in the distance. They make no effort to move. Deciding it best to move closer, our pelicans fly forward. As the distance between us decreases, the sparkles begin to manifest into delicate wings. These wings are of the solitary flying mammal.

We have found her; no question about it. Although, she appears to be in quite a questionable pose. Hovering roughly a hundred feet away, we discover the god hanging upside down from a branch. The Jauntla's eyes are completely shut. Shimmering wings fold over its body. Any animal expert can tell you what is going on. The Jauntla is definitely sleeping. She conserves desired energy to attack once more. Even I can tell at this point, that this is our best chance of destroying her.

"This has to happen now," my pelican affirms my course of action. "Marya, you know what to do."

As the three of us inch closer bit by bit, the pelicans land on an enormous tree nearby. This pine tree is gigantic. From the looks of the crispy branches, it's certainly sturdy and ancient. Thankfully, no noise is made as each bird's webbed feet stick. The Jauntla remains in deep slumber, blissfully unaware of our presence. This seems way too easy at the moment. Wouldn't she know we would follow her? Maybe she thought we would all return to the stadium or something.

Either way, this situation is certainly in our favor. Taking full advantage of this opportunity, Marya gingerly reaches for an arrow. Pulling it from her quiver, she inserts it into the bow. Her fierce eyes never leave the Jauntla. Yanking the string back, she puts complete focus into the aim. One eye shuts.

"What should I aim for?" she asks.

"The center," my pelican states without hesitation. White eyes glare through the cold night. "Aim right for her heart."

Chapter 41
Silent

Marya immediately obeys the advice, taking just a bit more time to prepare the arrow in the perfect location. Everything seems to be going as planned, but suddenly, something horrifying occurs. Marya releases the arrow, directly for the Jauntla's heart. All of us can do nothing but sit in anticipation. The arrow, however, merely passes through the creature. It's as if there is nothing there. As it travels through the Jauntla my jaw drops. *What in the world?* The Jauntla takes no notice of the projectile at all, just continues her peaceful slumber.

Amongst the sheer confusion, a spine-chilling echo booms. Before, there was a little creak in my mind, but I assumed I was just hearing things. Now, however, I realize I was definitely not. The crackling noise becomes far more boisterous. Every pair of eyes darts down to the unimaginable horror.

Another bat rests directly below us, preparing a giant fireball. The sphere of flames is almost at completion. Though all the others showed a magenta hue, this one is pure cobalt blue. Extreme shock shakes all of us, even the seemingly angelic pelicans. All of them squawk uncontrollably at the realization. If that's the Jauntla, then what did Marya fire at?

The first sleeping bat shimmers and sparkles a bit; very odd behavior indeed. After a few seconds, electricity charges the beast. The image slowly fades away into black nothingness.

I cannot believe I, or any of us, could have been that stupid. I did not come this far to be a complete idiot; yet that's just what I have become. The 'sleeping' bat was nothing more than a hologram; a fake decoy to draw us in for the kill. There is no way the Jauntla would have let us just bombard her in that state.

A fireball is surely complete down below us. The real bat screeches into the night. Before any of us have any time to retreat, the dark flame bursts through the tree. It takes down everything in its path. My pelican lets out a squawk of utter rage and horror. Unyielding heat terrorizes my senses. Bright flames now circle me as my pelican leaps off the branch just in time. I can't help but scream and close my eyes. Agony begins to overwhelm us all.

Amongst all this torture, I feel the horrendous heat subsiding. Looking up, I discover my pelican has skillfully flown us out of the chaos. This defies what I thought it could do.

A swift glance back portrays a giant blue flaming destruction. I look all around to only see Marya a few feet away. She has also escaped the fire. The sudden horror in my heart then sets in.

"Marya!" I yelp over the Jauntla's screeches. "Where's Gretchen?"

Marya's eyes dart around as well, with no sign of her anywhere. Upon further inspection, I now realize where she is; though I really wish I didn't. The sight I gaze upon next is certainly one I would like to forget.

Amongst the bright flames, I see Gretchen's pelican in frenzy. No human being is on top of it. Upon the ground lies Gretchen. She lies directly next to the gigantic bat, utterly paralyzed with fear. The Jauntla glares at her; neither gives a single blink. As my darkest fears become reality, the Jauntla aims one of her purple flames. The horrendous death of my friend is inevitable.

With Gretchen's pelican discovering her horrific fate, it dives downward. Hatred flows from its veins. There is pure focus and courage in its eyes. I don't think it cares if it doesn't survive. Barreling itself into the monster, it pecks with utter outrage. The Jauntla screeches in confusion, attempting to crunch the bird with her piercing fangs.

The last sight I see is Gretchen staring at me; the same eyes when the giant snake under the swamp constricted her. That, however, was an Obstacle; and this is real life. There is no coming back. All of us know that. Despite that horror, I still see the same message in those eyes; the message, 'Go without me.' I don't know if I can bear that again.

"NO!" I yell at the top of my lungs. Globs of tears fall from my eyes. The challenge with the snakes and mosquito is one thing; just a challenge. Now, however, the one person willing to risk everything for me may actually perish. There is no need to emphasize the rage and hatred now welling up inside my heart.

"Go down there!" I scream to my pelican. "You have to save her! Come on!"

My pelican does not budge, but continues to peer down. In a moment, the reason why becomes completely evident. All signs of hope are surely lost. The main part of the tree topples completely on Gretchen and her pelican. As if the flames had not been enough torture for them. It certainly does not take long to know the outcome. My friend and her avian soldier are no more. I swear the Jauntla smirks in the distance.

The Jauntla belches another ferocious screech, almost proud of her victory. This sets me off. There has never been as much fury in my heart as now. Looking over at Marya, I see that same feeling. The Jauntla has ripped the hearts out of both of us. Marya then fires arrows at the beast like a machine. She holds back nothing whatsoever. The Jauntla quickly avoids many of the attacks, but that many arrows are certainly difficult to stop. Despite her extreme agility, one arrow pierces her wing. She releases a loud shriek of pain. Another arrow pierces her miniature arm as well, producing more yells.

The Jauntla, sensing the danger of the situation, immediately spins around once more. This repeats the act inside the stadium. Marya, I, and both of our pelicans know what follows. Swift rotating and spinning accelerates, once again, producing a magnificent whirlwind. Gales envelop the area. Both of the pelicans take no time to respond. They soar high, establishing much distance between us and the ground.

Luckily, we fly high enough to just avoid deadly purple fire. It flashes along the winds, destroying everything in the area. I glare in pure horror as any remains of Gretchen now perish. All of the Obstacles we went through flash through my head. *Meeting her on the platform, listening to her story about Sharia, journeying into the deep temple in the jungle, dueling the giant mosquito; all of it we accomplished together, and now she is gone.*

The Jauntla once again wears herself out with that major attack. She requires a moment to collect herself. Eventually, she soars up to our location in the sky, preparing to battle once more. Our pelicans immediately charge toward another direction. Where they are headed I definitely do not know. Neither I nor Marya can utter a word; Gretchen is dead.

Chapter 42
Destroy

As the pelicans head into the black unknown, the Jauntla quickly gives chase. Neither of us needs to be reminded anymore. Both of us immediately rise up, preparing for the onslaught of fireballs; Marya with her arrows and me swinging my flail. The first purple death flame is hurled directly at me. There is no way I am going to miss this again. I lift my flail into the air. Heavy chain dangles in the wind.

The ball swings at a rapid, deadly pace. It certainly appears as if I wield a monster. Just as the fireball arrives, I let out a yell slamming it with the metal chain ball. It fades away to the side. I cannot believe I just did that. The flail has finally worked for me, and I couldn't be more proud.

The Jauntla seems quite disappointed at my new-found skill. She begins shooting fireballs at an alarming rate. Marya, mastering her archery, fires arrows with ease. Once the flail is already in motion, the rest poses no challenge to me. As fireball after fireball approaches, I bash each of them away into space. My feet hold firmly on the back of my pelican. Both of us evade every one of her attacks; all is going extremely well at the moment. The Jauntla is extremely upset, and is certainly not afraid to show it.

She screeches at the top of its lungs. Sharp noise bombards night sky. Once again this renders complete trauma to both of our ears. The pelicans are none too pleased with the sound either. Both pairs of white eyes squint painfully.

Deciding to cease long distance attacks, no more fireballs arrive. She then summons all of her strength, and charges directly toward us. Those devilish wings flap with increasing speed. It appears the Jauntla is surrounded in a vortex.

As the pelicans sense the quick approach, they nose-dive. My eyes widen in fear. We both keep a tight grip on their necks. I barely avoid the Jauntla's harsh tackling. My stomach twists and turns in me, causing me to almost throw up.

Thankfully, the pelicans begin to even out their seemingly vertical drop. It allows me to take a few deep breaths. Looking over the horizon, the sun begins to rise a little bit, replacing the darkness. The bright orange sphere arriving in the sky makes me sigh in relief. This fight won't be completely done in the dark. I doubt sunlight would be a bat's favorite thing in the world too. *Maybe there is a glimmer of hope after all.*

New-found sunlight also reveals where the pelicans have taken us; over a huge body of water, with any sign of land quickly disappearing in any direction. The pelicans even out their flight. The two of us are now directly above the water; surely close enough for that giant shark to jump and devour us all. Despite stupid fear, a feeling of freedom ignites inside me. Marya and I whisk along this beautiful ocean. My pelican shouts over the boisterous crash of waves.

"Marya," it wails in telepathy. "We have to split up! She'll definitely head for Alcott first, based on your ability to shoot long distance. Get out of sight for the time being."

The other bird lets out a loud call in response, as it turns, maneuvering away from us.

"You can do it Alcott!" Marya wails across the

waves. "Don't let her win!"

After that, they soar off into the distance, becoming only a miniature speck. My pelican and I glide over the ocean. The sun rises further bringing in much more light, with no sign of the Jauntla whatsoever. *Maybe she's taken a breather after that chaotic attack.*

All hope of that dream, however, is lost as the Jauntla screeches in uproar. She does not take long to locate us, evident by its descent in our direction. Taking a complete nose dive, the beast plummets directly toward the water.

I stand up once again. My pelican continues to speed away, oceanic hues shimmering through each heartbeat. Just as the Jauntla is about to smash the water, she levels out. It certainly did not take long for the monster to gain on us. Again, there is more obnoxious noise. She wants her presence known.

I start getting the momentum of my flail going. The spiked ball rotates all around for the worst. Just as I begin to get the hang of it, something miraculous occurs. Rising swiftly out of the water, the six Sphreams appear! My heart jumps in anticipation. I have completely forgotten about them. In the hotel, they had said that the true power of this flail could not be used without them. Extreme joy explodes my heart. Sphreams float directly around me forming a circle. The pelican and Jauntla both gaze in awe. Neither of them knows what is happening.

The Jauntla is filled to the brim with hostility. Her 'servants,' it appears, are ready to fight back. Sheer terror and anger swells.

Sphreams then begin to glow a magical white hue, each abandoning their original dark shade. There are six completely white balls surrounding me now. We glide toward the orange sun. Six beams of pure energy circle the pelican and myself, rendering my flail to shimmer stronger and brighter with each new rotation.

They then seem to morph themselves into the flail, barreling into it one by one. Each one practically becomes part of the weapon. I sense the flail's power increasing drastically, becoming a gigantic shining ball from all directions. As the last one does so, it abruptly yelps out a word…one word…

"Swing!"

With that, it merges into the deadly weapon. The final piece is now in place. My flail now radiates a glittery white majesty. It is truly the most spectacular thing I have ever laid eyes on. The Jauntla continues to stare in bewilderment, now actually appearing frightened of me. The realization then hits me; *wow, a god is actually afraid of me.* As I peer into the Jauntla's eyes, her hatred is tangible. Another fireball is manufactured briskly.

Before she finishes her creation, I raise the flail above my head. I begin to swing once more. The momentum grows viciously as the spiked ball rotates. This time, however, something is very different about my new weapon. As it twirls around, a sort of energy bursts within.

The spiked ball is now completely illuminated in strength. With each new spin, the energy increases. My trembling hands can barely hold it. Without any warning, the ball of light shoots off the weapon, charging straight for my enemy. The Jauntla's eyes again shoot wide open. A deadly force of energy now approaches.

All her agility is needed to evade the ball. Sadly, she is quick enough to avoid it as the ball of energy continues off into the horizon. Showing a satisfied expression at her intelligence, the Jauntla once again prepares a projectile. My timing and skills are worthy enough again. I cast the fireball aside and it fades into wind. Wasting no time, I begin to swing the flail with more determination. A giant energy ball forms, a little denser than the last had been.

As I swing harder, the energy leaves the metal ball. It barrels straight toward the Jauntla. She is indeed quite cunning, even on the ocean. She maneuvers directly to the left this time, dodging the ball easily; she seems to possess far too much agility for this to ever work. Disappointment quickly takes over my mind. *How am I going to do this if she can easily dodge everything?* Just then, a streak of joy hits my heart. I detect something soaring in the distance behind her. The Jauntla, however, seems to take no notice of this newcomer. My little burst of encouragement grows larger.

It is Marya!

Chapter 43
Energy

As she comes closer, I discover something in her hand. Her bow string is harshly pulled back ready to release its deadly arrow. Her pelican expresses the same determined look. Slits of eyes burst with fury. Without delay, I begin the rotation of my flail. I attempt to add more force than before. The sight of my friend once more gives me the courage to do so. The energy ball manifests at an alarming rate. It's bursting to attack once more.

The Jauntla, too, knows not to waste time. She immediately constructs another fireball. Just before the monster hurls it, I let out a quick grin; an arrow pierces the Jauntla's back. Now, the agony in her yell is far more evident than ever. Not because of the volume, but because of the sheer shock as she turns her head to spot Marya directly behind her. The fire ball she created then disintegrates, slowly evaporating into the air. The arrows do not cease. Marya continues unleashing them rapidly.

In extreme panic, the Jauntla initiates the attack I know all too well. Stopping utterly in mid-air, she begins to flap her wings. The vigorous rotation occurs at extreme velocity. Gusts begin to pick up as once again it constructs an enormous whirlwind. This time, however, things are far more complicated. As she spins round and round, the water flows into the winds, creating a deadly hurricane sensation. The newly created wind literally grasps the ocean water. It pulls it up into the sky with ease. The phenomenon resembles somewhat of a tornado or waterspout. Dark clouds now inevitably overtake the blue sky. A dreary horror state covers the scene.

A tornado is basically sucking up water from the ocean. My pelican glares baffled at the monstrosity, flying me away from it as quickly as its wings can flap.

Following purple fire flares up the waterspout. It overtakes it in deadly flames. I can only watch with awe. A water tornado transforms with ghastly heat, however that is possible. The Jauntla has created a death chamber waiting to invite all of us in. She now finishes with her artistry and flaps away from the manifestation with ease, practically immune to any of its force. She patiently hovers in one location. Her bat eyes watch how our journey will be destroyed.

The giant waterspout is extremely powerful, sucking in everything in its path. My pelican squawks in torment. Enormous winds are too strong for its wings. Looking far away, Marya's has the same issue, struggling to break free. We are utterly powerless against this horrific creation. If something does not move fast, we will be sucked in and burnt to a crisp.

Frantically glancing across the ocean, I discover Marya and the Jauntla come back into view over the monstrosity. Sheer terror jolts my heart. Marya's pelican's flapping does no good whatsoever. They slowly get taken into the vortex. Arrows are released at an alarming rate. Squinting, I see her pelican struggling with all its might.

All this toil is to no avail. The evil vortex continues to suck them in. The Jauntla adds to the torment, discharging fireballs to counterattack the arrows. From what I can detect, both seem to cancel each other out; nobody does any damage whatsoever. This is a good sign for the Jauntla, because all she has to do is hold out long enough. Marya is minutes away from entering her doom.

Suddenly, I see the Jauntla erupt in anger. She bursts out another screech from across the ocean. Fireballs are being shot rapidly. It's as if she has truly lost all patience whatsoever. It does not take long to realize that something has happened to the Jauntla. Once she turns in my direction, I discover her agonizing fate. Marya has pierced the monster directly in one of her eyes. This must cause her insane behavior; although not necessarily affecting the creature's aim.

We continue attempting to evade the whirlwind. Sadly, we cannot. Despite all effort, the whirlwind just overtakes my avian soldier. I then look straight ahead at the monstrosity coming into view. I can almost do nothing but gaze at the reason I will die. Thankfully, as I had expected, the ocean water begins to overwhelm the fire, taking the heat out of the flames. In not very long at all, the flames are completely doused. Nothing is left but a terrifying cylinder of water. I can only pray that Marya escaped.

"Come on!" I scream to my pelican. "You have to flap harder!"

"I can't do it," it screams, practically giving up right there. "The whirlwind's too strong. We should have never gone over the ocean. It's too late, Alcott, I'm so sorry."

"No!" I yell over the wind, not considering that answer for a second. "I did not come this far to let her win; fly faster!" I show no mercy in that order. The pelican seems to turn its head back, giving me a look of fear and sadness. It is a look a scared child might give a parent, wondering why the world is so cruel.

"Flap faster!" This time, though I do not enjoy doing this, I kick its rear as hard as I can. I need to give it determination and display urgency. The pelican lets out a very loud squawk of discomfort. This causes its wings to flap vigorously.

Harsh encouragement appears to be working, as it toils harder than I have ever seen before. To my surprise, it actually looks to be escaping the harsh winds. We might actually survive! My pelican holds nothing back. Eventually, less and less pressure forces on the two of us. We are able to glide at a normal pace. Because of my pelican's extreme courage and determination, we have escaped the whirlwind's grasp. Part of me can't believe that even happened.

"Thank you for pushing me, Alcott," my pelican says, a bit disappointed in itself. "I cannot believe I was about to give up." I merely pat its head in response, waiting to discover if Marya's bird has been so lucky.

To my horror, though, the next noise I hear is not pleasant; a blood curdling scream in the distance. Wails of terror indicate all hope is lost. They are surely of Marya and her pelican, taken into the unrelenting waterspout. Both of them dissolve into the middle. They are shot up into the dark clouds in no time.

Certainly not happy with her eye being shot out, the Jauntla shows no mercy in her next strategy. Flapping directly by the vortex, she rotates herself once again. This spinning, it does not take long to figure out, is not producing a whirlwind, but conjuring an abundance of deep purple fire alone. The dark flames once again shoot up. They burst up the waterspout. My eyes can only stare in utter horror.

The sight is far more terrifying, knowing that my friend is somewhere up there. It does not take a long time for dark thoughts to seep in. Marya's chances of survival aren't even close to slim. Complete anguish permeates me. I have just watched someone die; I can't do that again.

Looking toward the summit, I see a shadow plummeting. The dark figure falls at an alarming rate. It has emerged from the top of the waterspout, as if being chewed and spit back out. There is no mystery as to what the figure is; Marya's body falls from the sky.

My pelican doesn't need any direction. It gazes upon the same realization. Darting into action, it soars toward Marya. There is no hesitation or contemplation, just pure will. There is not much hope that she is alive, but we have to try.

To head off Marya's falling body in time, my pelican glides forward. It squawks the whole way. We then level out into a straight line. Her body comes closer into view. There isn't a lot of hope of success, but there is certainly no alternative. I slide over a bit in an attempt to give her some room on the bird. I hold my flail over to the other side, as well. The spikes could cause nasty effects should she land in the wrong place. This worked with me on Gretchen's bird before, but that had been extremely lucky. Could this even happen again?

As we meet the falling body in the air, Marya slams directly on my back. The sudden addition of weight causes my pelican to let out a yelp. I scream with the jolt of pain. Extreme pressure is certainly jarring, almost knocking the wind out of me. Rolling out from under, I slide her to the other side of the bird. I take a few deep breaths.

Staring at our new passenger, I see eyes firmly closed. There is no sign of movement. Luckily, she still has her quiver and bow. They are tightly grasped in her right hand.

"Marya!" I scream. "Marya! Wake up!"

Slowly, her eyes begin to flicker open. She's still alive! I cannot explain the joy bursting inside; I thought I would have to finish this show-down alone.

"Alcott…" she stammers, barely able to speak. "Alcott…I'm still alive?"

I smile vigorously and tell her she's safe now; though I surely cannot believe how. Honestly, I expected to be catching a dead body. The sight of the bow and eyes opening are nothing short of a miracle.

"Yes," I utter through tough breaths.

"We…got taken in by that…monster," she whispers, glaring at the towering waterspout. "Then, it caught fire!" Her eyes open wide. Terror obviously has overtaken her.

"My pelican," she continues, looking very distraught, "was burnt to a crisp. It instructed me to leap off its back to avoid the fire…I guess I made it high enough…" Hearing of the pelican's demise renders my own to shift its flying a bit. It must be physically shaken by the dark news. I can't say that I am not, as well.

"Yep," I say, now crying pretty hard. She was this close to being gone.

"Just high enough."

Sadly, the poor pelican went through the same grim fate that Gretchen and her pelican had; burnt to death in flames. I am not going to allow their agony to be in vain.

Another loud screech emerges from down below. We turn our heads to see what is going on. Looking down, the Jauntla seems to still be preoccupied with her eye. She screeches and flies around in a frenzy of pain. Marya obviously damaged her quite well, as the arrows still protrude from her body. If what I assume is correct, it won't take much more to do her in.

The pelican leers at the Jauntla. I've rarely seen this hatred before. Both of its friends have now been killed, and the only one left is itself. The darkness of its tone suggests no mercy…

"Finish her!" my pelican states. With that, it drastically swerves its course, darting straight for the Jauntla.

Carefully, now that there are two of us, I stand up on the pelican. The deadly chain is raised. With sheer focus, the spiked metal ball passes by Marya's head. More freedom allows the momentum to begin. The magical weapon still glimmers with the Sphream power.

"Get behind me!" I yell to Marya, making sure she doesn't get hurt. "I need to swing this pretty quickly to shoot; you need to duck or your head's coming off!"

"Okay!" Marya obeys without protest. She squats behind me. The waterspout slowly fades into nothingness now. Nothing is left but calm air as it eventually vanishes. With the monstrosity of nature now gone, gray clouds depart as well. Angelic morning sunshine gleams once again.

"Don't worry about the fireballs, Alcott, I got them covered. Do what you have to do," Marya shouts. An arrow is swiftly tugged back in her bow.

Now, we are gliding directly on the ocean's surface once more. Waves sharply clash beneath us. Everything is surely ready for our final showdown. Along with her new-found insanity, the Jauntla still seems to be in a state of panic. We continue gaining speed. Once we reach a certain range, she completely pauses. Our eyes lock.

Either she's going down, or we are.

Chapter 44
Soar

Immediately it perks up as if we set off some radar. Apparently eyes aren't needed much with its supersonic abilities. It has narrowed in on our location. As tradition, more fireballs are in production. Instead of flying directly at the beast, my avian soldier swerves around her, maneuvering in a circle. Beautiful light rays pouring down from the sun fill me with some hope.

Last time, I was alone. I had to maintain proper attention to both offense and defense. Now with Marya below me, I only have to focus on one thing; attack. The ball now spins dangerously above my head. Ghostly energy accelerates. The first fireball is hurled at us. It soars in the direction of my face. Still squatting behind me, Marya leans to the left of my legs. An arrow is released toward the oncoming projectile. Perfectly, it collides with its target. The fireball vanishes into abyss.

The energy is surely getting powerful. White rays of light pour out in all directions; the sight of it is truly magical and encouraging. The Jauntla seems to be shocked at the fireball's disintegration. Marya has actually not perished. That realization encourages her to shoot fireballs faster than ever before.

Marya easily counters them all, leaning to the left and right of my legs for the proper aim. I am invincible with my own personal archer. My weapon's power is definitely almost at its peak. Nothing the Jauntla does appears to be working. She surely recognizes that fact.

As we continue flying in a circle, the flail bursts with intensity. Before, the Jauntla easily dodged whatever I threw at her. Let's just hope things are different this time. Just as I prepare to fling the enormous manifestation of force, something unexpected happens. Honestly, I thought I had seen every tactic the monster could use. This is certainly shocking.

As if knowing the end is near, she utterly enters outrage. The monster charges directly at us with jagged fangs at the ready. There is definitely no time to dodge the onslaught. My heart races with horror. I cannot understand why the giant force is not being released from the flail. It doesn't appear to be able to hold any more power. A few more seconds must be all it needs, but I don't think time is on my side.

My pelican attempts to navigate away. However, the extreme velocity of the Jauntla astonishes all of us. It is then that I do the only thing I can. I spring off the pelican's back. My feet leave just before the Jauntla collides with it. Once in mid-air over the ocean, my flail finally releases the extreme energy. The power is sent straight toward the monster. Marya stares in awe. Just as the bat's fangs enter the pelican's neck, the extreme force slams into the beast.

It doesn't take long before I realize that I have smashed her head on. My body harshly smacks the cold ocean waves. Gravity thrusts me under. The extreme jolt of the water causes my stomach to almost burst. Dark water engulfs my senses. Salt floods my nose and mouth. The sharp impact causes me to cast my flail into the deep. I am now weaponless.

With all my might, I desperately paddle to escape the darkness; anticipation and anxiety overwhelm my mind. I finally reach the surface. The biggest breaths of my life follow.

Wiping my shining eyes, my still-hazy vision astounds me. The first thing I detect is the Jauntla shining a bright white. Sphream energy completely engulfs her now. My pelican seems to be heavily wounded. It hovers a few yards from it. Gushing shades of blood pour from fangs pierced into its neck.

Frantically glancing around, I see Marya now swimming in the water as well. Whether she jumped off purposely or not, I do not know. All I need to realize is that they are both alive. Each of us can do nothing but stare at the spectacle.

Light immerses the creature, resplendent and beaming. Marya looks just as amazed as I am. Somehow, we don't feel any need to shield ourselves, not that we could. Out of nowhere, the Jauntla explodes in a mash of lustrous energy. She destructs into the wind. Nothing is left but the wind and sea. The monster literally exists one second, and is utterly vanished the next.

Everything around me is completely silent. There is no sound coming from me, Marya, or the pelican. The only tones are gentle waves of the ocean, delicately bobbing the three of us up and down. Seagulls then wail in the distance of new-found morning. Waves swirl throughout the ocean. The sun shines brighter than ever; as well it should.

"You…" my pelican states, in nothing other than pure astonishment, "you did it; you've won." That statement is completely uttered in happiness. This matches the bulging feeling in my heart. I can't believe we actually did it.

As we delicately paddle in the ocean, all fear seems to escape me. *For all I know, there could be dangerous sharks. Anything could lurk under here; but I really don't care. I'm just too happy at the moment.* Glancing at Marya, I realize the both of us now have tears in our eyes. Neither of us knew what was going to happen, but what does it matter? Everything is unknown. For some reason, this is the most calming moment in my entire life.

Glancing about, land isn't visible. There only exists us, the bird, and the ocean. We all remain like this for a couple of minutes. No words are uttered to each other. Nobody needs to say anything; for we have won.

Breaking the silence, the pelican suddenly looks up into the sky, releasing a boisterous squawk of triumph. That is truly a magnificent sound to hear. Against all odds, we have actually defeated a god. That long and tiresome battle has all been worth it. There remains only one question in my mind; what is going to happen now?

Without any warning, my flail shoots up out of the water, still shimmering viciously with the Sphreams inside. I can only stare in bewilderment at my weapon's arrival. It rises above us all, soaring into the bright sky. Once it reaches a certain height, it shakes and hovers uncontrollably, as if something is desperately trying to get out of there. Instantly, six Sphreams catapult out. After releasing the white spirits, my flail plummets back into the deep ocean. The weapon sinks into the depths of darkness, seemingly never to return again.

The magical Sphreams make no attempt to speak. Each quickly resumes their position. This time, however, three circle my body. The rest do the same around Marya.

"What are you...what are you doing?" I shout, very baffled. Of course, no answer is given. They rotate now at a vigorous speed. Around and around they go, gaining velocity by the second. The extreme speed blinds me in a world of delusion. With no warning whatsoever, our bodies are thrust into the air. We leave my flapping pelican below. The Sphreams now apparently levitate us.

Getting one last glance, I detect a curious look on

my pelican's face. Through its pure white eyes, I cannot tell exactly what its expression means.

Marya and I both share the same concerned look. The ocean gets farther and farther away. We could be traveling into another galaxy for all I know.

***

Suddenly, my eyes dart open. I must have fallen asleep on something puffy. It almost feels as if I am sleeping on a giant piece of cotton candy. Reality jolts back. I desperately attempt to recollect what has occurred. *Was the whole brawl made up? If so, then how much?* I've had to ask myself that question every few minutes ever since this whole adventure began. Nothing makes sense anymore. The haze overtakes my brain. Peering around, I discover Marya sitting right next to me.

"What happened?" I desperately ask her.

"No idea," she replies. She rubs her forehead and looks around in confusion.

"Those Sphreams started carrying us up, and then all went blank. The last thing I saw was your pelican looking back at us over the ocean."

"So, it is all real," I state with wide eyes. I now get a true feeling for my new location. All around appears as if I am resting upon an enormous cloud. Delicate puffs of cotton spread throughout; bright blue cloud extends onward in all directions. Above us lies an atmosphere, the likes of none ever known before. Great blue majesty flows across the sky. Black spouts of stars poke through the skyline. Bright clouds hover in utter tranquility.

"I have to tell you Alcott," Marya states, just as mesmerized as me of the new land, "you were pretty brave back there."

"You too!" I immediately exclaim. "There's no way I could've hit her without your arrows at the ready."

Marya reveals a little smile. "Glad I could help." She looks around once more. "Where in the world could we possibly be now?"

I can't explain it precisely, but we're actually part of the sky; a breathtaking thing to take in.

"Is this a cloud?" Marya asks, grasping the puffy nothingness.

"Uhh...guess so," I reply. We both attempt to stand up. Shockingly, it holds our weight very well. Marya peers over the edge to discover no ground in sight.

"I just see sky all the way down."

"Wow," I respond, glancing over the edge myself. "What is this place?"

Just at that moment, something majestic happens. Out of seemingly nothingness in the sky, an abnormal creature manifests. This is definitely no animal I have ever seen before. Towering over us, the monster resembles a two story house. Prehistoric is one of the many adjectives to describe it. The slimy face and body mirror a turtle. A sturdy shell on its back looks perfect for carrying people. In complete form, however, I almost compare it to a dinosaur.

An extremely long neck extends. The magnificent creature appears in a state of tranquility. Many tails flow delicately from its rear. Both of us can only gaze in wonderment.

Its eyes drowsily begin to open, revealing two turquoise slits.

"Alcott..." the creature speaks in a jolting voice. "Marya..." I have never heard a purer, stronger voice in my lifetime. It seems incredibly quiet while boisterous at the same time.

"What brave souls you are," it speaks again, raising

its extremely long neck. "What brave souls indeed."

As both of us stand speechless, the creature lets out an extremely confident roar. The clamor vehemently echoes into the distance. This roar, despite the massive tone and volume, is quite soothing. It is almost peaceful, yet deadly; if that makes any sense at all.

"No one has conquered the horror which you faced. No one," it states once more, allowing more of its intimidating dark green eyes to show. In a halcyon whisper, it continues.

"By defeating the monster, you both have passed your third Obstacle. If I'm not mistaken, that means, does it not, that you have conquered the Obstacles."

Both of us stand flabbergasted. The Obstacles had completely slipped my mind. All I was focusing on was surviving. Nothing can describe what is going through my mind right now. The dreamy state quickly returns to me as I lose sight of reality. *Fighting the Jauntla was just a test?!*

"So," Marya asks, attempting to not faint, "who was that Jauntla?"

Just at that question, someone materializes across the cloud. The terror in our hearts remains at its fullest. The recognition of the person standing there jumps my heartbeat. Lustrous golden garb and magnificent apparel leaves no mystery; it is undoubtedly the Jauntla. The enormous monster we have been warring against, the woman that burned down helpless Gretchen, now stands before me.

Chapter 45
Shock

I immediately shout at her approach, raising my fists. This is my pathetic attempt to look tough. She, however, strides calmly toward us. A broad smile spreads across her face. I could not be more confused at the moment. The giant creature warmly hums.

"There's no need to battle," it lowers its face. "Your time to battle, for the time being, is complete." *How can that be so when my darkest adversary is here?* I don't lower my fists. No one can be trusted.

The Jauntla begins to expel tears. She moves closer to us.

"Never before," she states with a smile, "has someone had the courage, strength, and drive to accomplish what you two have done. You have taken on every Obstacle, and heroically fought your heart out every time."

I don't remotely know how to respond. *This is the giant bat that was trying to murder me.*

Just then, two more figures appear out of thin air. Their forms hover onto this cloud. Whisking up to us in the distance, I recognize Vitaly and Travis; two other people both solely intent on destroying me! Both portray a joyful, peaceful expression. This completely contrasts my terror. Marya and I swiftly back up, frightened to death of what is really going on. Everything is entering a parallel universe.

The Jauntla bellows to them. She waves her hand, motioning to the two. "These two over here were spies, ever since the Obstacles began. Their duty was of utter importance, as I'm sure you found out in the…last Obstacle." Her eyes twinkle with cunning.

"Alcott and Marya," Vitaly speaks. Her haunting voice remains the same. *This little kid chased me with a knife.*

"Ever since the first challenge, we knew there was something special in you. That determination isn't easy to find in humans."

"As you both conquered two, everyone was immensely astounded," Travis continues. "It was then time for the third and final Obstacle to begin."

"Sorry," Vitaly appears ashamed, "for the horrible things we did; it was purely to test your strength and belief in yourselves."

"Yes," Travis says, smiling the same grin, "and you did wonderfully."

"Alcott, there is one thing I told you that was not fake," Vitaly says, reaching her hand out to my shoulder. "By the pool, after your third challenge in the mansion, I told you you could do anything if you believed in yourself; and you have definitely proved you now know that."

"And," the Jauntla takes over, striding ahead of them, "you escaped the cellar, bravely fought off these two, and made it to the final battle, against myself. Nobody has ever done that before. And, to my complete shock, you actually won. My bat form is…not easily defeated," she states with a twinkle in her eye.

A large smile spreads across my face. Everything was all just a test. I am attempting to comprehend this news, but I still feel an incredible sensation. I have never been prouder of myself. Glancing over, I see Marya with tears. She certainly cannot utter a word. I couldn't have asked for a better partner. This high school girl proved the best soldier I could ask for.

"The true test," the Jauntla adds, "was that you were able to have the courage to fight me. I was your only safe-hold in this whole thing. Who else did you have to trust? Your whole world transformed into fantasy, and you had to put all faith in me. Yet, you both still had the fortitude to take me on and win. That, my friends, is true strength."

"What about..." I quickly ask. The harsh brawl flashes back in my head. "What about Gretchen? She deserves this as much as the both of us. I certainly couldn't have won without her."

The giant creature immediately answers my question. The grim tone is unavoidable.

"Gretchen, I'm sorry to say, did not pass three Obstacles," its booming voice echoes. "She has finished with only two passes." Complete sadness engulfs my heart. This sucks, and I definitely know it. Flashbacks of deadly snakes wrapping me down in the swamp enter my brain. *I was doomed and had practically just given up. This is when she dived down to rescue me. Though death in the challenge is not real, the sheer agony surely was. She saved me from the snake. Then, she was captured herself. The one word she said still rings out in my head. Gretchen's practically belting it out right now. "GO!" She wouldn't even let me try to save her.*

"What's going to happen to her?" I raise my head in apprehension.

"Just as what was told would happen, Alcott," the Jauntla states. "Gretchen has failed the Obstacles and has been returned to her normal life. Sharia must indeed pass on. Gretchen has no memory of any of this. *'Altering Fate'* never happened, and will never happen again."

"Can we at least say goodbye?" Marya's eyes mirror a puppy pleading for food.

"No," the sea creature whispers. "You will never

see her again."

Chapter 46
What's Next?

"So," I ask, jolting the elephant in the room. Part of me just wants to get off the topic of Gretchen. Lingering on her for too long will render me to tear up as well. "What happens now?"

"Well," the Jauntla speaks. She apparently takes over for the sea creature. "Since you have passed three Obstacles, it seems we have a contract to live up to. Some people are about to become very lucky."

Marya bites her upper lip. She's overwhelmed with emotion. After all of our triumphs and falls, we have done what we set out to do; victory has never been nor felt sweeter.

"Are you ready to truly leave this life," the creature assures the reality of the situation, "and offer it to someone else?"

After taking a quick glance at each other, we simultaneously agree. No doubt or reserve exists.

"Those you fought for," the sea creature shifts position, "will have no recollection of either of you; it will be as if you have never existed to them. I'm sorry, but that's the way it must be."

We both nod our heads in acknowledgment; we have expected and prepared for that. That certainly will be the scariest thing to bear. I guess we have no choice. If Gari living a long life means no memories of me, I guess I'll deal with it. There is one more thing, however, that I need to know.

"Wait," I ask. Every head turns. I just address them all. "Do we get to...see them again before we leave?"

No answer comes from anybody. The Sphreams suddenly appear on the cloud with all of us, scaring me half to death. Marya lets out a gasp at the sudden manifestation. All of them circle around the two of us, imitating the ritual below the ocean. This time, however, they spin at a much more rapid pace. The cloud, Travis, Vitaly, the Jauntla, and the giant creature begin to disappear. Sphreams all blend together in my eyes. All universes swirl into abyss.

***

Everything, as I'm certainly getting used to now, returns to dream land once again. The world transforms to a peaceful limbo. It is certainly peaceful, I think, for when I awake I cannot remember it at all.

"Hey Tom!" I hear a voice yell. I'm jolted out of my slumber. Glancing around, I find myself inside a very strange vehicle. It seems like a truck of some sort, with very many weird do-hickeys resting all over. I see a huge amount of space piled with letters and packages. *What in the world is going on?!* Staring out my window, I discover many cars parked all over the location.

My clothes seem very peculiar. I never remember putting them on. Looking on my chest, there is an emblem of some sort. Upon holding it up to myself, I discover that it reads, 'United States Postal Service.' *What in the world? When did I become a mailman?!* I hyperventilate as I attempt to regain sanity.

"Tom!" someone shouts again; it is at that point I recognize who beckons. The voice undoubtedly belongs to Antuna, now running right up to the vehicle. The door opens wide. I peer out to realize I'm parked directly outside of Gari and Antuna's house! Everything looks as it did before. An extremely beautiful house dazzles in shimmering sun rays. It's as if I have never left the place. Now just a few feet from my vehicle, Antuna speaks.

"Tom!" she yelps. "How are you doing this fine day?"

Since she looks at me directly, I assume that she is actually conversing with me. I don't remember my name ever being Tom. I must be truly insane.

"Uh…okay…" I stammer back. "How are you?"

She obviously is bursting with excitement. The woman blurts out the news in milliseconds.

"I'm wonderful! There's something miraculous that's just happened; Gari's disease is gone!" Her trembling hands grasp her mouth. She almost appears afraid someone will snatch the words from her.

That statement stops me dead in my tracks. Staring with a wholly dropped jaw, I can't even muster a response. *Could I have…actually done it?*

"What?!" I say, breaking myself from the trance. "Are you serious?"

"Yes," Antuna shouts back. "We went to the hospital for a routine check-up. They told us that the disease has vanished; practically into thin air! They've never seen anything like it." She's just as flabbergasted as me.

"That's great," I release a large grin. "I'm so happy for him."

I can't believe this is really happening. It really worked; I actually saved this little boy.

"Well," she motions with her hand. "Don't just sit there! Come on in and celebrate with us. There are plenty of delectable desserts inside."

"Oh…Okay…" I awkwardly say back. This mail

truck's door is quite enormous, and I almost stumble attempting to step out.

"Did you forget how to leave your own truck?" Antuna chuckles at my failure.

"I…guess so," I somewhat regain proper balance. After doing so, both of us head toward the household. Across the many vehicles in the driveway, I view a beautiful sun towering above. Not a single cloud is in the sky; even staring in the general direction makes me squint. Many different birds chirp in bliss. The day is perfect.

As I am guided through the front door, I find a giant party taking place. Streamers and balloons flow everywhere the eye can see. Beautiful colors and elaborate decorations cover the entire room. Tons of people are laughing. Everyone's conversing throughout my old home. Many heads turn.

"Hey Tom!" a couple of people shout. They must apparently know me. "How was work today?"

"Oh, you know…" I respond the best I can, "same old, same old."

As I continue around the house, I make more casual chit-chat. Everybody seems to know the mailman. I guess I should pretend I know them. Many people claim to have had very amusing stories with me. It is very interesting to listen to them speak. As they reminisce, I try to make it look like I have some idea what they are saying. It is comical really. All I can do is laugh in confusion.

I abruptly catch a glimpse of little kids across the room. This one child over there stands out. *He is the reason for everything that happened. If it wasn't for him, none of my great adventure would have even occurred; none of my triumphs, downfalls, battles, successes, or failures would have existed. Dueling great white sharks, mosquitoes, bats, answering trivia inside a deep temple, real life sword fighting warriors, escaping a cellar, and everything else, is all because of that chubby little boy snickering with his friends.*

Chapter 47
Reunion

"Gari!" I yell, rushing past the group of people. *Seeing him is such a magnificent thing; I didn't think I would ever do that again. It has been so long. Now here he is. Smiling as ever, he looks as if nothing was ever wrong in the first place.* "Gari, it's me, Dr. Alcott!"

He looks bewildered at my appearance...nervously replying back, "Hi…"

Why does he look so confused? I've lived here for quite some time. Now he acts like he doesn't even know me? Suddenly I catch my reflection in the mirror, jolting my heart as I gasp. Oh yeah; I'm…this Tom now.

"So," I try to change the subject, "when did you get the magnificent news?"

"A…few days ago…" he stammers. "We were going to get a doctor to live with me, when the scans showed my disease was gone!"

"That's awesome." My heart shudders. I must've been that doctor.

"So," I continue. "You never had any doctor live here? Does the name Alcott mean anything to you at all?" I pretty much know the answer to this question. I just need to hear it firsthand.

"No," he says. He's attempting to be courteous, but just appears apprehensive.

I can't lie; that last sentence cuts pretty deep. It was like an affirmation that my time here is done. It is hard to swallow, knowing that everything is gone. All of the memories we had together from the baseball games, to restaurants, to video games are all lost. That is okay, though. He will have the time now to make a lot more of those.

I just wish I could be in some of them.

"Would you like to learn how to sword fight?" he asks, swiftly handing me the controller.

"Of course I know how to sword fight, I've been doing it for a long tim--" I say, taking myself back. Whoops. "I mean, of course I'll take you kids on! How do you play?"

So, I have a lot of fun sword fighting all the little kids. It's so great to find Gari having many friends to play with. As each of them attempts to learn how to play, I give some interesting pointers. Perhaps the little scamps can beat Gari one day. Of course, flashbacks of extreme duels in the arenas keep flooding my brain. I'm not afraid of them anymore. After supervising the chaos, a voice rings in my head.

"Alcott," the whisper echoes. From all I have been through, random ghostly voices are just the norm.

"Alcott...the time has come...you have fifteen seconds..." With that, it vanishes. A cacophony of party conversation takes its place. There is definitely no doubt in my mind. I know exactly how to use them.

Pulling Gari away from spectating, I plainly state one last thing. "Don't you ever stop looking at the horizon." I smile as I fully realize my next statement to be true. "It's yours anytime you want it."

No response is given. He just leers into my soul, showing a mix of confusion and understanding. Both seem to battle with each other in his mind.

With that, the world once again turns into a sea of utter darkness. I'm left victim to the endlessness.

Chapter 48
Uncharted

My eyes flicker into reality. I feel myself resting upon soft and grainy texture. Wiping my eyes off, I raise my upper body. I swiftly discover that I am lying on sand. Specks of it cling to every inch of my body.

From the discovery of my black skin, I know I am back to my normal self. As I peacefully lie on the sand, the last scene floods my mind. *It was difficult being unknown to those two. It is also pretty terrifying, despite all I have been through. I suppose I knew that would happen.*

I gaze up into the shimmering, blue sky. This is literally the brightest I've ever seen the sun. No evidence of clouds. *Life definitely has not turned out as I had expected it to. I was just a doctor. Now, I have no idea what I am.* All of the Obstacles flash through my head as well; I wholly doubt that's ever going away.

Enjoying the peaceful beach, I merely take in the aspects of this world. Seagulls call, pelicans dive for fish, and crisp waves crash against the shore. It makes me sad to believe I will depart this life soon. It feels like there's still too much to see. My heart beats faster. I almost fear I'm going to hyperventilate again. My palms sweat. Panic grips every part of me. *Am I really ready to leave everything?*

Gari then emerges into my mind. The image of that kid stops it all. *This must be what he had to go through. If he could charge into death, so can I.* My heartbeat returns to normal. I'm utterly terrified, but that's okay.

"Alcott," a recognizable hero wails. The voice is of

a true warrior. This girl fought with me until the end. Marya waves me over to her direction.

Lifting myself off the comfortable sand, I squint over there. She rests atop something magnificent in the ocean. Upon further inspection, there is no doubt. Marya's on top of the sea creature from the cloud. The majestic monster looks more gigantic from this angle. The slimy dinosaur gleams in sun rays.

Its fins slowly bob up and down. Shiny waves bash against it. Tails wag to clear themselves of water. As I cautiously approach, the creature begins to speak...

"Alcott," it speaks in its eerie tone, "are you ready to die?"

Yeah, like I get a choice now. Despite the scene on the beach, everything alters. Death somehow is not scary at all.

"Before we leave," it rotates its head toward the ocean, "if you would like, we can take one final view of this world. Marya has agreed to do so. What do you say?"

"That sounds great," I respond with a smile.

Jaunting up to the magnificent creature, an enormous fin is extended. It allows me to climb up on it. Initially walking into the ocean, the temperature is quite chilly. Waves harshly slap my legs. As I continue up the slimy, bluish fin, my leg completely slips off. Before I know what's happening, I'm plummeting into water.

"Ahhh!" I scream. Wintry water clutches my limbs. That certainly is not fun at all!

My body begins to adjust to the temperature. It actually becomes quite relaxing. As I eventually emerge, getting a foothold in the sand, I can't help but laugh. Marya snickers uncontrollably too. The creature even looks to give a slight grin, towering in the sunlight.

Now completely drenched, I successfully make it up

the fin and take my place next to Marya. Its back is certainly quite comfortable; sleeping on this thing actually appears appealing.

"So, where did you go?" I ask Marya, very curious to learn if her experience had been similar to mine.

Marya lets out the biggest smile. She looks at the ocean waves.

She leers at ocean waves. I have absolutely no idea what's going through the young woman's mind.

"I didn't go anywhere," Marya finally says. "I was allowed a glimpse into the life of the man I killed. This time he gets to live. All his friends and family aren't crying anymore and thankfully don't have me to blame for ruining their lives." Tears flood down her cheeks as she rotates towards the horizon.

We watch bouncing splashes of foam. As the sun gleams high in the sky, waves slam roughly onto the shore. That feeling that Gari talked about is definitely inside me now. *Adventure is coming; there is no doubt about it in my mind. It calls for nobody but me.*

Once I sit firmly aboard, the creature extends its long neck to the fullest. Along with that, it belts out a massive roar. This powerful sound is stronger than any done before. It echoes as far as we can hear into the cliffs.

With that, the creature begins paddling out toward the ocean, abandoning the pretty beach behind. We accelerate forward. The ocean slowly engulfs all of us.

A dazzling clash of waves whirls amongst the sand. This makes my heart beat a little faster. I never fully embraced the beauty of the ocean's majesty until this very moment. I've never been more excited.

"Was the water cold?" Marya giggles once more.

"Maybe you should find out," I reply.

"Wha--?" Marya attempts to say as I swiftly kick

her off the creature's back. She plunges into the deep blue. I let out a quick smirk at my action. It swiftly erupts into full-on laughter.

Marya shouts obscenities. Her body rises to the surface of the freezing ocean.

"Alcott! I'm gonna kill you!"

"Too late!" I shout with unyielding amusement. "We're already dying!"

The girl shivers in the freezing ocean while I lay back on the sea creature. It decreases its speed, aware of the now missing passenger.

"Alcott," the creature yelps into my mind, "I would appreciate it if you did not remove passengers along our journey."

"What are you going to do about it, Mr. Long Neck?" I state with a snicker, extremely surprised at my courage.

"Hmmm," the sea creature contemplates. Green slits of eyes glare at me. The next sight astounds me. The sea creature rolls its extremely tall neck backwards. Its head extends toward me. Now locking eyes with its upside down face, I am utterly speechless. My jaw drops. Blobs of slime overtake a scaly nose and cheeks.

Could this be what looking at a dragon is like? The creature grabs my shirt with its sharp teeth. Without any warning, I'm rising up into the air. I can only shriek at the top of my lungs as the creature lifts me up. I tower above the ocean around me. My stomach bursts with pressure.

The creature slams me into the unyielding depths. Plentiful water plunges up my nose. Salt drives into my senses. I still can't help but smile.

Being thrust into deep water is something I've become quite accustomed to. It does not pose much of a threat. Darting up to the surface, I discover the giant creature chuckling in the sunlight, proud of its feat. Marya proves no different, cracking up across the waves.

"That's what you get, jerk!" She bursts into laughter.

Suddenly, my eyes catch sight of the horizon. The line of sky meeting ocean mesmerizes me. Reality kicks in my heart once again. There is a bit of fear, leaving everything I know to be true. *Every time I thought that happened before, I just woke up. Everything returned to normal. Not this time.* This is no bad nightmare; I'm surely aware of that now.

As if transformed in that second, all worry vanishes. Anticipation takes its place.

Something is waiting. I know that to be true, more than I had ever imagined before. More sights to see, more journeys to go on, and definitely more battles to be faced.

I think back to my nightmares. *Fear overtook me and I gave in to every horror.* I can't help but snicker at my behavior. *That pathetic man turned into this guy I am now. I never believed this new guy could be me.*

"Are you ready, Dr. Alcott," the creature wails, "or do you have more shenanigans to pull?" I swerve among waves. Marya climbs aboard once more.

I breaststroke over to the creature. Marya bends down upon the enormous shell. She extends her arm down to me. There's only one sensation remaining in my heart. Only two words can do this feeling justice.

I lunge for her arm and grasp it.

"Let's go!"

The End